Hallmark
PUBLISHING

An Unforgettable Christmas

NEW YORK TIMES BESTSELLING AUTHOR
GINNY BAIRD

An Unforgettable Christmas

Print ISBN: 978-1-947892-45-3
eBook ISBN: 978-1-947892-59-0

www.hallmarkpublishing.com

Table of Contents

For John

Chapter One

Angie hurried Pepe out the door of their modest third-floor apartment and into the chilly stairwell. He wore his coat, hat, and mittens, and had his Batman backpack slung over his shoulders. But, lunch. *Where's lunch?*

She halted midstride, calling out, "Hang on! We forgot your lunchbox."

Pepe turned his big, dark eyes in her direction. He'd been racing ahead and had already made it to the second-floor landing. "But, Mo-om, I'll miss the bus."

He was right, and she knew it. She didn't have time to drive him in to school today. She rapidly descended the steps after him, taking care with her footing in her new cranberry-colored pumps. They matched her bag as well as her necklace and earrings. When combined with her jolly Santa Claus pin, the fun accessories added a pop of color to her otherwise drab work outfit.

"Okay," Angie said, relenting. This was what her son always wanted—to purchase lunch with the cool kids in his first-grade class. "You can buy today."

Pepe fist-pumped in the air. "Ye-es!"

"But eat your lunch before the ice cream," Angie

warned, knowing the tempting dessert was what he was secretly after.

She followed him down the stairs, marveling at how much taller he'd grown since September. He'd been the new kid in his class but appeared to be settling in. He'd never had trouble making new friends.

Pepe reached the building's front door as Angie stepped up behind him, shoving it open. A sharp blast of wind greeted them, and icy droplets prickled her face. She cinched the belt on her coat and tugged her hat down over her ears, shivering in the cold.

Pepe held out his hands, catching the tiny flakes in his mittens. "Woo-hoo! It's snowing!"

"Yeah. How cool is that?" Angie's gaze swept the street where she spied the school bus approaching, its windshield wipers swishing.

As she and Pepe scurried that way, Angie's mother parked her gold-colored sedan at the curb abutting their apartment building. Elena climbed from the passenger seat, and her short, layered, dark hair was instantly speckled with little white dots. Beneath her puffy blue coat, Elena's nurse's scrubs were adorned with cartoon storks carrying pink and blue baby bundles in their pointy beaks.

"Grandma!" Pepe waved his arms, as Angie escorted him toward the now-waiting school bus. "It's snowing!"

Elena grinned. "Yes, yes! I know."

Angie hugged Pepe's shoulders, giving him a quick kiss on the head. "Have a great day at school. If it closes early, don't worry. Grandma and Lita will be here," she said, mentioning Pepe's great-grandmother. When Angie was small, she'd been unable to call her maternal grandmother by her preferred name, *Abuelita*, Spanish for little grandmother. "Lita" was all toddler Angie could manage, and so the endearment had stuck. Pepe now called Alma "Lita," as well, even though she was technically his *bisabuela*.

The bus driver opened the door, and Pepe surprised Angie with a question. "Can Bobby come over?"

"What?"

"Home from school? We can play in the snow."

Angie knew Bobby was Pepe's new special first-grade buddy, but things like that needed to be arranged ahead of time. Besides, today was impossible. "I'd have to talk to his mom," Angie said apologetically. "Maybe tomorrow, all right?"

Pepe puffed out his bottom lip as Angie greeted the bus driver, "Hi, Mr. Jackson!"

"Morning, Ms. Lopez! Looks like a snowy one."

"Indeed."

Pepe climbed the school bus steps with a dour look, but moments later he was smiling again. He took a seat beside another boy, waving at Angie through the school bus window.

Kids.

Angie whirled on her heel, checking her watch. She'd need to get going in order to pick up the Christmas wreath she wanted for the shop. She caught up with her mom, who was removing a couple of reusable shopping totes from the trunk of her car.

"What's all this?" Angie asked Elena, rushing over to help her.

Elena handed Angie one of the heavy bags, and Angie spied sketch pads and paintbrushes inside it. "More art supplies for Lita."

"How nice of you. She's running low," Angie answered, surmising Elena must have stopped at the craft store yesterday evening on her way into the hospital.

Elena worked the night shift as a labor and delivery nurse, and Angie worked days as an accountant at a jewelry shop. Elena slept while Pepe was in school and also kept an ear out for Lita, who was still largely self-sufficient and could get herself around reasonably well by using a combination of her wheelchair and a walker.

Angie nodded at Elena as they climbed the apartment stairs, carting their armloads of supplies. "Today she's doing birds."

Elena smiled. Lita loved painting birds nearly as much as she adored painting butterflies. All were colorful creations and masterfully done for a woman who'd only begun painting much later in life.

Angie unlocked their apartment door, letting her mother inside. "How was your night?"

"Long, but good." Elena heaved a breath. "We had a last-minute C-section. That's why I'm running late." When Angie's brows rose in concern, Elena added, "The mom's *very* tired, but fine."

"And the baby?"

"A perfectly healthy little boy." Elena shut the door and winked. "*And* his perfectly healthy sister."

"Twins? What fun!" Angie grinned and eyed the clock on the stove. "Uh-oh. Gotta dash." She reached for the canvas bag on the kitchen table that contained her lunch and a few other personal items she carried in to work.

Angie saw Lita seated in her wheelchair at a card

table in the nearby living room. The stylish older woman's chestnut-colored hair was pulled back in a bun, and she'd tucked a bright pink orchid into it. Lita's fashionable costume jewelry and her beautiful floral scarf complemented her lilac-and-turquoise outfit. The woman leaned forward, busily outlining something on the sketchpad in front of her. Lita raised her eyes to view a cardinal perched on the birdfeeder outside the living room window, its spectacular crimson plumage visible through the pelting snow.

"Bye, Lita," Angie called. "Have a great day!"

The older woman looked up and smiled softly, giving Angie a parting wave with her pencil.

"Leaving already?" Elena asked. "What's the big rush?"

"I've got to make a quick stop on the way in. Sam's big sale is today," Angie replied, referencing her boss.

"I thought that was last Friday. Black Friday?"

"That was one of them." Angie tucked her purse into her canvas tote and slung the bag over her shoulder. "The first part of Sam's one-two punch."

"His what?"

"It's a two-part sale. Beginning with Black Friday and ending on Cyber Monday."

"But it's a jewelry store," Elena complained. "Not a tech shop."

"Folks can print out discount coupons online."

Elena frowned at this. "That means you'll be working late, I suppose?"

Angie gave her mom a peck on the cheek. "Hope not!"

"You already worked extra last week," Elena said. "You went in on Saturday too. To train the new girl."

"She's a woman, Ma. Close to your age."

"What does that mean?"

Angie wryly twisted her lips. "Mature."

"Good. Maybe she'll be able to talk some sense into him."

"Who?"

"Sam!" When Angie stared at her, Elena continued, "Help him see that there's a *world* beyond work. People have lives...commitments..."

Elena initially had been pleased by her daughter's employment at Singleton's Jewelers. But before long, she'd started questioning aloud whether the job was the right fit. Sam Singleton worked extremely hard. Those who worked for him were expected to work hard, as well. Which would have been fine, in Elena's opinion, if that didn't sometimes entail extra hours. Extra hours without extra pay, since Angie was in a salaried position. Then, there were the additional hours Angie put in processing her accounting reports at home.

Angie honestly didn't mind her demanding schedule. She slept better at night when her tasks were wrapped up for the day and not lingering overhead to be tackled tomorrow.

She sighed and buttoned her coat. "I'll try to be home by seven, okay? We can all have a nice dinner together then."

When Angie turned to go, her mother said, "I don't know why you continue to work for that man. We don't need the money that badly. I can take on extra shifts until you find something else."

Angie knew that Elena was just being proud—and protective. The truth was, they did need the money.

She and her mom were both saving up to purchase a house: some place really nice for Pepe to grow up in.

"I don't *want* another job, Ma." Angie turned from where she stood on the threshold. "'That man' is my boss. And in many ways, he's a good one."

"Ha!"

"I mean it," Angie insisted. "He pays me well, and the hours aren't bad." She winced at her amendment. "Normally."

"Maybe if you explained you have a family—"

"I can't risk being unprofessional," she countered. "Not with so much at stake." Her gaze flitted to the refrigerator crowded with magnets and a combination of Pepe and Alma's artwork. Pepe's latest report card hung there, too, and he'd received very high marks. They were all settling in here. What's more, Pepe was *thriving*.

"Besides, Sam's not really *that* awful. Not really. Not once you get to know him." Angie shrugged. "He has potential! You know, like a diamond in the rough."

Elena studied her daughter and then her tone took on a teasing lilt. "And just who do you suppose will do the shaping and polishing? You?"

Angie blushed hotly. "Me? No! That's...that's not how I look at Sam. He's my *employer*. I wouldn't dream of—" She paused and drew in a breath, surveying Elena. "Just what are you hinting at?"

Elena's mouth dropped open. "I can't believe it. You actually *like* him."

"Of course I *like* him. As a person. In a way," Angie stammered. "The way any person would like another individual. Person to person. Not that we're really that personal with each other. Sam and I, I mean."

Elena's eyebrows arched and she got that sage look in her eyes. "You never mentioned that he's handsome."

"I'm not saying that now," Angie added, feeling weirdly caught out. Naturally, she'd noticed Sam's good looks. Who wouldn't? The guy was tall and built, with short, dark hair and deep blue eyes.

That only made Angie observant, not interested. The thought of adding one more item to her already crammed to-do list, like becoming romantically involved with someone, frankly made her exhausted.

She added, "It's not like that, okay?"

Even if she *had* had time for dating these days, which she didn't, she clearly wouldn't entertain notions of going out with Sam. He was her boss, for goodness' sake.

And no matter how Angie defended him to her mom, Sam was also a little stuffy. Although he was just three years older than she was, with his firmly set jaw and that determined stance, Sam gave the impression of being much older.

Angie couldn't begin to imagine him on a date. The man appeared to have absolutely zero interest in fun, which was fine with Angie. She wasn't angling to have fun with Sam, anyhow.

"Anyway, I've got to go!" Angie tugged the door open, shaking off Elena's weird suggestion. *Me and Sam. Ha, ha.* Not *happening.* Then, she scurried down the stairs and out into the blustery cold.

Sam Singleton strolled down the sidewalk through

the drifting snow, the crisp morning air adding an extra spring to his step. Holiday garlands circled the lampposts lining the road and each held an green pennant, decorated with holly sprigs and joyfully welcoming folks to Hopedale, Virginia. On each pennant, two fluttering white doves held an unfurled banner in their beaks showcasing the town's motto: *Where love springs eternal.* This was partially in reference to the thermal springs in the nearby Hopedale Valley Springs Ski Resort. The slogan was also meant to inspire greater business among couples visiting the area on romantic getaways.

When the Hopedale Chamber of Commerce first proposed the new motto, Sam had privately considered it hokey. Nonetheless, he'd grasped its marketing potential. Since love and the sale of elegant diamond engagement rings went hand in hand, Sam had been among the first to vote in favor of the change from the old town saying: *Home of the Hopedale Honey Bee.*

Sam ambled along, passing shuttered storefronts. Only the Main Street Market had its interior lights on. He could see a few folks milling about through its big front window. The quaint grocers had a café section selling fresh-baked breads, muffins, and pastries, and offering an assortment of imported coffees to early birds. Mostly, those patrons were individuals like him: people with jobs downtown who were on their way into work. Sam prided himself on being the first to arrive at work each day and the last to leave in the evening. Although his staff was small, as the boss, it was fitting for him to set the example.

He crossed the street at the corner before reaching Harris Hardware. Pete Harris's granddaughter,

Hannah, ran it now. She took over the place right around the time Sam's dad, David, retired from his long career as a clerk there. David had never aspired to a higher education than high school. He'd reserved ambition for his one and only child, Sam. Precisely why Sam had been shipped off to Ashton Academy as a boy. Those were times he preferred not to think about. What Sam enjoyed was focusing on his current goals, including his typical checkerboard trajectory to work. This customary path gave him a keen appreciation for all of Hopedale, a quaint Blue Ridge Mountain town with a high walkability score.

One could live quite well here and accomplish most daily errands getting around on foot. He did just that, as he lived in a cool condo complex beyond the historic area. Local residents had kicked up a fuss when the sleek five-story chrome and glass building had gone in, but he truly hadn't understood what the hubbub was about. The building was eco-friendly with many green initiatives in place, such as solar panels on its roof, and it didn't stand out *all that much* against the thicket of woods it bordered.

Sam traversed Main Street again before reaching the library. The red brick building with a low tin roof had been fashioned from the small train depot, which was once operational in town back in the day when westbound passenger trains still stopped there. The cozy reading area inside, comprised of a semicircular stack of carpeted steps, was positioned by a plate-glass window overlooking the tracks. When Sam was small, his dad used to take him there sometimes to pick out books and watch the trains rumble by. That was all before Ashton, when he got too grown-up for train watching anyway.

Sam passed the post office and tamped down his hat, hunching his shoulders against the wind. He hoped the weather wouldn't deter shoppers today and, as he drew nearer, he saw he had no worries. A healthy crowd had gathered outside Singleton's Jewelers with its impressive front window display and that stunning marque hanging overhead. Sam loved the way the dot in the letter "i" in Singleton's was shaped like a glistening diamond.

His new television commercials advertising Sam's Signature Diamond Collection were doing especially well. *A Singleton's Signature Diamond Says Forever.* Sam grinned to himself, envisioning the way that line rolled across the television screen: stylized gold font shimmering against a darkened background, with the diamond-shaped dot of the "i" in Singleton's giving a little twinkle. He and his advertising director had designed a total of five ads, each one featuring a touching marriage proposal.

He'd requested Angie's input on that, since he had very little idea what women considered romantic. His past relationships had been companionable rather than affectionate, as neither he nor his former partners had entertained much interest in forming a bond that was too deep. His last girlfriend, Rebecca, was a banker and no-nonsense like Sam. When they'd broken up due to her job transfer out of state, neither one had shed a tear.

Sam approached the crowd gathered outside his shop, giving a cheery wave. "Morning, folks! Thanks for coming out."

People nodded and smiled, taking cover from the pelting snow under open umbrellas. Sam gauged the crowd to number roughly thirty individuals, and he was encouraged to see so many eager shoppers anticipating the store's opening. This could be his most profitable sales event—ever.

He grinned at the expectant faces as he edged his way through the crowd. Sam recognized several patrons as regulars, but there were newcomers as well. There was a time when he knew almost everyone in Hopedale by name. Then, the fancy ski resort had gone in nearby, and the tiny mountain town had boomed. Not just during tourist season, either. People were discovering what Hopedale's residents had known all along: This was the ideal, picturesque place to settle down and raise a family. The excellent reputation of the school district served as an additional draw. Due to Hopedale's fine medical facility and its adjacent hospital, retirees were discovering Hopedale, too. All this growth had been good for business. Sam's business, in particular. He'd had to hire an additional sales associate just last week.

Sam stood under the awning outside his shop's front door and slid his key into the lock as happy anticipation skittered through him. He could just feel it. Today was going to be a memorable day.

Chapter Two

ANGIE GRINNED AT KEN LARSEN as he handed her the pretty Christmas wreath at the festively adorned Holly and the Ivy Nursery.

"Thanks for helping me pick this out," Angie said. "I love it." She accepted the heavy item and it sank in her hold. The wreath was made from fresh greenery, and its pine scent was heavenly. It sported a big gold bow, a collection of pinecones, and a tasteful assortment of waxy white holly berries. The piece was simple yet elegant, and would make an ideal addition to the seasonal decorations at the shop.

"Anytime." Ken wore a blue flannel shirt, jeans, and sturdy hiking boots that suited his tall, muscular frame. He had dark blond hair, a neatly trimmed beard and mustache, and his attractive features were weathered from spending lots of time outdoors. "Need help loading that in your car?"

"No, thanks. I've got it." Angie strutted awkwardly toward the door, and Ken held it open for her.

"Where are you going to hang that?"

"At work," Angie responded, a little out of breath.

Ken's eyes shone. "'*A Singleton's Signature Diamond says forever.*'"

"Yep." Angie grinned. "That's the place."

"Well, then, that wreath is perfect."

Angie paused to peer over her shoulder as snowflakes began to pelt her. "What do you mean?"

"It's a romance wreath, didn't you know?" Ken chuckled. "Loaded with mistletoe."

"Huh?" Angie stared down at the wreath in her grasp. Ken was right. She'd mistaken the mistletoe for holly. It was no wonder Angie had struggled to get a passing grade in her high school horticulture class. She laughed in reply. "Well, I guess the mistletoe will do."

Hmm. Maybe a mistletoe wreath was the right thing to hang above those Singleton's Signature Diamonds. What could be more fitting?

"Might want to be careful," Ken teased. "Some of its magic might rub off on you."

"Ha ha."

Ken waved goodbye from the doorway and, as he did, he called out, "Say hey to Sam for me!"

"Will do!" Angie answered, popping the trunk of her SUV. She wrangled the wreath into the back, feeling a scratch against her left leg just above her knee. She glanced down in a panic to see one of the prickly pinecones had snagged her tights.

Great. What an ideal way to start her day.

Twenty minutes later, Sam strode into the showroom of Singleton's Jewelers, spotting his new hire, Pam King, standing at the ready. Dressed in pleated black slacks, a cream-colored turtleneck, and a coordinating houndstooth blazer, she looked ready to take on the work day.

"Good morning, Mr. Singleton."

She'd come in on Saturday for intensive employee training, which had involved practice ringing up sales, returns, layaways, repairs, and special orders, while under Angie's supervision. Like Sam's other employee, George, Angie didn't typically work weekends, but Saturday had presented a special circumstance, and Sam had asked Angie to step in to train Pam on the software used at the register.

"Really." He shot her a smile, attempting to put her at ease. "Sam is fine."

She nodded and tucked a strand of her auburn hair behind her ear. "Sam."

Sam narrowed his gaze at Pam, deciding to test her knowledge. It was crucial to him that his staff took their roles here as seriously as he took his own. New employees were no exception. "Now. What are our ABCs of salesmanship?"

Pam straightened her spine and recited as if from rote. "A is for *assertiveness*: greet the customer first thing..." She hesitated and then added, "In pleasant and welcoming tones!"

Sam nodded encouragingly, and Pam continued, "B is for *buying* opportunities. Present more than one purchasing option."

"And C?" Sam asked, holding up one finger like an expectant instructor.

"Clo...*closing* the deal?" she managed.

"Excellent. Let's see if we can put that plan into action, shall we?"

Pam blinked and said, "Yes, sir. Sam."

Sam hoped he hadn't been too hard on her, but a certain professional attitude was paramount to success. Angie and George certainly understood that. Everyone at Singleton's wore multiple hats. Angie was primarily his accountant, but she regularly filled in on the floor, as did George, his craftsman. Sam was always prepared to roll up his own shirtsleeves and do whatever it took to get the job done for the benefit of the shop.

His high expectations—both of himself and others—had led to great things for the store. Nobody at Singleton's worked on an individually commissioned basis. He divided the profits equally in bonus checks at the end of each quarter, because he believed all of them were a team, and he wanted his staff to function as such.

Sam's gaze skirted the room, catching Angie behind the display case for his Singleton's Signature Diamond Collection. She'd removed his prize bear painting and was wrestling with an oversized wreath, attempting to place it on the painting's hook.

"Angie," he asked, walking toward her. "What have you got there?"

She met his eyes with a sheepish look, and Sam noticed that the wreath was composed mostly of mistletoe. "Er...just adding one final, holiday decoration to the store."

"Today?" This seemed awfully last-minute. Angie had already done all her holiday decorating prior to their Black Friday Sale, and she'd done a stellar job of it. Sam scanned the painting she'd removed and leaned against the wall. It showcased two black bears clambering over a moss-covered boulder, and was his personal favorite. "But why put it here? Why can't we put this nice wreath in the break room?"

Angie glanced over her shoulder, her wavy brown hair swishing behind her. "The *bears*," she whispered, leaning toward him, "and Christmas? They really don't go together." She gave an apologetic frown, but somehow she didn't look sorry.

"What's wrong with my *bears*?" Sam contended. He tugged at the knot in his tie when he realized his voice had risen. "I happen to love that painting."

Angie's eyebrows knitted. "Then why don't you keep it at home?"

"Because," he said, as though it were obvious. "It doesn't exactly fit in there."

Angie wryly twisted her lips as if to say, *Sure, like it fits in here.* Fortunately, she held her tongue.

"I hired you to be my accountant and not my interior decorator, you know."

Her cheerful face lit up. "Guess you got more than you bargained for."

When she spoke like a sprightly elf, it was impossible to be mad at her. At the same time, Sam hadn't been consulted about this latest change. He was, after all, the boss.

He stared straight at Angie and she stared right back. Without even blinking. Sam grunted and picked up his painting, determined to return it to its rightful place. "Nobody asked me about this," he said. "And I don't approve of the substitution."

Angie's mouth dropped open and then she closed it as the heavy wreath sagged in her arms. "Well, I do," she said forcing a perky smile. "I'm betting our customers will, too."

Sam stopped, holding his painting in mid-air. "Why are you being so stubborn about this?" he asked with an amused grin.

"Because I..." Angie blinked and appeared to collect herself. "View it as an improvement." Sam could almost hear her mental wheels turning. She was a very sly woman, Angie Lopez.

"An improvement?"

From the corner of his eye, Sam saw Pam goggling in their direction trying to pretend she was looking the other way. Wisely, she hadn't said a word.

Angie must have read Sam's intrigued expression, because she seized this as an opening.

"You have to admit that the more modern-looking display cases are an *improvement*," she said with a leading lilt.

"Well, yes." Of course she was right. Angie was frequently right. She presented her ideas so cheerfully that it was impossible not to give them careful consideration. Particularly when her proposals positively benefited the shop, which they always did.

"Plus, our new seating area is a boon."

Sam studied the white leather bucket seats and the low coffee table Angie had installed by the front window, avoiding her gaze. It was the perfect place for customers to sit and peruse their purchasing options in a more relaxed way while savoring a sip of gourmet coffee from their wonderful new machine. Naturally, Angie had been right about those things, too. "Customers seem to like it," Sam agreed.

"*And* the shop looks nice and Christmassy!"

Sam hadn't understood how much Angie loved the holidays until the season rolled around. The day after

Thanksgiving, she'd clipped that little Santa Claus pin to the lapel of her jacket, and she'd worn it to work every day since.

"Yes, yes," he conceded. "You've done a great job." Sam intuited that this was a battle he wasn't winning. What's more, it really wasn't worth the fight.

He grumbled and set down the painting, reaching for the wreath in Angie's grasp. It was so large she could barely hold onto it. From her previous failed efforts, she clearly couldn't hang it on the wall herself, either. Sam positioned the wire on the back of the wreath on the hook that had been used to hold the bear painting, then he stepped back to survey the wreath. He privately admitted that the mistletoe wreath was a nice accompaniment to his Singleton's Signature Diamond display. Its piney scent was fresh and festive, as well.

Angie beamed with satisfaction, her eyes on the wreath. "Ahh. Lovely."

Sam folded his arms without uttering a word. Angie knew she had his begrudging approval. He wasn't going to gush about it.

"Oh," Angie said as an apparent afterthought. "Ken Larsen said to tell you hello."

"Ken?" Sam furrowed his brow, thinking of his old childhood friend. "Oh, that's nice." He and Ken had been tight for a while, but over the years they'd drifted apart. Things like that happened to folks as they grew older. Both Ken and Sam had their own businesses now, and Sam was happy to hear Ken's nursery was flourishing.

"Howdy, folks!" George Lee breezed onto the sales

floor from the private entrance in back, removing his snow-dusted coat and hat.

George, a confirmed bachelor, was in his late forties with raven-black hair and warm golden skin. In contrast to Sam's more measured temperament, George possessed a perpetually sunny attitude. He was a dedicated employee and always eager to lend a hand. He was also an expert at resizing rings, polishing gems, and repairing damaged jewelry. His one and only fault seemed to be that he could never arrive to work on time.

Sam checked his watch in frustration. "Down to the wire, George."

"Traffic's in a snarl everywhere." George smiled bemusedly and unwrapped his scarf. "Christmas shoppers, I suppose."

Sam wished he could convince his free-spirited employee to be more punctual. But George seemed to have a very different view of time than Sam did. Sam didn't believe in wasting it. "Please hang up your things and get ready. All hands are needed on deck."

"No problem." George scanned the room, his eyes landing on Pam. "Well, *hello*." George grinned, adjusting his round, rimless glasses. "You're new."

A hint of color swept Pam's cheeks, and Sam wondered if it was on account of George being an eligible and attractive guy, or whether she was simply nervous about her first day at Singleton's. Pam, who was in her fifties, had confided to Angie during her training that, apart from being laid off from her last job at a travel agency, she had also recently divorced. Angie had shared this information with Sam while urging him to go easy since she was "in transition." Of course he'd "go easy on her." Sam was never anything but reasonable and fair. What did Angie think he was, some kind of heartless ogre?

"George Lee. Great to meet you."

"Pam King. Same here."

George turned toward the Singleton's Signature Diamond Collection section, perusing the new wreath, and then said to Sam, "Nice touch!"

Sam cleared his throat. "Yes, well. Let's everybody stay focused here. We've got a big crowd outside, and our potential for record-breaking sales is high. I want you all on your toes today. No mistakes, missteps, or missed opportunities. After all..." He grinned around the room. "It's Christmastime."

Angie tugged at her hemline, glancing down at her leg. Then, she let out an unexpected cry. "Oh! Let me, um..." She hoisted the bear painting into her hands, holding it up in front of her. "Just tuck this away in back."

Sam addressed George. "Could you—"

"Help her?" George offered. "No problem."

"It's all right. I've got it."

"You're sure?" George asked her.

"Yeah, yeah." Angie scuttled toward the break room. "I'll be right back!"

Sam's gaze trailed after her, and he realized she'd been dropping hints about removing that bear painting practically since the first day she'd gotten there. Which had been almost three months ago. In that short time, Angie had managed to persuade Sam to make a number of "improvements" to the shop's décor, giving it what she called *more sophisticated appeal.*

Angie was bent on making Singleton's Jewelers upscale yet inviting, the cozy kind of retail space where clients liked to linger. When people felt relaxed, Angie reasoned, they were more apt to buy. Part of her relaxation technique involved having subdued classical background music piped in. At the moment, the subscription music station played cheery Christmas tunes instead.

In any event, Angie's tactics appeared to be working. When combined with Sam's keen business acumen at directing advertising, they were taking the shop to the next level, making it one of the more successful enterprises in town.

George excused himself to go and hang up his coat, and Pam peered at Sam like a deer frozen in somebody's headlights. Sam hoped he hadn't been too harsh on her during her orientation. He'd only given her the basics in a matter-of-fact fashion. Angie was always urging him to use a softer touch. But "softer" wasn't Sam. Soft didn't get the tough jobs done. Or turn record-breaking profits, year after year.

"Is there, um...something else I need to do?"

"Just prepare yourself for the hard sell." Sam exuded warm confidence, silently willing Pam to absorb some of it. He liked Pam and wanted her do well. He simply didn't need any major gaffes occurring today. Not if he could preempt them by giving extremely clear and concise directions.

"It's just like I told you during training. Nine times out of ten, people don't know what they want until you tell them. They're just in here looking around for something nice. Sometimes for themselves, but generally as a gift for someone else. Which is why..."

His smile broadened. "You encourage them toward this end of the store." Sam's arm swept across the back section of the showroom, where their highest-ticket items resided: vintage pieces and the like. Next to his Singleton's Signature Diamond Collection, his Singleton's Classic Choice ensemble was Sam's pride and joy.

"Hard sell," Pam reiterated, wringing her hands together. "Sure." She drew in a deep breath and released it, and Sam issued a confident smile.

"You'll do just fine," he told her, hoping he was right.

Sam's gaze darted to the store's front window, which displayed a lovely array of emerald and ruby jewelry, artfully arranged amid a colorful Christmas display. Nestled in fake snow, a quaint snowman with little wooden arms held the fourteen-carat-gold chain of a gorgeous ruby pendant necklace shaped like a heart. Other fabulous pieces were arranged on silken pillows in open jewelry boxes, and a miniature Christmas tree made of silver wire dangled several pairs of breathtaking red or green teardrop earrings from its branches.

A big sign on the front door read *Holiday Sale*. Beyond it and through the front widow's glass, Sam saw that the crowd gathered on the sidewalk had doubled since he'd arrived a half hour ago. Some folks held up umbrellas as snow cascaded around them, covering the hats and coats of other unsheltered patrons nearby. It was almost ten o'clock and nearly time for the shop to open. And now both George and Angie had disappeared on him.

Just as he thought that, George materialized.

Angie, on the other hand, was missing.

Angie leaned the painting against her desk, examining the snag in her tights. In all the back and forth about the wreath with Sam, she'd nearly forgotten about it, and it looked pretty bad, all right. It would look even worse if it continued to run all the way down to her ankle! She yanked open one desk drawer and then another, hunting for the bottle of clear, quick-dry nail polish she kept on hand for emergencies. It would keep the snag from running further. But that elusive little bottle was nowhere to be found.

When the jostling motion of the drawers jiggled the painting that was leaning against her desk, Angie carefully gripped the frame and slid the piece behind her desk, stabilizing it between the back of her desk and the wall. That was all she needed to do, break that silly painting somehow. At least she'd finally convinced Sam to take the hideous thing down.

She couldn't fathom why he liked it so much. It was very naively done, almost like one of those paint-by-numbers jobs or something someone might find in a hunting lodge. It was totally out of place in a jewelry shop, and it appeared to be even more of an eyesore when compared to the rest of the cheerily decked out store, which Angie had labored to make look stylish and seasonal. She'd tried to get Sam to remove the bear painting prior to their Black Friday sale, but he'd said, "What on earth will I hang in its place?"

Luckily, today, Angie had an answer for that.

She thought of poor Pam suffering through the

ABCs of salesmanship. Angie thought Sam had given up on that spiel, but he apparently kept it mentally handy. He merely hadn't used it on her and George in a while. George had worked here long enough to know how to deal with Sam, which basically meant with his characteristically good humor. Angie had learned her own tap-dancing routine. Sam wasn't a bad person, but he did have a tendency to get prickly. Particularly on sales days.

Angie rummaged though a bottom drawer, spying a bottle of Valentine Red nail enamel in the corner. She snatched it up and quickly uncapped the bottle, dabbing a swab of the gooey liquid on the snag. *Oops.* She applied too much, and now a big, goopy blob stuck to her tights. Angie dabbed at it with the napkin that had been sitting with her coffee on her desk. Next, she picked up a file folder and rapidly fanned her leg. Unfortunately, this wasn't the quick-dry kind of polish, and the color wasn't optimal, but this temporary solution would have to do.

"Angie!" That was Sam's voice bellowing from the showroom, and it seemed to be getting closer. "Five min..."

Angie slammed shut her desk drawer seconds before Sam emerged on the threshold to the office. "What's going on?"

Her heart pounded, and she fanned her face with the file folder when Sam's perusal caused her to blush. His exceptionally well-cut dark gray suit sported fine navy pinstripes, and he'd donned a starched, light blue shirt and a red-and-navy silk tie with it. Sam stood just under six feet tall, and Angie was only a few inches shorter than him in heels.

She winced and slid the file folder onto her desk. “Just fixing a little disaster,” she said, hoping it would be her last one of the day.

“Good morning!” Sam boomed cheerfully, holding open the front door and ushering a steady stream of patrons into his shop. “Welcome to Singleton’s Jewelers.”

Angie was amazed by the horde crowding into the suddenly cramped interior of the jewelers. She’d never seen this place so packed. Sam had apportioned an awfully big budget for advertising this season, and apparently, it was paying off.

“Happy holidays,” she said, greeting a pair who appeared to be mother and daughter. “What can I help you find today?”

Pam was poised behind one of the counters, already answering a customer’s questions, and Angie was relieved to note she’d relaxed a bit. Pam would catch on quickly. She had previous retail experience from before the travel agency, so she was used to working in sales. George’s job wasn’t normally on the floor, but today he was needed to answer questions any potential buyers might have about getting their purchases adjusted.

The mother-daughter pair was shopping for bridesmaids’ gifts for the daughter’s upcoming wedding, so Angie showed them sterling silver bracelets they could get engraved with each bridesmaid’s name. As they spoke, a pretty solitaire diamond ring sparkled on the young woman’s hand,

and Angie recognized it as one of Sam's Signature Diamonds. He'd commissioned each one personally from a well-known jewelry designer in New York and had apparently spent months putting the stunning collection together. Angie understood why new brides-to-be oohed and ahhed over the gorgeous gems in their elegant settings. Though sometimes very subtle, each ring had a signature detail that made it one-of-a-kind and distinctive from the rest.

Just then, Sam sidled up next to Angie behind the counter, capturing her attention. "It's Mr. Jeffries," he whispered. "He'd like to speak to you."

Angie peeked across the room at the tall, slim man with silvery hair. He only occasionally came into Singleton's, and just to look around. Everyone knew Paxton Jeffries was likely rich enough to buy every diamond in this place. He'd been the land developer who'd proposed the Hopedale Valley Springs Ski Resort, and he'd ultimately brought it to fruition.

"I'm kind of busy right now," Angie said softly. She noted that Pam was free. "Maybe see if Pam can help him?"

"No, Mr. Jefferies asked specifically for—" Sam scooted a little closer, and his pants leg brushed against Angie's tights. The warm friction of the glancing blow was unexpected and intimate. It was an innocent mistake, of course. So why, then, was Angie's pulse racing? She thought of Elena's earlier insinuations about her romantic interest in Sam, and heat flooded her cheeks.

Sam's neck flushed red and he immediately backed up. "Oh, sor—"

That was when Angie saw the streak of red nail polish on Sam's slacks. "Eek!"

Sam gaped in horror at the usual sight, staring down at his leg and then at hers. "Oh no," he muttered quietly. "You're *hurt.*" His genuine concern caused her heart to thump.

"No, no," she assured him in a whisper. "It's just—"

He issued a low reply, apparently unable to hear her. "What?"

Angie stared up at him, lost in his spellbinding gaze. The shade of his shirt brought out the brilliant blue color of Sam's eyes. *Gosh.* He smelled good, too. All masculine and spicy—like scented soap, or maybe cologne. Angie's mouth went sandpaper-dry as she wondered why she'd had those thoughts. Maybe she should blame Elena for planting ideas in her head. She'd never had such notions about Sam before. It was just like she'd told her mom. Apart from the connection she and Sam shared on the job, there was absolutely nothing personal between them. And, couldn't be. Wouldn't be. *Ever.* "I, er..."

"I think it's settled," said the older woman Angie had been helping. She fingered the elegant silver cuff bracelet and passed it back to Angie. "We'll take eight of these."

"Eight?" Angie asked, her voice a squeak. "That's great!" She self-consciously tugged a tissue from her jacket pocket and attempted to stealthily swipe at Sam's pants leg below the counter and out of the customers' view, but he slapped her hand away.

"Are you all right, miss?" the customer asked Angie. "You seem a tad preoccupied."

Sam yanked the tissue from Angie's hand and

dabbed at his own slacks, but little white flecks from the tissue adhered to the sticky polish on his expensive trousers. "Great." Sam let out a low grumble, and Angie's heart hammered harder.

The mother and daughter exchanged startled glances. "If this isn't a good time," the woman said, "my daughter and I can take our business elsewhere. Come along, Elizabeth—"

"No, wait!" Angie sent the woman a pleading look. "Please, wait. I'm so sorry," she said contritely. "I didn't mean to seem distracted. My manager and I were just having a little discussion about how much of a discount to offer you."

"Discount?" the woman asked, intrigued. "You mean, beyond the twenty percent?"

"Oh, yes," Angie stated.

"It's an extra ten percent off for return customers," Sam added without missing a beat. He smiled politely at the woman and her daughter. "I'm sure I've seen you in here before. It's Mrs. Stewart, isn't it?"

The customer's face lit up. "Why, yes."

Sam reached across the counter extending his hand. "Sam Singleton. So nice to see you again." He nodded at Elizabeth. "I hear congratulations are in order?"

"I'm getting married in January," the pretty blonde announced proudly.

Sam smiled. "What a great way to start the year."

Angie caught Pam's eye when she glanced their way. "Ms. King, would you mind ringing up these nice customers? They'd like to have eight of our silver cuff bracelets personally engraved."

Mrs. Stewart shared a worried look. "How long will that take?"

"Not much time at all," Sam assured her. Sam called out as George ambled by. "Oh, George. Could you help Pam with processing this order? The Stewarts will need a delivery date for some engraving."

George tipped his chin in a professional manner. "Of course."

As the Stewarts slipped away with George leading them toward Pam at the register, Sam glowered at Angie. His earlier concern had turned into actual aggravation. His employees were expected to arrive at work dressed professionally. Not covered in some kind of paint. "Angie," he whispered. "*What* is on your leg?"

She grimaced tightly. "Nail polish."

Now he'd heard everything. "How did it wander all the way down there?"

Angie's eyes went wide, and Sam strangely felt his heart ping. It was a tiny ping. Barely noticeable. Certainly uncalled for. And, yet...it was there.

"I, well, um..." She nervously licked her lips, and Sam was shocked to think of them as lovely. Angie's entire face was a portrait of loveliness, in fact, from her creamy tan complexion to her bold, dark eyes.

A Christmas song played in the background. The one about kissing by the mistletoe.

Noooo.... Sam's mind was *not* going there.

"Long story, all right?" Angie heaved a sigh and then her smile brightened as she cast a look at Mrs.

Stewart paying her bill. "At least things worked out okay?"

"Hmm, yes." Sam observed his stained slacks. "Except for one thing."

She gazed at him apprehensively, and Sam felt another jolt—like an electrical current buzzing straight through him. He'd worked with Angie all this time and had never fully noticed her sweet womanly scent, or that charming sparkle in her dark brown eyes.

"This *was*"—Sam coughed into his hand when his voice grew husky"—a brand-new suit."

"Oh, gosh, Sam," she said, out of the earshot of others. "I'm *sorry*. Really, I am. I can pay to have it cleaned."

As if he couldn't afford to do that himself. "No worries," he said, brushing aside any unsettling feelings of attraction. "I'll do it." He straightened his tie, reining in his emotions. Naturally, he was a man and Angie was a woman. He'd just never noticed how pretty she was. He had no idea why he'd noticed that now. Then again, they had never stood so close. And they wouldn't have, had it not been a simple accident. Which absolutely wouldn't happen again. He would make sure of it.

Angie walked from behind the counter, concealing her damaged tights with her hand. "Mr. Jeffries," she said brightly, striding toward the older gentleman. "So sorry for the delay. Thanks for waiting."

Chapter Three

Angie thought that six o'clock would never come, but thankfully, it finally did. Pam left shortly afterwards, and Angie couldn't blame her for being wiped out. What an extremely busy day. George slipped toward the break room as Angie closed down the register. "'Night, George!"

"Thanks, Angie. Hope you have a good one." He shot her a warm grin and shrugged on his coat. "Get some rest tonight."

"I'm planning on it. You too." She strode into the office she shared with Sam to find him leaning back in his chair, resting his laptop on his thighs and propping his feet up on his desk, the red streak of dried nail polish on one of his pants legs visible.

Sam's suit jacket hung over the back of his chair, and he'd loosened his tie and rolled up his shirtsleeves. He smiled over his shoulder when he saw Angie standing on the threshold. "Oh, hey," he said, noticing her. "I was just going over our midday receipts, and if the afternoon sales were halfway as good, this will turn out to be a banner day."

She yawned. "Night, Sam."

"Huh?"

Angie glanced out the darkened window where

steady snow continued to fall. She'd received a call from Elena about school closing early, but Elena had told Angie not to worry, she'd be there to meet Pepe's bus when he got home.

"It's night," she confirmed. "Pitch-black outside, and I'm afraid it's quitting time."

"But you still haven't run today's reports."

She knew Sam could garner the basic data from scanning today's receipts in their automated software, but he needed Angie to run the more sophisticated analyses of how today's sales ranked historically and how their inventory had been affected so the store could restock.

"Would you mind if I did that from home?"

"But we all worked so hard. I was hoping to learn the numbers—"

"You will. I promise. By nine o'clock. Just let me fix dinner and tuck Pepe into bed first." She set her purse on her desk and searched the rest of the office for her canvas tote. She located it on a hook in the hall, and then slipped into her coat and tugged on her hat and gloves.

"Thanks for getting that wreath, by the way," Sam said, surprising her. "I had several shoppers comment on it. You were absolutely right. Better than the bears."

Angie smiled, thinking there was hope for Sam yet. It was just like she'd told Elena. He was a diamond in the rough. Though it was *not* Angie's job to do the polishing. "I tucked the painting behind my desk," she informed him. "For safe keeping until after the holidays."

"Great thought," Sam answered. "Afterward, we can hang it right back up."

Angie winced internally, wondering what else she could come up with to hang there next. "Sounds good!"

Sam studied her in a thoughtful way, and Angie's heart thumped. "Meanwhile, we have mistletoe." She knew he hadn't meant that flirtatiously. Still, her cheeks warmed.

She laughed to conceal her blush. "Believe it or not, I thought the mistletoe was holly."

"Seriously?" Sam asked, seemingly charmed by this. "Ha-ha." He set his feet on the floor and angled forward. "Speaking of the Holly and the Ivy," he said more seriously. "My dad's birthday is coming up..."

"Oh, yeah?"

"Yeah." Sam paused a beat. "So, I was wondering if you could help with that?"

Angie eyed him, growing uncomfortable. "Help how?"

"Well, maybe pick out a gift?" Sam routinely asked Angie to purchase things for suppliers and advertisers, but he'd never asked her to run a personal errand before. This felt a little like crossing a line.

"Er, I'm not sure, Sam. What did you give him last year?"

"A Christmas Cactus."

"And the year before that?"

"A Peace Lily."

"And the year prior?"

"A Hawaiian Umbrella Bonsai."

"Do you always give your dad plants?"

"Pretty much, yeah." Sam read her look. "What? My dad loves plants."

"Well, then. Buy him another." She tried to inject a bright note in her voice. "Something you haven't given him before." She located her keys in her coat pocket, attempting to close the subject. "After all, any present will mean *so much more* coming from you."

"Not if it's an ugly tie he won't wear!" he hollered after her as she walked away.

Angie's skin prickled with agitation, but she tried not to let it show. Her tone was polite but firm as she turned toward him before reaching the door. "Goodnight, Sam."

"Come on, Angie," he said, pleading. "*Have a heart.* It's the holidays."

A muscle in her jaw tightened. It was bad enough that he was asking her to do something outside of her job description, but now he was trying to use her love of Christmas for emotional blackmail. "So then, *Sam*," she said, her nerves standing on end. "Show some holiday spirit."

Angie sucked in a breath when she realized how harsh that had sounded. She was tired, overwrought, and hadn't meant to snap.

Sam frowned, obviously reeling. "Fine. No worries. I'll get the gift myself."

Angie felt horrible for mouthing off to her boss. She needed this job, she really did. Here it was three weeks before Christmas, and she could have jeopardized everything. "Sam. I'm so, so sorry. I honestly didn't mean—"

"It's all right," he answered without meeting her gaze. "Go on. Just go." He waved her away. "You can work on those reports in the morning." Although he was playing it tough, Angie could tell she'd hurt his feelings. And hurting Sam was the last thing she'd intended to do.

She swallowed past the burn in her throat, wishing she could make this whole stupid conversation go away. That she and Sam could wipe the slate clean and pretend this day had never happened. The last part of it, anyway.

"See you tomorrow," she said, hating the warble in her voice. Then she tugged open the outside door where whistling winds and torrents of snow greeted her.

Sam returned to the office and sank into his chair, a dispirited melancholy taking hold. He and his dad weren't exactly close, and now Angie had probably guessed that. There'd been an odd tension between him and Angie that Sam wasn't used to, and it left him feeling all churned up inside. Perhaps he shouldn't have requested her help with a personal matter. But seriously, she didn't have to make him out to be Mr. Scrooge.

Sam reflected on the day and the close interaction he'd had with Angie when she'd gotten that silly nail polish on his slacks. It had only lasted seconds, but he'd briefly been drawn to her in a quite unprofessional way. Even if Angie had ruined his slacks, she hadn't done that on purpose. She certainly hadn't done anything to invite his romantic interest. All she'd ever done was play the consummate professional, trying to improve things around here, and he had repaid her by making an inappropriate request—and then losing his temper when she'd reasonably declined to get involved.

He scanned the small office area, his gaze snagging on a red rectangular object on Angie's desk. She'd left her purse behind. Sam leaped to his feet, deciding he could still catch her. He should probably issue an apology, too. Angie's substantial contributions to his business had helped make it more successful, and Sam understood that. While he probably could have done it without her, he wouldn't have done it nearly as well. He didn't want Angie leaving here tonight without knowing that.

Angie was nearly to her SUV when she heard Sam's voice. She'd had to walk carefully because the entire parking area was extra slippery.

"Angie! Wait!"

She turned and squinted at him through the driving snow. Sam had dashed outdoors after her in his shirt and tie without even wearing his coat. He held her purse in one hand.

"You forgot this!" he called, holding it up and waving it toward her.

He scuttled her way, and Angie tried to stop him. He was cutting in her direction at a fast clip and striding directly toward a patch of black ice. "Sam! No!"

But it was already too late. Sam's expression morphed from urgent to startled and his face contorted in shock. "*Whoa! Oh-ooooh!*" His feet slid out from under him, and he slammed down on his back, his head hitting the pavement—hard.

Fear gripped Angie's chest and her heart thundered. She teetered across the slick parking area in her heels, fretfully rushing to him and kneeling by his side. In the frigid evening, the snow drove down harder. "Sam! Sam, are you all right?"

But he was passed out cold and unable to answer.

Angie cupped her hand to her mouth and hot tears sprang to her eyes. As annoyed as she'd been with him, she never would have wanted this. *Oh, gosh. Oh, no.* Angie's pulse whipped into overdrive while she frantically scooped her purse off the ground where it had landed next to Sam. With trembling fingers, she popped it open and yanked out her cell, pressing in three numbers.

A dispatcher answered immediately. "9-1-1. What's your emergency?"

"My boss! He fell," Angie replied, choking back her sobs. "Fell and hit his head on the ice, and I can't... can't wake him up. Please, please hurry!"

Chapter Four

SAM WOKE TO STEADY BEEPING noises and the heaving and exhaling of medical machines. A tight cuff wound around his upper arm, and a small paddle-clip pinched his right index finger. He opened his eyes, emerging from a dark fog into the bright, blinding aura of hospital lights.

"Well, hey there," a gorgeous woman said. "How are you feeling?" She observed him with warm brown eyes. Dark hair spilled past her shoulders, and Sam saw she was dressed in street clothes. Not a medical worker then... *My wife?* His heart beat harder as he questioned whether he'd really gotten that lucky. Then he spied the woman's empty left ring finger and realized he hadn't. *A girlfriend, maybe?*

Surely, he'd recall if he were deeply involved with someone. And yet, somehow all of his emotional connections seemed hazy. Sam didn't really get a sister vibe from this woman, but she seemed to know him awfully well.

She tenderly took his free hand, giving it a light pat. "You gave me quite a scare, Sam."

Sam?

He struggled to find the correct words. He could speak, surely. But why was she calling him Sam?

That didn't sound right, did it? And, who on earth was she? "And you are?"

"Angie." He was immediately caught up in her spell, like she was some bewitching enchantress, captivating him with her gaze. *Definitely not my sister.* Sam doubted she was a kindly neighbor, either. When he didn't respond, she cocked her chin. "Angie Lopez," she further explained. Then, her brow furrowed. "Don't you remember?"

Reality slammed up against him and the back of his head throbbed. It was just the two of them hemmed in by a hospital bay. From the surrounding commotion on the far side of the drawn curtains, Sam surmised he was in an emergency room. *But where?*

He stared back at Angie, his pulse pounding. Suddenly, the beeping of his heart monitor increased, its pulsating sound underscoring the urgency of his query. "Are we involved?"

"No, er, I mean, not..." She paused to swallow hard. "Personally."

"So, you're not my girlfriend? Or—"

"I'm your accountant," she said, cutting him off. She blinked then forged ahead. Apparently, this conversation was difficult for her. "You're not...not married. Or even engaged, according to your father." Her face bloomed bright red. "Not even a girlfriend."

"I see." Sam weighted this information, considering what she'd told him. "You and I are work colleagues, then?"

"Yes. At Singleton's Jewelers?" She uttered this last part more as a question than an answer while she continued to scan his features. "You do recall working there?"

Sam raised his head off his pillow. When it throbbed, he eased it back down again. Sam mulled the name over, the familiarity of the surname ringing true. "Who's Singleton?"

"Who's—" Angie drew in a short gasp and squeezed his hand. "Sam. Sam Singleton! That...that's *you*."

He squinted at her, thinking hard. While Singleton sounded right, the Sam part didn't quite hit the mark. *Samuel? Samson? Sammy?* "You're sure?"

Angie backed away from his gurney. "Hang on just a sec," she said with apprehension. "Let me go and grab our nurse. And...and..." She nervously tucked a loose strand of hair behind one ear. "Maybe your doctor, too."

"That sounds like the right idea," Sam said with a shaky smile. Then, he stared up at the ceiling where a patch of plaster was starting to crack. It looked just like his brain felt at the moment. There was a fissure there—something broken. Sam scanned the full length of his body with his eyes, taking in the hospital gown and the entrapments of the medical machines. Apart from some serious aches and pains, he physically seemed all right. Sam tried to recall what had landed him here and in this state, but all his mind came up with was a great big blank.

Sam lay on his gurney in the emergency room, waiting on Angie's return. She said she'd be back after he'd been examined, and Sam had been poked and prodded by dozens of doctors, as well as subjected to several tests. Convinced his vitals had stabilized, he'd finally been untaped and unclipped from the monitors. There were just a few more folks he needed to talk to then he would be free to go. Only, he hadn't a solid clue where.

The curtains to Sam's hospital bay parted, and a middle-aged man with disheveled brown hair and a bushy brown mustache ambled up to his bedside. The man wore chinos and a crimson pullover sweater, which revealed the knot of a necktie beneath its crewneck. The ID badge draped from his lanyard identified him as Dr. Andrew Benson.

Dr. Benson held a clipboard in one hand as he reached the other out toward Sam.

"Andrew Benson." He gave a firm but pleasant smile, shaking Sam's hand. "Feel free to call me Andrew." He scooted over a chair, preparing to sit. "Do you mind if we have a word?"

Sam eyed the fellow uncertainly. He'd been asked the same litany of questions repeatedly and had supplied identical answers every time.

"That's fine," Sam finally said, and the doctor took a seat.

Dr. Benson studied him with serious brown eyes. "Do you know why I'm here?"

"I'm assuming it's because you're employed by the hospital."

Dr. Benson chuckled, but Sam didn't find this the least bit amusing. "That's reasonable thinking on your part."

"Thinking doesn't seem to be my issue," Sam replied with frustration. "It's remembering."

"I'm the hospital staff psychologist,' Dr. Benson explained. "Maybe I can help you with that."

"Yeah? How?"

Dr. Benson pulled a pen from his pocket and scribbled down a few notes. "Let's start by discussing what you do recall."

Sam wished he had something to offer, but he didn't remember much prior to waking up in the hospital and he said so.

"I mean, before that," Dr. Benson prodded.

Sam did his best to concentrate, but accessing his memory databanks was like staring at an empty whiteboard. "Nothing."

"Do you know what year this is?"

Sam repeated the information the attending physician had provided him after Angie had called him in.

"And you know this because...?"

"That's what I was told when I came to."

"Okay." Dr. Benson flipped over a page on his clipboard and wrote something else down. Next, he unclipped a small oblong card coated in plastic and passed it to Sam. "Does this fellow look familiar?"

Sam, accepting the card, saw it was a form of identification: a driver's license issued by the Commonwealth of Virginia. The adult man in the photo had dark hair and light eyes. His firmly set jaw indicated a seriousness of purpose, and Sam sensed a Type A personality, the sort who grew impatient waiting in line and who liked things done at the snap of his fingers. According to the birthdate, the man was thirty-five years old. He read the name printed on the license and then looked up.

"Samuel David Singleton?"

"How did that feel?" Lines of compassion creased

Dr. Benson's face, but Sam had no clue where he was going with this.

"What?" he asked uncertainly.

Sam returned the license to Dr. Benson, and the doctor set it down on a small rolling table holding a filled jug of ice water and Styrofoam cup.

"Saying it out loud?"

Sam stared at Benson in confusion. "I guess, like, I can read?"

"You don't connect with that name in any way?"

He raked a hand through his hair and then stopped when his fingers graced the tender area in back. "I...I'm not sure."

"How about the picture?"

An inexplicable panic spiked through him, causing his blood to pound and his head to throb. Now Sam understood what Benson was hinting at: that he was this Singleton guy. The one that Angie had mentioned. "Samuel doesn't sound right."

"Sam, then?" Benson pressed. "Maybe, Sammy?"

Sam felt a slug to his chest like something heavy had slammed into him. "Wha...what did you say?"

Benson angled forward. "Sammy?"

Sam's pulse raced as a voice called to him from far away. It was a woman's voice, soft and sweet. The sound resonated like a melody, haunting the farthest recesses of his brain. *Sammy.*

Dr. Benson watched him closely, observing his shaken look. "Did you remember something?"

Sam blinked hard and a fuzzy picture formed in his mind, almost like an old, faded photograph. Then a second photo followed, and then a third...each one yielding gradually to reveal the next, like a cartoon flipbook portraying the past in extra slow motion, or the flickers of individual movie frames across an old-timey screen.

A beautiful dark-haired woman, with dimples in her cheeks and a winning smile, traipsed across the lawn behind a little boy. She wore a shirtwaist dress and loafers, and the child was dressed in denim overalls and a little red and white T-shirt as he toddled along carrying a toy truck in his hand.

A dog barked excitedly behind them, yapping and taking playful bounds toward the sandbox, where the child was headed. It was summertime and warm. Freshly cut grass was cool and springy beneath small bare feet, and there were sweet-smelling wildflowers by a swing set. The boy gurgled and peered up at the sky, and blasting bright sunlight shone in his eyes.

Oomph. Sam's head spun, and the hospital bay turned upside-down.

"Sam?" The psychologist perused him worriedly. "What happened?"

"I saw something." Sam tried to catch his breath. "I think I was the boy."

"A childhood memory?"

"I...possibly," Sam said, still feeling winded.

Dr. Benson poured a cup of cold water and handed it to him.

Sam drained it quickly, the odd snippet of memories tripping through his mind. "I think...I was with my mom, and—Duke," he said, awestruck that he'd hit upon his former pet's name.

Dr. Benson nodded as Sam set down his cup. "How old do you suppose you were?"

"I don't know. Little. Maybe three or four?"

"That might have been the very first memory you had."

"Yeah? Well, what happened to the rest of them?"

"I'd like to administer some tests, if you don't mind. I'll basically be asking questions about when you were little to see how much you can remember up until now."

Sam nodded. Any memories were better than none at all. At least he hadn't experienced a total hard drive crash, which was what he'd feared at first.

"I'll also be testing your anterograde memory," Dr. Benson said. "Your current ability to create and maintain new memories. Based on our discussion, I expect the outcome of that line of inquiry to be positive."

"So, you're saying...things I'm learning now, I'm not apt to forget?"

"That's my hypothesis, yes, but to be thorough, we'll need to test it." He surveyed Sam kindly. "Okay?"

"Okay."

Sam watched as the doctor stood and slid a drawer out of the rolling table beside his gurney. "This is what I'm after," he said, flipping up a small mirror on a spring inserted inside the table drawer. Dr. Benson rolled the table toward him, then gradually spun it around so the mirror faced Sam. Then he positioned it over the gurney and in front of him, so Sam could get a good look at his own face.

"Man." Sam goggled in shock at his reflection. "You weren't kidding." His gaze roved over the driver's license on the table, and he compared its photo to the image he saw in the mirror. Sam stroked his chin, surprised to find it bristling with beard stubble. He leaned closer to the mirror, noting the beginnings of a five o'clock shadow. His eyes were a much brighter blue than they appeared on the ID, but his jaw looked just as determined.

He experienced an embarrassing flush of pride when he realized he'd turned out to be an okay-looking guy. "It really is me." He dragged a hand down one side of his face, and then he scrunched up a bunch of his dark brown hair in his fingers, wincing when the action caused his hand to tug at the sore area on his scalp. The doctors had explained that his main injury was a concussion due to his fall, combined with bruising and swelling at the back of his head. The concussion had caused his loss of consciousness and was now contributing to his confusion.

Sam flipped shut the mirror and slid the drawer back into the table.

"So, I'm Samuel David Singleton," he said to Dr. Benson. "Otherwise know as Sammy, or Sam?"

"That's right."

Worry filled Sam's brain and fear clutched his gut. How could he be someone and completely lose all sense of himself? It was like waking up in an alternate reality, when he had no recollection of what the first realm had been. "How much of my memory have I lost?"

"That's what I'm here to help you find out."

An hour later, Angie stood in a private corner of the ER lobby with Dr. Kate Mullens. The kindly older doctor had short spiky gray hair and tired brown eyes.

An exhausted smile withered her features when she spoke. "The results from the CAT scan and MRI are encouraging. We don't believe there's any permanent damage from Sam's concussion. The current swelling in his brain should go down over time."

Angie addressed the doctor. "And Sam's memory?"

"Our hospital staff psychologist spoke with Sam. It's his opinion that Sam's suffering from focal retrograde amnesia."

Angie fretted, thinking this sounded dire. "I'm sorry?"

"There are two kinds of amnesia that can be associated with head trauma like his," Dr. Mullens patiently explained. "Anterograde and retrograde. At times, both conditions can coexist. With Anterograde amnesia, the patient loses the ability to create and maintain new memories, but that doesn't appear to be Sam's problem. He passed his new memory retention tests just fine.

"It's very rare for an individual to lose everything," Dr. Mullens continued. "Retrograde amnesia is temporally graded. Most patients lose their more recently formed memories first. Some lose only the past one or two years. Others can experience a lapse of decades. But, in most cases, the patient's earliest memories, such as those relating to childhood, are spared."

Angie stared at her aghast. "How much does Sam remember?"

"His parents. His childhood home. His dog." Dr. Mullens sadly shook her head. "Certain things that are bound to have changed dramatically over time."

Angie's head reeled and her heart pounded,

imagining how tumultuous this must be for him. She couldn't fathom the sad confusion of not recalling huge chunks of your life. "Yes," she said softly. "Sam lost his mother years ago."

"And his father?"

"He's still around."

"That's good. We'll need to call him, so Sam can be released into his care."

This assertion gave Angie pause. The older man was soft-spoken and warm, but physically, he was ailing. Suffering from severe arthritis and using a cane. "I'm not sure Sam's dad is up to caring for someone else. He's elderly now. On disability."

"A sibling perhaps?" the doctor queried.

Angie shook her head.

"A good friend, then?"

If Sam had any, Angie hadn't heard him speak about them. Sadness pinged in her soul, as her heart went out to this lonely and complicated man. Sam had so much potential, and yet he'd kept himself walled off. From everyone, it seemed, including his father.

"I don't know of anyone I can call," Angie admitted regretfully.

"You could try looking through the contact list on Sam's phone?"

Angie knew what his contact list looked like. All business connections or service industry people. The only personal numbers he had belonged to his three employees, including Angie, and his dad, David. "Unfortunately, that's not of much use," she said, responding to Dr. Mullens. "Sam's had me make a few calls for him while we were at work..." Angie's chin trembled, when she grasped the situation. Big, blustery Sam Singleton literally had no place to go.

"Well, it's highly unadvisable for him to go home alone," Dr. Mullens added. She studied Angie a moment while a fake Christmas tree on the admitting desk twinkled in the background. "You seem to know Sam well..."

Angie blinked "No, I couldn't— I mean, I have obligations, and a family."

"Just until his memory heals?"

Angie was worried for Sam, of course she was. But she couldn't just take him home. Her place was tiny. And Sam was, well...*Sam.* Her difficult boss. How would she handle having him at her apartment? And how could she juggle his care while still trying to tend to Pepe and Lita?

"How long might that be?"

"I wish I could tell you he'll be better by Christmas." Dr. Mullen's shoulders sagged. "But I can't make any promises."

Angie thoughtfully fingered the Santa Claus pin on her jacket lapel. "I see." After a moment, she looked up and met the doctor's eyes. "You must have some protocol. Some way to deal with these..." Angie fumbled for her words, "unusual situations."

Dr. Mullens sighed resignedly. "We could call in social services. See about placement in a group home. There are also convalescent care options at our affiliated facilities, assuming Sam's insurance will cover them."

That sounded abysmal. Putting Sam with a bunch of strangers and right around the holidays.

"But it really would be best for Sam's recovery

for him to keep to his regular routine as much as possible. He'll need a few days of R&R to recover from the head blow, but—after that—getting back to work should be a boon." When Angie's brow shot up, Dr. Mullens said, "Sam's procedural memory shouldn't be affected. He'll still probably be able to perform his job. Doing so, and being back in his regular environment as much as possible, might even help with jogging his memory."

Angie thought of elderly David and how hard it would be for him to know Sam had been sent to an impersonal group home or an industrial care facility. If Angie took Sam in, she could say it was at her insistence, so David wouldn't feel guilty about not being able to look after Sam himself.

Angie's blood pumped harder when she realized she was caving. She guessed Sam's care elsewhere would be competent, but even under the best circumstances Angie knew in her heart that Sam wouldn't experience nearly as nice a Christmas as he could with her and her family. Although her place was small, she could make room.

"I could take him home temporarily," she hedged. "But long-term—"

"Let's hope there won't be a long-term. All right?" Dr. Mullen's warm smile surprised her.

"But if there is..." Angie sucked in a gasp, wondering how she was going to handle this. One week or two? Okay. Much more than that seemed impossible.

"Why don't we just take this one day at a time?" Dr. Mullens urged. "I'll need you to fill out some forms so I can write the discharge papers." She pulled a business card from her lab coat pocket. "Here's my number in case you have any questions during the next forty-eight hours. I've written the name and number of a brain trauma specialist on the back. I'd like you to contact him for a follow-up visit later this week."

This all sounded overwhelming to Angie, but at least she knew this put Sam on an optimal path for his recovery. And, if Angie could do anything to help with that, she was determined to. Even if he was at times a bit of a brash boss, Sam had given Angie a job when she'd needed one badly. She'd been able to relocate her family to Hopedale and get Pepe into better schools. Without fully understanding it, Sam had made her life better. Now, she wanted to help him.

"There's one more thing," Dr. Mullens said. "Some of the changes that have occurred over the years are going to be difficult for Sam to process. When he learns about things like losing his mom, that's going to be hard."

Angie's heart ached for him. "Of course."

Dr. Mullens shook Angie's hand. "Sam's lucky to have a friend like you."

After completing the paperwork she was requested to, Angie returned to the emergency room holding Sam's bag of personal affects, which one of the nurses had given to her. Angie had Sam's wallet and phone in her purse, since she'd been asked to hang onto them when he'd been admitted. The hospital psychologist had borrowed Sam's driver's license for his interview and said he'd leave it with her boss in the ER.

Angie stopped Sam's attending nurse, Maryanne, who was hustling down a corridor pushing a rolling IV poll ahead of her. "Is he ready to go?"

"As soon as he gets dressed." Maryanne eyed the clear-plastic bag in Angie's hand with Sam's name on it. "I see you've got his stuff."

"Yes, thanks."

"I'll be there in just a moment to help you," the nurse said. "You can pull your vehicle around to the discharge door. Sam will need to leave in a wheelchair." She read Angie's worried look and responded. "Hospital protocol."

Angie nodded and strode toward Sam's hospital bay, tugging back the curtain. The moment she did, her heart caught in her throat. Sam was gone! There was no trace of him anywhere. Only his license remained on the table.

Angie snatched up the license and scurried out to the nearest desk and its huddle of busy medical professionals. "Excuse me?" she said, capturing the attention of a couple of nurses in scrubs. "Sam Singleton?" She held up his license to show who he was. "Has he been taken somewhere?"

Maryanne, returning from her errand, appeared rattled. "Mr. Singleton's gone? But where?"

A bulky young man wearing scrubs and a tattoo on his arm looked up from a computer behind the desk. "I saw him walking that way," he said, pointing down a hall to the right. "I thought he was going to the bathroom."

"Bathroom," Angie said on a hopeful breath. "Right."

She and Maryanne hurried in that direction, and Maryanne rapped on the door, which was slightly ajar. She shoved it open the rest of the way, and she and Angie were greeted by an empty, dark space.

"Oh no!" Angie gasped and covered her mouth, her heart hammering. Was Sam so distressed that he'd taken off? He wasn't even dressed. Still in his hospital gown.

"I need to put in an alert," Maryanne said, stepping away.

Chapter Five

SAM LUMBERED DOWN THE COLD stone steps, gripping onto the chilly metal banister for balance. *Twenty-six years? No way.* There was no way at all Sam had lost more than half his life. And yet, he had. He stumbled on a riser and shored himself up, his breathing heavy. He didn't even have a game plan, just the notion he should go. He was a grownup, a business owner. Somebody supposedly in charge of his own life.

And now, he was being told he'd need to be discharged into another person's care? The nurse who'd had Sam sign his discharge papers had been purposely vague on the details. She'd just been told that someone had been assigned to take Sam home and look after him. Assigned? Like he was some sort of charity case? And what about Angie? Why had she totally disappeared? She said she'd return after speaking with the doctors. Then, she'd completely gone AWOL on him. Well, who was going AWOL now? Sam was, that was who!

He reached the exit at the bottom of the emergency stairs and shoved open the door. A shrill alarm began blaring immediately, and Sam shielded his ears with his hands. Bright red lights were flashing, too. The wind blasting back through the door ripped at Sam's thin cotton hospital gown, causing gooseflesh to rise on his bare legs and arms. He stared out into the snow, utterly panicked, as a wailing ambulance pulled up to the rear of the building, dragging to a halt. His head felt light and his knees wobbled as he stumbled backward, clutching the doorframe.

That was when the harsh reality hit him. He had nowhere to go and no way to get there. Snow came down in droves, covering the hospital parking lot and crowning the tall, glimmering lampposts hedging its borders. The icy ground chilled his feet through his hospital socks, as frigid winds whipped around him. He had a home, he was sure of it. Only the address was on the license he'd left back in the ER, and he had no wallet or phone. No way to call a car service or a cab.

And what about his mom and dad? Where were they? Why hadn't they come for him? Didn't they care? Did he have no one?"

"Sam." A female voice called out behind him, and Sam glanced over his shoulder to see Angie standing in the stairwell, her face etched with worry. "What are you doing?"

"I can't stay here."

"I know." She sent him a petitioning look. "Come away from the door."

"Why?"

"Because..." Her teeth chattered as she hugged her arms. "It's *freezing*."

All at once, Sam felt horrible for exposing Angie to the elements. Of course she was chilled. It was blistering cold outside. He yanked shut the door, and the alarm fell silent.

Angie drew in a breath as the stairwell behind her became flooded with hospital personnel. “Let’s go back upstairs.”

“Angie, I...” Sam’s voice grew rough, “don’t know who I am anymore.”

“It’s all right. I’m going to help you.” Her eyes glimmered with compassion, and Sam felt instantly bathed in their warmth. “Come away from the door, Sam,” she said again. “Why don’t you come back upstairs with me?”

“And then what?”

“We’ll talk about things,” she said. “Formulate a plan.”

“You and I together?”

Angie nodded, and Sam had the deep instinct that he could trust her. “Yes.”

A couple of orderlies scampered down the steps and positioned themselves on either side of Sam to help support him. Without intending to, he sagged in their sturdy hold. He was weaker than he thought. A lot more confused, too. He wasn’t sure of anything or anyone anymore, he realized with a jolt.

Except for one person: Angie.

Minutes later, Sam sat on his hospital gurney awash with shame. His attempted escape had caused a huge disruption at the hospital, and from the look in Angie’s eyes, he’d caused her extreme worry. “I’m really sorry about what happened earlier. I don't know what got into me. I guess, I..." Sam hung his head, "panicked."

"Hey." When he looked up, she continued speaking in calming tones. "I know you did, and I don't blame you. You've had quite a shock."

"I don't know why you're here, or why you care." Sam felt his voice grow scratchy. "But, in any case, thank you."

"Sam," she said with a serious gleam in her eyes. "I'm honored to be here. Freak accidents happen. We can't always know why." She pursed her lips when her eyes watered. "But please don't do anything like that again."

"I'm sorry," he said in a rush, and his heart broke just a little. She was such a kind and generous woman. While he didn't know much, Sam understood it was a rare blessing that she was in his life. "I won't."

"Now that we've got that clear." Angie sniffed and wiped at the corner of her eye. "I think we need to talk about arrangements."

This was the part Sam had been fearing. Angie was about to tell him the name of the caretaker who'd been assigned to his case. It was likely someone from social services because his parents weren't here. Sam's throat constricted when he considered one explanation for their absence.

"Angie," he said tentatively. "About my folks? Are they...?"

"I'm so sorry." Her face fell. "Your mom is gone. She has been for years."

"I see." A raw burn twisted in Sam's chest and his stomach lurched. "And my dad?"

"David's just fine." She shared a soft smile. "But

he's getting older now and isn't in the best shape to care for you."

"I don't need someone to care for me," Sam said proudly. He swung his feet over the edge of the gurney and his head grew woozy. His palms shot to the mattress and he used both his arms to steady himself when his torso sagged.

Angie rushed to him, placing her hands on his shoulders. "Sam!"

He gazed up into her mesmerizing dark eyes, suddenly lightheaded again. "I guess I moved too fast."

"Just take it easy. Catch your breath."

But that was awfully hard to do with his heart beating double-time. Angie still gripped his shoulders in a manner that was reassuring, yet firm. She wasn't going to let him go until she was certain he had full command of his faculties. Sam sensed her strength and devotion. Even without any memories to assist him, it was easy to see that Angie was a caring person. Someone who was supportive and strong.

"You promised," she reminded him sternly. "No more running away."

"I wasn't running. I was merely attempting to stand."

Angie smirked. "Standing's not necessarily a bad idea. Sooner or later you'll have to get dressed." Her gaze traveled to a clear bag of Sam's personal items that rested on the gurney beside him. "I'm not taking you home in a hospital gown."

"Home?" he asked with surprise.

Angie's cell rang and she held up her hand, withdrawing the phone from her purse. "Hang on a minute," she whispered prior to accepting the call. "I'd better take this. It's Pepe."

Pepe. Nickname for Jose. Somehow Sam knew this. He also intuited rather quickly that "Pepe" was pretty important to Angie.

"I'm sorry, hon. I know," she cooed cajolingly into the mouthpiece. "I had an emergency after work and am running late. That's right." Angie's gaze roved over Sam then she sneakily turned away. "She also told you that other thing?" Angie added in a whisper, though Sam overheard her. "Well, great. We'll be home in a bit."

We'll?

"That was just—" she began.

"Pepe," Sam supplied. "Boyfriend?" He didn't know why it should matter, but his heart sank a tad at the thought.

Angie giggled. "Son."

Sam did a double take. Angie didn't look old enough to have a child, much less one mature enough to converse on the phone. "How old is Pepe?"

"He's six now."

Sam's heart hammered. Despite his huge memory gap, he did recall what being a kid was like. Though the majority of his life seemed like one big fog, he could spy glimmers of things around the edges. Yet the images were fuzzy, so he couldn't quite make them out. The only recollections that came out crystal clear were those having to do with his apparently happy childhood.

He'd had great parents and an awesome dog. A very jazzy eighth birthday party celebration, too. It had been thrown in a bowling alley at night, with psychedelic lights pulsating. He'd received all five Power Rangers as gifts from his folks, and had invited his best friend, brown-eyed and golden-haired Ken, to sleep over afterward.

"Sam? Sam, did you hear me?" That was Angie's soft voice, recalling him to the present. "I said it's time to get dressed so I can take you back to my place."

Sam's mouth dropped open. "Your place?"

"Dr. Mullens says you shouldn't be alone while you have amnesia. You especially need to have someone else looking after you while you're recovering from that head trauma."

"I can look after myself," Sam said. Then another wave of dizziness hit him. He hated the idea that he'd been checked out to an individual like a worn library book. At least Angie didn't act put upon, though he still couldn't help but feel he'd be imposing.

She eyed him askance and said, "The discharge papers have already been written. And, anyway, it should only be for a couple of days. Dr. Mullens is very optimistic about your recovery."

"Dr. Benson said it could take weeks," Sam said. "There's even a rare chance that I'll never—"

"Let's think positive, hmm?" Angie lifted the bag off the gurney and handed it to him. "Come on, let me help you to that chair." She indicated the one in the corner of the bay. "It'll be easier for you to get yourself dressed over there."

The way she said it was like the issue had been settled. Rationally, Sam understood that it was. He couldn't stay in the hospital forever, particularly since he had no life-threatening ailments or injuries. He also sounded short of other places to go. How could he have advanced this far in life without maintaining one single meaningful friendship? Sam supposed he was lucky to have Angie taking pity on him. He'd just have to get better in a hurry so he wouldn't become a burden to her for too long.

Sam peeked into the hospital bag, finding a neatly folded suit, shirt, and tie inside it. An expensive-looking pair of men's leather shoes was beneath them. "So, I'm Sam Singleton?" he said to Angie, repeating the information Dr. Benson had told him. "Owner of Singleton's Jewelers?"

"That's right," she reinforced. "And I work there with you. Along with George and Pam. Pam's new." Sam hated seeing the glimmer of hope in her eyes because he knew he was going to disappoint her. "Do you remember either of them?"

He tried focusing with all his might, but no familiar faces came to mind.

"Me neither, huh?" she asked a bit sadly. She had an undeniably pretty face. If Sam didn't recall that, chances were slim of him remembering anything.

"I'm sorry. I've tried, but—apart from what I told Dr. Benson—nothing else is coming back to me."

"It will," she said, and Sam wasn't sure whether she was trying to convince him or herself. "Just give it time. After all, it's the holidays." She smiled sweetly, and his heart pinged. The tiny tug on his heartstrings felt strangely familiar. "When miracles happen."

Sam was momentarily lost in her dark brown gaze. "Miracles, right." He found it a miracle that he was here with her and that she was offering to help him. Sam recalled his early Christmases and that feeling of hopeful anticipation that returned each year. With

Santa coming, it seemed like anything was possible. Even the attainment of the greatest wish.

Angie motioned Sam off the gurney, and he inched forward.

"That's it," she urged gently. "Just set your feet on the floor. One at a time."

He did, and the earth didn't move beneath him. *Good. That's progress.* Sam looked up at Angie and smiled, gratitude coursing through him. "You're sure you're an accountant and not a nurse?"

She grinned in return. "My mom's the nurse at my place. You'll meet her soon enough."

"That's so great that you live with your mom."

"It works out for the four of us."

"Four?" Sam questioned.

"There's my mom, Elena, and me...Pepe and Alma, too." She smiled fondly. "Alma is my grandmother. We call her 'Lita' from Abuelita."

"Wow. Four generations in one household. That's fantastic."

Angie took his elbow and led him to the chair.

Sam gingerly took a seat, gripping the hospital bag with his clothes in it. Next, a worrying thought occurred. With all those folks at her place, would she have room to accommodate an extra guest? He peered up at her, once again concerned he was putting her out. "If adding one more person to the mix is too much..."

"Don't be silly. It's all arranged. Besides, they can't wait to meet you." She playfully cocked an eyebrow, and Sam's neck warmed. Angie had a strange affect on him that was at once comforting and confusing. In his lost state, he couldn't help but think that she was like a guardian angel sent to him from above. A very beautiful guardian angel with a smile from heaven and a heart of gold.

She slipped beyond the curtain, giving Sam privacy to change. "I'll be right out here if you need me."

Sam thanked her and began to get dressed. But, when he pulled his trousers from the bag, he saw one of his pant legs was marred with a dark red lacquer and what appeared to be bits of... He lifted the clothing to examine it more closely. Tissue paper?

It was such an odd sight, Sam couldn't help himself from exclaiming out loud. "What in the world happened to these pants?"

Chapter Six

ANGIE LOPEZ LIVED IN A mid-sized apartment complex on the west side of town near the hospital. As Angie drove them there in her SUV, they passed a couple of strip malls. One hosted a brand-name grocery store and a chain pharmacy, along with a pet supply place, and a mom-and-pop type Italian restaurant. The other held a sub shop and a couple of big box stores, the sort that sold huge amounts of stuff in bulk. One of these had a dedicated garden center, which weirdly caught Sam's attention. There were also a couple of industrial-looking eateries with glowing neon signs, which he somehow recognized as fast-food joints. The scenery was oddly out of place, yet familiar. Even the six-screen movie theater seemed like somewhere he had visited before. Although he couldn't recall viewing any specific pictures.

Looming in the background, beyond these small city lights, Sam detected the rugged outline of an abutting mountain range cutting through the snow-dotted darkness. The area appeared rural, yet well equipped enough to meet the demands of daily living. Angie told Sam that his shop was in the historic district downtown, where towering lampposts lined the streets and the charm of yesteryear still bubbled up like the effervescence in a champagne bottle. She had an oddly poetic way of putting things, but Sam enjoyed the way she talked and being in her company.

And yet, in an uncomfortable way, Sam felt beholden to her. He was apparently her boss, so the fact that he'd been released into her care was more than a little awkward. If Sam could think up a better solution, he'd be happy to arrive at one. Apparently the folks at the hospital had studied the equation too and come up with the same answer. Angie Lopez was all Sam had left. His dad was too elderly to care for him, and Sam didn't appear to have any close friends. What kind of guy was he anyway? *One who evidently had no life beyond work,* Sam reflected, answering his own question.

Within a quarter of an hour, they arrived at Angie's place. The three-story cinderblock building was painted pale yellow with black shutters, and the parking lot presented a standard allotment of parking spaces facing her unit.

Angie unlocked her third-floor apartment door, and a stir of commotion rang out beyond it.

"It's them!" That small, childlike voice must belong to Pepe. It was followed by the commanding tones of a middle-aged woman.

"*Cielos,* Pepe! Help pick up those newspapers!"

"*Pero, no.*" This lady sounded older. The grandmother? "*Mis pinturas!*"

"Welcome to my humble abode." Angie grinned and pushed open the door, which led directly to the crowded kitchen. Colorful knickknacks were everywhere, and Christmas-themed potholders and a dishtowel draped from the stove. Refrigerator magnets held child's artwork and some much more sophisticated pieces showcasing birds and butterflies, swamping the front surface of the refrigerator-freezer. The side that faced the door was loaded with drawings and paintings, too. Sam also noticed a recent grade school report card along with a school photo of a boy. The image matched the face of the pintsize kid bounding into the kitchen from the living area, which contained a sofa, a coffee table, two armchairs, a wide-screen television, and a card table set off to one side where somebody had been painting.

"Woo-hoo!" the boy shouted. His dark eyes shone brightly as he peered up at Sam. "I have a roommate!"

"No, Pepecito, I told you." Angie set her tote bag in a kitchen chair. "Sam's not staying in your room. He's sleeping on the couch."

Pepe puckered his lower lip. "But I have room on the bottom bunk."

Sam stooped low so he could greet the child at eye level. "Hello, little buddy. My name's Sam."

"My name's Pepe." The boy grinned from ear to ear. "But you can call me 'little buddy' if you want to."

A nice-looking lady in her fifties walked toward Sam and extended her hand. She was dressed in light green hospital scrubs with ABC blocks on them. "I'm Elena Miller, Sam. It's so nice to meet you."

An elderly woman wearing a colorful scarf and accessories glided their way in an electric wheelchair. She grinned happily at Sam. "*Bienvenidos*. Welcome. My name is Alma Garcia, but everyone calls me 'Lita.'" Next, she cut a sly glance at Angie and rasped softly, "*Es muy guapo, Angelita.*"

Sam must have studied Spanish at some point

because he somehow knew that "guapo" meant handsome. His face steamed at the compliment and then he shook Alma's hand.

She hung onto his an extra minute, her dark eyes sparkling. "I do speak English," she offered in a heavy accent. "Spanish, too. Of course."

"I might know Spanish?" he offered.

"*Fantastico.*" Alma grinned and squeezed Sam's hand, and he instantly lost faith in his linguistic abilities.

"Not sure?"

"It's okay," Angie told him. "Lita's English is excellent. She's been on the mainland for many years."

Pepe grinned up at the adults, observing the scene.

"Is Pepe fluent?" Sam asked Angie, and she shook her head.

"Fluent in understanding, yes. He doesn't like to speak it all that much, though."

Elena nodded in agreement. "Angie was just like him at that age. Kids don't like being different. She wanted to fit in."

"It's true! But then I regretted it." Angie chuckled at the memory. "I wound up having to learn Spanish along with the other kids in middle school."

"I'll bet you got good grades, though." Sam smiled at her, and Angie blushed.

"I did. It's true." She shrugged, glancing around. "Okay. Let me show you the apartment."

They left the others in the kitchen, where Elena had offered to reheat dinner for Angie and Sam. Elena and Alma had eaten earlier with Pepe to keep the young boy on his schedule. Alma stayed in the kitchen to visit with Elena while overseeing Pepe's homework at the kitchen table.

Angie led Sam through the living area and down a long hallway, briefly pushing open the doors to three bedrooms. The one with bunk beds and Batman posters all over the walls belonged to Pepe, and the larger one with twin beds belonged to Lita and Elena. An en suite bedroom across the way held a double bed and a private bath. Sam gleaned that was Angie's room.

"Ma, Lita, and I can use my bathroom," Angie said, "while you and Pepe can share the one in the hall."

Sam nodded as they returned to the living area, noting that things were neat and tidy, but—everywhere he looked—nooks and crannies were packed with stuff. Photo albums crowded the bookcase holding the television... Magazines, a few of them in Spanish, littered the coffee table... Stacks of paperback novels, piled sideways, filled the lower shelves of the end tables on either side of the sofa. Framed family photographs hung on the walls with others in standing frames tucked into spare spots all around. Sam pointed to a faded black-and-white photograph of a wedding couple, which appeared to be decades old. The pair was extremely dashing. The woman was a stunning brunette, and the dark-haired man wore a pencil-thin mustache. "Is that Alma?"

"Yes, with my grandfather, Jose."

"Pepe's the nickname for Jose, isn't it?" Sam asked, curiously recalling this.

"Yeah, it is."

"So you named your son after him?"

"My husband and I both liked the idea of preserving

our heritage." Angie nodded and shared a soft smile, gazing back at the photograph. "My grandfather lived long enough for him and Alma to celebrate their fiftieth wedding anniversary."

"My."

"I know. Pretty remarkable, right? My parents weren't so lucky." She briefly pursed her lips. "Neither was I. My mom and I both lost our husbands young."

"I'm sorry," Sam said, his heart aching for her. The death of a parent was tough. That was a recollection Sam carried in his bones. But the loss of a spouse was something he'd never had to endure. After speaking with David on the phone at the hospital, Angie had assured Sam he'd never been married. He'd apparently not been seeing anyone seriously, either. At least, not as far as David knew. Then again, David and Sam weren't in very close touch.

"It was an accident," Angie said. Her expression registered pain at the memory. "Both my dad and my husband Jack, Pepe's father, were in the car."

Sam's heart sank. "Oh, gosh...Angie." Instinctively, he reached out for her but stopped himself, dropping his hand to his side. "The two of them, together?"

She set her chin, but there was anguish written in her eyes. "It was a drunk driver. They were on their way home from one of Jack's baseball games."

"Your husband played?"

Angie's features softened at the memory. "Minor leagues." Her smile trembled, and for the second time, Sam fought the urge to hold her. He had no clue where this inclination was coming from because he and Angie had never been romantically involved. Then, he realized maybe it wasn't a romantic inclination at all. Perhaps he'd simply been moved toward compassion and caring. Sam wondered if he was innately a compassionate and caring sort of man. From all indications, including the nearly nonexistent contact list on his cell phone, he didn't think so.

"My dad never missed a game," Angie further explained. "I wouldn't have missed it, either. But Pepe was down with an ear infection that night, so we stayed home. Otherwise, we might all have..."

Her voice trailed off and she looked away. "Anyway," she said, much more solidly, turning back toward him. "That was a long time ago."

While Sam had gleaned that Angie was strong, he hadn't known how brave she was. It must have been torment to live through a double loss, and yet she had. He guessed she hadn't told him about her family life when they worked together at the jewelers. They'd more than likely been on cordial professional terms, rather than friendly. The intimacy of Sam being in her home was probably prompting Angie to share more personal details. Then again, it was pretty hard to ignore them with all the photographic evidence around.

Angie gestured toward another snapshot of a dark-haired, dark-eyed, athletic-looking guy in a baseball uniform on the wall. He had his arm around the shoulders of an older man with salt and pepper hair, who Sam took to be Angie's father.

"That's Jack with my father, Edward," she explained. "My dad was a college professor who taught Spanish. Jack's family was Cuban on his dad's side."

"Hence the Lopez," Sam surmised.

"Hence the Lopez," Angie concurred. "Jack and I

were very much alike. We had a lot in..." She stopped herself, seeming to realize she'd wandered off track, revealing more than she'd intended.

"Looks like they were close," Sam commented kindly. "Jack and your dad."

"Yeah. They were." Angie answered on a wistful note, and then she seemed to collect herself, her mood brightening. "Come on, let me show you the linen closet where you'll find some blankets and a pillow. A bath towel, too."

"You mean, I'm expected to bathe?" Sam teased.

She smirked. "Shower, at least."

"Aye-aye, captain!" He gave her a salute. "You run a tight ship."

"Yes, I do, sailor," she said, playing right along. "And I expect you to fall in line."

Sam couldn't resist a grin. Somehow, he didn't mind Angie bossing him around. She was obviously in her element here and glad to be home. They'd come straight from the hospital because Angie had wanted to check in with her family. She'd insisted they needed to eat dinner as well. Afterward, she'd drive Sam back to his place so he could pick up some things for his temporary stay with her. Angie was being very generous with her resources and time, and he genuinely appreciated it. He felt so helpless too, though, like there was something he should do.

"I don't want you to treat me like a guest," Sam said sincerely. "Put me to work. I'm sure I've got some skills buried in here somewhere." He paused in thought, and then said jokingly, "I can probably even swab the deck."

Angie chuckled at his attempt at humor. "I'm sure

you could. But nobody's assigning you duties just yet. For the next couple of days, your number one task is to rest. After you see that specialist and he puts you in the clear for regular activities, we can talk about what comes next."

That sounded so reasonable he decided not to argue with her. Particularly as she'd said it with that very determined look in her eyes. Her eyes were quite enchanting, too. Extremely dark and lovely, and just as warm as her smile. Sam wondered whether he'd ever noticed this before, or whether he'd simply been oblivious to Angie's beauty.

"Will you at least let me do the dishes?" he parried. "K.P.?"

"Not tonight, I won't," she stated firmly. "But another time? We'll see." The way her eyes glimmered looked almost flirty.

"Another time," he said hoarsely. "Sure."

She opened the linen closet and tugged out sheets, two blankets, and a pillow. "I'll just set these in the living room in a chair," she said, her arms loaded.

"Here," Sam said gallantly. "I can take those from you." But when he reached out, he stumbled and had to catch himself on the doorframe to the bathroom.

Angie bit her bottom lip. "You'd probably better sit down. All this moving around has been too much for you."

"But I've scarcely done a thing," he protested, the room still reeling.

"You hit your head pretty hard," she told him. "And here I am, giving you a tour."

Sam inhaled then exhaled slowly, steadying himself

on the doorjamb. “I’ve appreciated it, though,” he said, still catching his breath. “Getting the lay of the land.”

Fear and worry filled her eyes. “Maybe we shouldn’t go to your place tonight? Perhaps sometime tomorrow would be better?”

Sam wanted to stay strong and tough things out. Insist he was fine. But he knew he wasn’t. The last thing Angie needed was for him to pass out on her halfway to his condo. Or even when it was just the two of them there. “Maybe you’re right,” he finally agreed.

Angie shared a practiced grin. “I’m always right.”

“I doubt that.” Sam’s eyebrows arched. “Very seriously.”

“Oh?”

“Nobody’s right one hundred percent of the time.”

She squared her shoulders at the challenge. “My record’s pretty good. You made quite a few improvements to the shop at my suggestion.”

He studied her big dark eyes. “Is that right?”

“Yes. Absolutely.”

“Something tells me you enjoyed telling me what to do.”

“Did *not.*” But even as she said it, the corners of her mouth twitched. “I was merely good at offering recommendations.”

“We never butted heads?”

She hesitated just a fraction of a second too long. “No, not once.”

He captured her in his gaze, wishing again that he could know what their relationship had been like. They seemed to get along well now, which made Sam question whether they’d always been this comfortable with each other. It was hard to know with Sam not recalling how he'd behaved at the jewelry shop. Instinctively, he guessed he must have stayed professional. And yet, there was some kind of undercurrent between him and Angie that didn't precisely feel brand new.

"It's a miracle we managed to work together."

The blankets in her hold seemed to grow weighty. "A miracle. Yeah."

A fine blush swept her cheeks, and Angie looked more beautiful than ever, standing there in that tasteful gray suit, with that run in her tights, while wearing those absurdly high-heeled red shoes. Sam noticed the Santa Claus pin on her lapel, and the jolly old elf seemed to wink at him.

"Thanks for taking me in here," he said with a mixture of embarrassment and indebtedness. "As soon as we see that specialist and can come up with a better solution, I'll be out of your hair."

"Let's take this one step at a time, all right? For the moment, this is where you need to be. Your dad was glad to hear about it, too. He wants to see you." She stalled a second. "When you're up to it?"

"Maybe we can stop by tomorrow when we head out to my place?" Sam released his grasp on the doorframe, gathering his reserves as his pulse thrummed in his ears. She appeared so domestic standing there, clutching his bedding and a pillow. It made Sam wonder why he'd never had a wife. Someone like Angie to care about, and care for. Someone who would take care of him, too. And not because he'd stupidly gotten a concussion and landed in the hospital, but because she wanted to.

"Why don't we see how you're feeling?" She self-consciously licked her lips, and Sam's voice grew husky.

"All right." A small wisp of her hair fell across her cheek, and it took everything he had to resist reaching out to tuck it behind her ear. She smelled so good. Womanly. And not at all like winter. More like lilacs in the spring. Sensation overwhelmed him, and he felt warm all over as her beautiful brown eyes transported him to another place and time.

"Dinner's almost... Oh!"

Sam glanced toward the front of the hall and saw Elena standing there wearing an apron and holding a wooden spoon. It was only then that he realized his extremely close proximity to Angie. How he'd been standing right over her and hovering closer, almost as if angling for a kiss. He hadn't done it intentionally. It had just...happened.

"I'm sorry," Elena said, her cheeks flushed. "I didn't mean to interrupt."

Angie's face turned crimson, and Sam's neck burned hot. He mentally kicked himself extra hard. He was here as a houseguest and physically recovering from head trauma, not at Angie's on a date. Perhaps his head was more jumbled up than he'd understood. The rapid pounding of his heart told him that his emotions had gone all topsy turvy, too.

"It's okay, Ma," Angie said, turning on her heel. "We were just grabbing Sam's linens for later."

"For later," Sam echoed ridiculously, feeling his throat clog.

"Of course." Elena waved her wooden spoon. "I hope you like *arroz con pollo*?" she asked him as he emerged from the hall.

"That's chicken with yellow rice," Angie explained over her shoulder, her cheeks still burning brightly.

"Yes, yes. I know," Sam said, collecting himself. "And thanks! It smells delicious."

Chapter Seven

A SHORT TIME LATER, SAM AND Angie sat alone at the kitchen table. Elena had excused herself to go and get ready for work, and Alma had accompanied Pepe into the living room to watch a bit of television.

As Alma trailed the child in her wheelchair, Angie called after her.

"No *telenovelas* while Pepe's around!"

Alma raised her hand in an understanding wave as she glided away.

"*Telenovelas*?" Sam asked as aromas from the delicious meal wafted toward him. He smelled saffron rice, baked chicken, and olives. Perhaps a hint of smoked paprika, too. His stomach rumbled, and Sam realized how hungry he was. It probably had been a while since he'd eaten.

"Spanish soap operas," Angie said with a grin. "Lita loves them. They're just not suitable for children," she added, dropping her voice into a whisper.

"Ahh," Sam replied with a chuckle. He scanned his full plate heaping with yellow rice, green olives, and chicken. Small strips of cut pimento added color to the dish that was as pretty as it promised to be delicious. "This looks amazing." He reached for his fork, feeling ravenous, but Angie stopped him, taking his hand.

He met her gaze, confused, and she smiled softly and said, "If you don't mind...a little blessing?"

"A blessing? Sure." Something tugged at the back of Sam's mind, an odd familiarity about saying prayers before eating. Then, he recalled his pretty dark-haired mother saying grace around their family table, and his heart caught in his throat. She'd been a good woman, his mom. Tender. Caring. That much he recalled. It was hard to believe she was really gone.

Angie bowed her head and squeezed Sam's hand. "May the Lord make us truly grateful for what we're about to receive."

She squeezed his hand again, and they both said, "Amen."

"My parents used to say a blessing," Sam offered when Angie opened her eyes. "Back when I was little."

"Did you all go to church?"

Sam squinted in thought. "I think so." Then the image of a tall-steeple church arose in his mind. "Yes. I'm pretty sure of it."

"Do you attend services now?" Angie blushed. "Oops, sorry."

"That's okay," he said good-humoredly. "Sometimes I forget that I can't remember, too." They both chuckled at this. "How about you and your family? Is church a regular thing?"

"We go to Hopedale Presbyterian on the east side of town."

"Presbyterian? I would have thought—"

"Catholic?" she guessed correctly. "No. My dad was Anglo—and *very* Presbyterian. My mom said she didn't care where we went to church as long as we attended somewhere, and so I was raised protestant."

Angie motioned for Sam to begin eating, and he gratefully lifted his fork, taking a bite of the fantastic food. "Wow, this is good."

"You're probably just hungry."

"I am," he agreed. "But, still, this is amazing. I'll have to pay my compliments to the chef."

Angie shyly ducked her chin. "Thank you."

"Wait a minute. You made this? I thought it was your mom?"

"I made it this morning—early. Before getting Pepe ready for school."

"What time do you get up?"

"Normally?" She thought on this. "Around five."

"Whoa," Sam said, impressed.

"Elena's pretty exhausted when she gets home. I try to leave something cooking in the crockpot or have a meal waiting, something that can be reheated easily. By the time I get home, I'm often too tired too cook."

He studied her a beat, his admiration for this remarkable woman growing. Angie carried so much on her shoulders, and yet she didn't complain.

"I don't mind it, really," she said, taking a bite of her dinner. "I like being organized, and it helps free up more of my evening for spending time with Pepe."

Elena appeared dressed in her coat and hat, walking briefly through the kitchen on her way out the door. "I'll see you both in the morning," she said in cheerful tones, and Sam noted that was the pervasive mood around here. Happiness seemed to fill the small space and creep into the apartment's every corner. He heard

Alma and Pepe laughing merrily in the next room, the musical sound accentuating the homey atmosphere.

"Does your mom always work nights?" Sam asked once Elena had gone.

"Yes, at the local hospital." Angie smiled. "She's a labor and delivery nurse."

"That sounds exciting."

"She loves her job."

"Do you have any brothers or sisters?" he asked, continuing to clean his plate. He'd never tasted anything this good, he was sure of it. The flavorful rice had a bit of stickiness to it, and the chicken thighs and legs were extra tender and tasty, the meat virtually falling off the bones. When combined with the Spanish olives and smoky paprika, the meal created a party of delicious Caribbean flavors in his mouth.

"I'm the only one." She smiled prettily. "My mom and dad used to joke that one perfect angel was all they needed."

"Angie from Angela?"

"*Ahn-hel-la,*" she said, pronouncing it with a Spanish lilt. "When I was little, they used to call me, Angelita, or little angel."

"Angelita." Sam grinned, recalling how he'd likened her to an angel in the hospital. "I like that."

"Well, I *didn't,*" Angie said, but she was chuckling. "Like we talked about earlier, kids don't like being different, especially in school. It wasn't like things are today, where Pepe has tons of Hispanic kids in his class. Back then, I stuck out like a sore thumb as being the only one with a 'foreign' mother." She took a sip of her ice water before finishing. "Since my parents filled out my enrollment paperwork, I was 'Angelita' all the way through high school. I couldn't wait to get to college and Anglicize my name." She shrugged sheepishly at the admission. "I told everyone I was Angie then, and so...here I am today!"

"Here you are." Sam drank her in like a thirsty desert accepting warm rain. Angie was so remarkable and interesting.

She blushed under his perusal and reached for his empty plate. "Can I get you some more?"

"Oh, no. Thank you, but no," Sam answered, feeling delightfully full and happy. It somehow seemed a very long time since anyone had cooked for him. This made Sam wonder if he was any good at cooking for himself, or if he was one of those stereotypical bachelors who always ordered takeout. "Thank you for the dinner, though," he told her. "It was truly delicious."

"You're welcome." She stood and began clearing the table, and Sam scooted back his chair. "Oh, no, you don't," she told him. "You stay right there."

"But I can't just watch you work."

"Then, don't." She glanced into the living room. "Pepe!" she called loudly. "Teeth-brushing time!"

"But Mo-om," came his whiny reply.

"I mean it," Angie responded. She peered toward the sofa where Pepe sat beside Alma in her wheelchair and spoke authoritatively. "You've gotten to stay up past your bedtime already."

Pepe reluctantly dragged himself off the sofa and headed to his bedroom to change into pajamas. The moment he'd gone, Sam saw Alma cagily lift the remote from a sofa cushion and flip to a different station where a couple embraced amorously on the screen while kissing below a full moon at the seaside.

Angie met Sam's gaze and lowered her eyebrows. "*Telenovelas.*"

Sam chortled. "I see."

"After Pepe's in bed, maybe you'll want to freshen up?" She studied Sam's long, lean frame and his rumpled suit. "I'm not sure I have anything to fit you."

"That's okay," he answered. "I'll be all right in this until tomorrow when we stop by my place. In the meantime," Sam said, trying to rub the soreness out of the back of his neck, "a hot shower sounds good." His bones ached all over and his head pounded mercilessly.

Angie shared a worried frown. "We should probably give you some more acetaminophen, and I can prepare an ice pack for you while you're cleaning up."

"Thanks, Angie," he said, grateful she was being so kind to him. "I'd appreciate that."

Angie tucked Pepe into bed and lightly kissed his forehead. "Goodnight, sweetheart. Sleep well."

"Do you think we'll have school tomorrow?"

"I'm not sure." Angie's gaze darted toward the snowy window. "But probably not."

"Woo!" Pepe's eyes rounded. "Can I play in the snow with Sam?"

"I'm not so sure Sam will be up to playing outdoors." Angie smiled and thumbed Pepe's nose. "But maybe you and I can build a snowman?"

"You don't have to work?" Pepe asked, sounding hopeful.

"I will in the morning, but I'm taking the afternoon off." She heard the shower in the hall bath turn on through the thin walls of the apartment. "I have a few things to take care of regarding Sam. But afterward? There'll be plenty of time for playing outdoors, *and* for making hot cocoa."

Pepe excitedly gripped the covers, pulling them up to his chin. "When can Bobby come over?"

Bobby, gosh. In the flurry of today's activities, Angie had forgotten all about the promise she'd made Pepe this morning. "Maybe later in the week? Once things get more settled around here?"

"More settled for Sam?"

Angie nodded. "That's right."

"Mom?"

"Yes, Pepe?"

"Why doesn't Sam know who he is?"

"He knows, Pepe. He just can't remember a lot of things."

"But why?"

"He fell and hit his head pretty hard."

"That's why he's here? So you can take care of him?"

"Yes."

Pepe's dark eyes welled with affection. "You're a good mom."

"Thanks, Pepe." Angie's heart warmed and she hugged her son. "You're a great son."

When Angie pulled back, Pepe asked her, "When will Sam get better?"

"Soon, I hope!" Angie tousled Pepe's short dark hair. "Now get some rest, all right?"

Angie quietly shut Pepe's door, leaving it open just a smidgen. Then she went into the living room and got to work making up the sofa bed for Sam. In one way, it seemed odd to think that Sam was spending the night at her place. But then, in another, this was obviously the most logical choice. Besides, it wasn't like Angie was putting up the old Sam. This new Sam was different: more interested in learning things, including about her. Angie's cheeks warmed when she recalled the way he'd looked at her at dinner and how she'd become so caught up in his gaze while standing in the hall. But those were ridiculous thoughts to have. Sam wasn't intrigued by her romantically; he was simply curious to fill in the blanks regarding his missing history. Why then had he kept bringing the conversation back around to her?

The Sam Singleton she knew didn't ask her intimate questions, or pry into her personal life. He mostly talked about business because business was what he knew. Even when he had asked for her input on marriage proposals for his television commercials, he'd done so in a removed and tactical way. Sam claimed he wasn't the romantic sort, and Angie easily believed that. It was hard to imagine him bringing a woman flowers or pulling her into his arms... Angie's face heated when she realized she'd done just that. When she'd been gathering his linens earlier, there'd been this telling moment between them, and she had this barely perceptible longing for his embrace. But that was crazy! Unthinkable. Angie considered briefly that she was acting like the one who'd bumped her head, not Sam.

The door to the hall bathroom opened and a narrow column of steam emerged from behind it, seconds before Sam appeared wearing his untucked dress shirt and marred work slacks. His dark hair was damp and a smattering of beard stubble dappled his manly face. He stroked his cheek and chuckled.

"I suppose I'll need to pick up a razor from my place."

"How was your shower? Good?"

"Great." he sighed, and then he padded across the carpet barefoot. "Here, let me help with that," he said, tugging at the other end of the blanket as Angie stretched it across the foot of the mattress. "I can't stop thinking that I'm putting you out," he said, raising his eyes to hers.

"Now, stop." She tossed him a pillow, and he caught it. "We've been through this, all right?" She smiled softly. "The moment your memory comes back, you'll be free to go."

"You should never have said that."

"Why not?"

"How do you know I won't keep pretending?"

"Sam!" Angie gaped at him. "You wouldn't dare."

"I'm just sayin'..." He shrugged in a teasing manner, still gripping his pillow. "The food's pretty good, and the accommodations are cozy..."

Angie picked up the second pillow she'd grabbed from the closet and lobbed it at him. Sam caught it just in time.

"It's good to see you haven't lost your sense of humor," she said, holding his gaze.

"So, I was a pretty witty guy?"

"You were..." Angie hesitated. "Clever, in a certain way."

"Clever?" Sam frowned, apparently not liking the sound of this. "Hmm."

"Yeah," Angie answered emphatically. "You were a master at promotion, offering *the single best deal in town*."

"That's catchy."

"You wrote it."

Sam stewed on this a moment before asking, "Angie?"

"Huh?" He smiled, and her heart thumped.

"Thanks. I mean, for this...the hospital. Everything."

He observed her in a way that made Angie wish she knew what he was thinking. Was he wondering about how their past relationship had been? Questioning whether they'd ever been attracted to each other? He'd clearly never shown a romantic interest, and she'd never aspired to becoming intimately involved with him. It was just like she'd told her mom. There was nothing personal between them, even if they had shared that uncharacteristic moment when he had made her head spin and her heart pound.

Angie turned away when her face warmed. "Let me just go and grab that ice pack," she said, hurrying toward the kitchen. "Then we should both probably get some rest."

Chapter Eight

SAM OPENED HIS EYES TO bright light pouring in through a window. And, *yikes!* Something was sitting on the end of his bed. It was a little boy in Batman pajamas.

"Well, hey there, little buddy," Sam said in groggy tones.

Pepe shot him a toothy smile. "You're a sleepy head."

Sam sat up part way, propping himself on his elbows. *I'm in Angie's apartment, that's right. With Pepe and...* He turned his gaze toward the window and tugged the covers up to his chest. *Alma.*

The older woman gave him a cheery grin from where she sat sketching at the card table by the window. The sun blazed brightly outside, bouncing off fresh-fallen snow.

"*Buenos días.*"

"*Buenos días.*" Sam deferentially ducked his chin, wondering how long he'd had company in the living room. He shot a look toward the kitchen but didn't spot anybody there. Plus, the kitchen lights were turned off. Although, he did smell coffee.

"Is your mom around?" Sam asked Pepe.

"Nope!"

"And your grandma?"

Pepe staged a yawn. "Sleeping."

Alma said something to Pepe in rapid Spanish, then Pepe addressed Sam.

"She said, Mom's gone to work, but she'll be back at lunchtime."

"Lunchtime," Sam said uncertainly. "I see."

Alma twinkled in Sam's direction. "*Un cafelito*?"

Café? "Uh...coffee! Coffee. Right." Sam sat up more fully, checking to make sure his shirt was buttoned. "Sounds good. *Por favor.*"

Alma smiled at Sam's feeble attempt at Spanish while Pepe tilted his head. "How do you know Spanish?"

"Well, I don't...don't really. Just a little."

Alma nodded encouragingly. "*Un poco.*"

"*Muy poco,*" Sam said with a chuckle. "*Sí.*"

Pepe scooted closer to Sam on the bed. "Did your mommy teach you?" he asked with big, innocent eyes.

"No, no. I don't think so." Sam worked hard to bring an earlier memory up to the surface. "We had a teacher in elementary school. Someone who came around once a week, I think. She'd scribbled with crayons onto paper plates, then held each one up so we could learn our colors."

Pepe jumped up and down on the mattress, his knees tucked beneath him. He yanked at his Batman pajama top, pinching up some of the fabric. "What's this?"

Sam focused in concentration. "*Azul*?"

Pepe bounced excitedly and pointed to the dark bat design covering his chest. "And this?"

"*Negro.*"

"What about—"

"Pepecito!" Alma called, capturing the boy's attention. "Enough," she said gently and in English. She set down her pencil and gestured toward the kitchen. "The coffee's by the stove," she said to Sam. "Cream in the refrigerator." Then she glanced at little Pepe and urged him to go along and help Sam in the kitchen.

When Angie returned home just after noontime, she couldn't believe the domestic ambience. The sofa bed had been folded and put back away, and Lita's card table had been moved into the center of the room in place of the coffee table. Sam, Lita, and Pepe were all seated around it playing Parcheesi.

Sam heard Angie shut the door and he looked up, pleasantly surprised. "You're back."

Angie set her tote bag in a kitchen chair, surveying the scene. "I was about to ask what you all have been up to, but I can see."

"Parcheesi is Sam's favorite game," Pepe informed his mom.

"Yes, but Lita's killing us at it." Sam shared a good natured-grin, and Angie had to blink to believe her vision was real and not some kind of illusion. When she'd worked with Sam at Singleton's Jewelers, she never could have imagined him juxtaposed in her crazy-busy life. Just like she couldn't have fathomed her being any part of his seemingly cold and impersonal world. And yet, here he was. And, strangely, even in yesterday's work clothes and sporting that beard stubble that had grown even more pronounced this morning, Sam didn't look out of place. "How were things at the jewelers?" he asked as Angie entered the living room.

"I explained to George and Pam about what's going on," she said. "They said they hope you're feeling better and that they're happy to hold down the fort."

"I'd like to see them," Sam said. "And the shop."

"We can go in tomorrow after you see Dr. Sullivan." Angie's smile brightened. "I got you an appointment at nine o'clock."

"Thanks for doing that," Sam said, clearly touched. "Hopefully, he can fix whatever's wrong with my noggin."

"I'm hopeful he'll have good news, too. Or that he'll at least give us some tips on how to better handle things." She studied Sam a beat and then asked kindly. "No more progress with the memory today?"

"Sam had a Spanish teacher," Pepe piped in.

"Oh yeah?" Angie eyed Sam.

"In early elementary school," he said. "I'm still tapping into some of those childhood memories. But nothing from beyond the second or third grade."

Angie frowned sympathetically. "Well, at least you've got something. And that's something to work with. When we visit your dad this afternoon, perhaps he can help supply more missing information."

"He's still in the same house? The house where I grew up?"

"Yeah."

"Well then, maybe seeing that will help, too."

"We also might find some clues at your condo," Angie said.

"Along with some more comfortable clothes," Sam joked.

"I'm sure you've got jeans and sweaters somewhere," Angie agreed.

Then, she glanced cheerily around the room. "But first, who wants lunch?"

A short time later, Sam slid his key into the door lock on his upscale top-floor condo. He was filled with trepidation—he couldn't help it. He was walking into a home he wouldn't even likely recognize as his. What if he'd left things a wreck with dirty socks strewn about and damp towels lying on the floor? Angie's place was cramped, but neatly picked up. Would she think less of him if she discovered he was a slob? Sam slid open the deadbolt then cracked the door open a smidgen.

"Um, maybe I should go in first and look around?"

Angie started to question him, but then apparently she got it. "Oh! Oh, sure. I'll just wait right here in the hallway." The condo corridor was pretty grand, so Sam didn't feel bad about leaving Angie standing in it for a brief minute. Gorgeous teak root tables with smooth glass tops held art deco vases of fresh-cut flowers. Floor-to-ceiling windows let a flood of light in from the clear blue sky hanging over the parking lot. The sun had come out this morning, but the temperature was still too low to allow for any melting snow. And more of the white stuff was predicted for later.

Sam pressed the door ajar slightly and stepped through it, heat warming his neck. He had no clue what he'd find, and the answer pretty much surprised him. *Whoa.* This was the most tricked-out bachelor pad Sam could have imagined. A sleek black leather sofa with matching armchairs sat before a gas log-burning hearth that had an expensive-looking black-and-cream-colored marble surround with an intricate earthy pattern. Polished oak floors gleamed beneath strategically arranged rugs boasting monochrome geometric patterns. The low coffee table had a chrome base and a glass top, mimicking the design of the much larger glass-topped dining room table that had high-backed black leather chairs and seating for six. He wondered if he'd purchased the dining set with ambitions of entertaining, but he had no memories of mirthful gatherings in this room.

Sam glanced toward the kitchen, which was divided from the living area by a island flanked by high bar stools and could serve as either a food preparation spot or an additional eating area. The entire place was awash with light and stainless-steel appliances gleamed in the compact yet efficient kitchen that included a handy wine rack and an impressive farm sink with brushed-chrome fixtures. The ample cabinets were painted a creamy color, and a white subway tile pattern formed the backsplash above stunning marble countertops, which picked up the black-and-white tones of the fireplace surround but also contained interesting splotches of earthy browns, rusts, and reds.

The rear wall of the room was essentially a huge glass window overlooking a forest, where the wavering pines were covered with snow. Beyond those, he spied the hazy purple-and-blue outline of the abutting Blue Ridge Mountains. This was truly a fabulous place.

But where was the television? Sam found it hard to believe he didn't have one. Then, his gaze snagged on the large cream-colored console to the far side of the living area, which looked like it had been fashioned out of reclaimed wood. He carefully approached it and swung its doors open. *Aha!* A satisfactorily large wide-screen television sat inside, along with controls to what looked like a Bluetooth enabled sound system, which also had its own remote. Surveying the ceiling and upper portions of the walls, which housed track lighting, Sam saw that a cache of high-end speakers had been strategically installed.

"Sam?" That was Angie, calling from the hall. "Everything okay in there?"

"Yeah! Hang on one sec." He took a quick peek through the bedroom door, finding a king-size bed with matching end tables and stylized lamps. A chrome-and-glass writing desk with a swivel leather chair was aligned along the back window. Sam noted a remote on it, guessing that was for opening and drawing the curtains at night. He was incredibly impressed by the design of the place, even if it did seem a little cold. There wasn't much artwork to speak of, only some framed prints that looked like they'd come from art museums and a couple of accent mirrors. There were no photographs anywhere.

"I'm sorry, Angie," he said, returning to the front door. "You can come on in." During his quick perusal of the place, Sam had also found a half bath by a laundry area on the far side of the kitchen and a lavishly appointed master bathroom adjoining his bedroom. There were also a couple of doors to what he assumed to be closets, but he didn't want to leave Angie standing outside his condo forever.

She stepped into the condo unwrapping her winter scarf. "Wow," she said, glancing around.

"I know." he chuckled in amazement. "I even impressed myself."

Angie walked toward the back of the room taking in the view. "This is stunning, Sam. This whole place looks like something out of a catalogue. Square footage wise, you probably have as much room here as we do at my apartment."

When she put it like that, he found the assessment a little embarrassing. These were awfully large living quarters for only one person.

She strode to the island dividing the kitchen and living area, and ran her hand along its smooth marble top. "This kitchen is amazing. Did you do much cooking here?"

When Sam gave her a vacant look, apology filled her eyes. "Oh, sorry... I... It's just that sometimes I forget. You know?" She walked into the kitchen and slid open a drawer. Then, she shut it and opened another one.

Sam observed her with interest. "What are you doing?"

"Searching for clues." She looked up and grinned. "I think I found some!"

Sam walked over to where Angie stood as she withdrew a fistful of takeout menus from the drawer.

He grimaced at the evidence. "I guess I wasn't much of a cook."

"That's okay," she said, laughing. "We all have our strengths."

"Yeah?" He leaned back against a counter and folded his arms. "What are mine?"

"Well," she said, thumbing through his takeout selections. "It looks like you order from pretty good restaurants, for one. Hey, the Panda Palace!" she said, holding up a dark red menu. "I love that place."

He chuckled in reply. "I'm guessing I must, too."

She pulled open another drawer that contained silverware and a whole bunch of prepackaged chopsticks. "I'm thinking that's a yes," she said, smiling at him.

"I wish I remembered eating Chinese food, but I don't," he said. "I don't recall eating anywhere but at home as a kid. And even those memories are sketchy."

"Yeah, but at least they're there."

"Yeah."

Angie continued her examination of his condo as Sam watched her peek into cabinets, and even in the refrigerator. "You definitely didn't do a lot of eating in," she told him. "There's almost nothing in your refrigerator."

They both still wore their coats, and it was getting toasty in here. Angie apparently noticed that too because she unbuttoned her coat before striding toward the laundry area.

"Where are you going?" he asked.

"To see what's back here... Oh-ho!" Her voice rang out from around the corner, and he followed after her. "A home gym," she proclaimed, pressing open a door.

Sam saw it was a pretty great one, too. There was an elliptical machine, a treadmill, and a stationary recumbent bike. A set of free weights and a pressing bench were positioned off to one side. A smaller flat-screen television had been mounted on the wall opposite the door.

"Gosh, Sam. You could charge a membership fee."

"Ha-ha."

"Seriously, though. What a place!" She peered into his eyes for a prolonged moment. "Maybe you should exercise?"

"What?" he asked, taken aback.

"It might help you rememb—" She stopped herself just as quickly as she'd begun. "You're right. It was a bad idea. At least until we get the doctor's okay." She twisted her lips in thought. "Maybe if you just sat on the bike?"

"Angie..."

"Come on."

"Seriously?"

"Yes. Dr. Mullens at the hospital said something about you getting back into your routine as soon as possible. You don't have to pedal, just—hop on!"

Sam stared at her, flummoxed, but she held his gaze in that determined fashion.

"Humor me."

"Okay! All right." He threw up his hands then unbuttoned his coat as well. But he was still warm, so he decided to remove it altogether, handing it to Angie. She waited patiently as he got on the bike, watching him like a hawk.

"Well?" she said after a beat.

But Sam got nothing, except... *Argh, that hurt.*

"Sam?" Angie asked worriedly, noting his contorted features. "What's wrong?"

"When I was six," Sam said hoarsely, "and learning

to ride a bike. You know the first time without training wheels…"

"You remember that?"

"It was a pretty messy memory," Sam said with a frown. He tapped his two upper front teeth. "These are capped."

"Oh no." Angie appeared immediately sorry she'd forced this upon him. "Okay," she said, grabbing him by the elbow. "Let's get off the bike."

When Sam complied and took back his coat, Angie said regretfully, "That was a really bad idea."

"No, it was a good one. It could have worked, hey."

"What we need is a breakthrough. Something that gets you past those childhood years."

"Maybe going back to work will help?"

"Yeah, and also seeing your father. Let's go and pack up some of your things so we can head over there."

Angie couldn't believe Sam had, not one, but two walk-in closets, and both were chock full of clothing. There were also two large tie racks on the wall and built-in drawers for folded and personal items, like socks and underwear. She guessed he had enough merchandise to front a small men's store.

"Who knew you were such a clotheshorse?" she said, staring at him wide-eyed.

The tips of Sam's ears tinged red as he surveyed the rows upon rows of hanging suit coats, slacks, shirts and sweaters. "It does seem a bit excessive."

"You can probably get by with a couple of fresh

suits for the jewelers," she told him. "We can come back and grab more of your things, once we've heard what Dr. Sullivan has to say." She hunted around on the high shelves until she found a carry-on suitcase. She lifted it out of the closet, setting it on Sam's bed. "In the meantime, you'll probably mostly need a pair of jeans, a few shirts, and a casual sweater or two. Maybe also a sweatshirt... Something like that."

"Jeans, right." Sam's eyes scanned the contents of one closet, and then the next. Afterward, he started pulling open drawers. "That's strange."

"What is?"

"I wonder if I sent them out to the cleaners."

"Blue jeans?" Angie puzzled over how a guy could have dozens of professional outfits, yet nothing to relax in. "You're kidding?"

He looked at her so helplessly Angie's heart ached for him. "Look," she uttered with confidence. "I'm sure we'll find some around here somewhere." But, twenty minutes later, when the most informal pants they could locate were a pair of chinos, they decided to give up.

"At least we found some sweatpants and a sweatshirt," Angie said brightly. "And we've got your snow boots and parka, in case you decide to go out in the snow."

"I'm definitely going out in the snow," Sam said. "I already promised Pepe."

"What? When?"

"This morning. When you were gone. He and I are going to build a snow fort."

"Oh, now, Sam... I don't think that's such a good idea. Not until after you've seen Dr. Sullivan."

"Says the lady who just told me to exercise."

"I said to mimic exercising. Sit on the bike. That was clearly part of your regular routine." Angie squared her shoulders. "Building snow forts was not."

Sam's eyebrow arched. "How do you know?"

Angie huffed a little breath at his good-natured teasing. "As soon as you get Dr. Sullivan's okay, I'll be fine with you playing in the snow with Pepe." Then she softened, meeting Sam's eyes. "And, thank you."

"You don't have to thank me. It was Pepe's idea."

Angie laughed heartily at this. "Thought so!" She pressed on Sam's overstuffed suitcase, attempting to shut it.

"Here, let me..." Sam leaned toward her and reached for the zipper.

She glanced up and their noses nearly collided as the side of Sam's hand brushed hers. Angie's heart hammered as she stared into his deep blue eyes, the warmth of his skin seeping into hers. He really was a great-looking man, and so much kinder than she'd understood. His offer to build a snow fort with Pepe had been truly generous and sweet. Even if Pepe had been the one to suggest it, Sam didn't have to go along with the little boy's whim. "I...er..."

"Angie, I think...I've—" Sam set his lips in a firm line and gave an expert tug. "Got it!" Then—*zzzip.* He closed the suitcase, exhaling sharply. "Whew! That was close."

Angie swallowed past the lump in her throat. "Yeah," she said, feeling a little lightheaded. What had she imagined? That Sam was going to say something personal? About the two of them, or maybe her?

He searched her eyes. "Are you all right?"

"Yeah, yeah. Just fine." Angie turned away to hide her blush. She nabbed his hanging bag off the doorframe and bundled his parka in her other arm.

"You're sure?" Doubt resonated in his voice, and she wondered if he'd felt that hint of electricity between them, or whether it had all been in her mind.

"Um-hmm!" she answered, smiling brightly.

"Well, good." Sam grinned in return and picked up his suitcase. "Let me just grab my laptop, and I'll be ready to go."

Chapter Nine

ANGIE PARKED HER SUV IN the short driveway of the cute stucco bungalow on a tree-lined street. It was a nice neighborhood comprised of a mixed style of houses and sidewalks, which—at the moment—were covered in snow. She turned toward Sam in the passenger seat, guessing his emotions were in a whirl. It had to be unsettling seeing the home you grew up in and having huge gaps in your memory. "How are you feeling?"

He peered through the windshield at the small covered stoop and the snow-dusted flagstone path leading up to it from the drive. "It's a lot smaller than I remember."

"That's typical," she told him gently. "Your perspective has changed. When you were a boy, naturally a lot of things seemed larger."

"Yeah." Sam set his chin, appearing to ponder something. "It's weird that I remember my mom here."

"I'm sorry, Sam."

"No, no." He smiled softly. "It's good." Sam unhitched his seatbelt, viewing the house again from top to bottom, and then from side to side. It almost looked like he was hoping it would speak to him and bring back more recollections.

Angie shut off the ignition. "Still nothing beyond your eighth birthday?"

"I don't even remember a whole lot of things before that," Sam admitted. "They're patchwork memories, like different pieces of a quilt, but they don't neatly fit together." He shared a melancholy smile. "I do remember Duke, though."

"Duke?"

"Our little beagle. He was the best bud a boy could have."

"Pepe wants a dog, but we can't have them in our apartment." She rested her gloves on the steering wheel and spoke wistfully. "Maybe someday."

"Someday."

She turned to find Sam studying her.

"He's an awfully good kid, that Pepe of yours."

"I know, thanks."

"Lita and your mom are pretty awesome, too."

Angie pursed her lips. "Why do I get the idea that you're stalling?"

Sam thumbed his chest. "Me?"

"Yes, you," she said, chuckling and giving him a playful push on his arm.

Sam surprised her by reaching out and taking her hand, pinning it in place against his coat sleeve. "What if it's bad?" He tried to disguise it, but there was a slight tremor in his voice. "This thing between me and my dad?"

"Sam—"

"You told me yourself that I rarely see him," he went on, his voice husky.

Angie reassuringly squeezed Sam's glove. "The important thing is that you're seeing him now, all right?"

"But—"

"Sam." When he met her eyes, she continued. "It's okay to feel anxious."

"I'm not anxious," he said, but his raspy tone gave him away. "I'm just...uncertain. Not sure about what I'm going to feel when I see him."

"Well, I know what David's going to feel when he sees you."

"Oh?"

"Love, Sam. A parent's unconditional love."

"For a prodigal son," he said bitterly.

"You don't know that."

"I do know I must have messed something up." Slowly he released his gentle hold on her. "Lots of things maybe."

"Well, even if you did," Angie said, "I don't think that's what you should focus on today."

"No? What should I focus on?"

"Saying hello to your father. David's missed you, Sam. And he was worried sick about you. Incredibly worried. While you were in the ER, he phoned the hospital six times."

Sam frowned at this news. "I'm sorry I put him through that."

"He'll feel better once he sees you." Her eyebrows arched when Sam laid his hand on the door handle. "You ready to go?"

"Sure," he said, swallowing hard.

When David answered the door, Sam didn't recognize the older fellow with cropped gray hair at first. It took a moment to square his recollection of a younger, more robust dark-haired man with the figure before him, who was much thinner and hunched forward, steadying himself on a cane. Although, David's heavy-rimmed glasses were identical to the pair Sam remembered. "Dad?"

David stepped forward and pulled Sam into a hug right there on the stoop in the blistering cold. "Sammy," he said, his voice cracking. He tightly hugged his son's shoulders. "Welcome home."

Sam returned the hug, feeling awkward about it. He couldn't say how long it had been since he and his dad had embraced, but he gathered that it had been a while. David released Sam and glanced at Angie.

"Ms. Lopez," he said, clearly recognizing her from a previous introduction. "It's nice to see you again."

She smiled and shook David's hand. "Please, call me Angie."

"You were so good to keep me informed from the hospital," he told her. "Thank you."

A cold gust of wind blasted snowdrifts up onto the stoop, and David flushed with embarrassment. "Just look at me keeping you two out in the cold! Please, come in."

He stepped back and made way for them to enter the small, cramped space. Sam's first impression of the house was that it was dusty and probably hadn't gotten a decent cleaning in years. It was cram-packed with furniture and potted plants were everywhere. The small dining room to the right of the foyer contained a table with four chairs, a coordinating china cabinet, and a sideboard holding assorted ferns and cactuses.

The living room to the left housed a worn plaid sofa with one matching armchair and an old leather recliner by a lamp beside the window, where a large hibiscus stood. More potted plants sat on low shelves by the other windows facing the front yard. Additional planters stood on the floor, and Sam didn't have to visit the kitchen to guess there'd be at least one aloe plant perched on a countertop.

The TV on an antiquated stand was the old tube kind, and low bookshelves were packed with fraying paperbacks that looked like they hadn't been touched in years. While there was no coffee table to speak of, there were end tables on either side of the sofa holding brown ceramic lamps with yellowed shades. And a huge, glass-fronted curio cabinet near a rear hallway held three full shelves of trophies and ribbons.

Something tugged at the back of Sam's mind and he had an image of his pretty blue-eyed mother gripping his shoulders with an encouraging grin. "Swim fast, Sammy!" she said, her curly brown hair falling in ringlets to her shoulders as dimples settled in her cheeks. "Swim fast!"

Heat warmed Sam's eyes, and Angie whispered softly. "Hey, are you all right?"

He pulled himself into the present, seeing David hobbling through the dining room toward the kitchen after offering to make some coffee. "Sorry."

Angie's gaze tracked to the curio cabinet. "What's

all this?" she asked, walking over to it to examine its contents more closely. "Awards?"

"For swimming," Sam said, still in a foggy state. "Yeah."

"Sam was a champion swimmer," David said, returning to the living room. He'd apparently had the coffee prepared and ready to go and only had to switch it on. "Top notch in his league." The old man's eyes twinkled with pride as he addressed Angie. "He won a full scholarship to Ashton Academy his last four years."

Sam felt like someone had socked him in the gut, and he doubled over. Somehow, Ashton Academy had a bad ring to it. Yet, by the way his dad spoke of it, it sounded like a respected institution. If only Sam could remember *something* more. About that school. About everything. Being at the mercy of these capricious memories made him feel futile. Incompetent. Out of control.

Angie worriedly took his arm. "Sam?"

"I'm okay. I just, um..." He glanced apologetically at her and then his dad. "Think I'd better sit."

"Of course, please." David attempted to amble over to help him, but Sam held up his hand. "Make yourself at—" David called himself up short, laughing at the absurdity of the comment. "I was about to say—"

"Yeah." Sam grinned gratefully. "I get it. Thanks."

Sam sat on the sofa and Angie sat beside him, while David gingerly settled himself in the recliner. David was clearly suffering physically, Sam guessed from arthritis.

"You say Sam went to Ashton Academy?" Angie asked David. "Was that a boarding school?"

David nodded. "Private boys' school and the best in the state. Sammy got a fine education there, didn't you—" David stopped short, his forehead furrowing. "I'm sorry, son. Ms. Lo—" He glanced Angie's way. "I mean, Angie says you don't remember?"

"Not a lot of things, I'm afraid." Sam exhaled sharply. "I don't remember Ashton Academy. That's for sure."

"And after that?" David asked, his tone wrought with concern.

Sam shook his head. "Nothing until waking up in the hospital."

"Not even your shop?"

"Not even that," Sam said glumly.

"Gee, son." David sat back in his chair with a distressed look. "That's a shame." Next, he spoke to Angie. "Singleton's Jewelers is Sam's pride and joy. He built that business from the ground up. People said he couldn't do it, that there was no call for that kind of high-end store in our town, but Sammy proved them all wrong." He pensively studied the ceiling then added, "That new ski resort going in also helped."

"Hopedale Valley Springs," Angie supplied.

"Yes," David nodded in agreement. "That's the one. Paxton Jeffries started it. Paxton's a big land developer around here."

"I know Mr. Jeffries," Angie responded pleasantly. "He comes into the shop once in a while."

"Bet he could buy your entire inventory," David said with a knowing chuckle.

Angie grinned in reply. "Probably so."

David eyed her kindly. "What do you do there, dear?"

"I'm Sam's accountant."

"Have you worked there long?"

"Just since September."

David returned his attention to Sam. "How are you feeling, Sammy? Any better?"

"Yes, thanks. Sitting helped."

David glanced around the room. "Then how about coffee?"

"Let me come to help you," Angie said, getting to her feet.

When they were alone in the kitchen, David whispered to Angie. "What did the doctors say about his recovery?"

"They're hopeful his memories will come back. They just don't know when."

"Poor Sammy." David pursed his lips and poured the coffee. "I hate seeing him like this."

"Do you think after coffee you can show us around? Maybe if Sam sees his old room that will trigger something?"

"Of course," David agreed, pulling creamer from the refrigerator. "Everything's just as he left it. I haven't changed a thing."

"Mr. Singleton—"

"Ah-ah," he warned with a grin. "You call me David."

Angie smiled at this. "David. I'm so sorry for the loss of your wife. Would you mind telling me how long ago that happened?"

"Oh my. It's been years now. Sammy was only nine. He went off to Ashton after that."

"Oh! Oh, I see."

"It wasn't that I didn't want to care for the boy," David confessed. "I honestly..." His hazel eyes glistened. "I was just at a loss, that's all. With Jocelyn gone and me working full-time... And, well, we didn't have family in the area."

"That's all right," Angie said kindly. "You don't have to explain anything to me." At the same time, she wondered if David had ever explained things to Sam.

"He was well cared for there," David said in a manner that sounded like he was trying to reassure himself. "Made lots of friends."

"Did he?" Angie asked, surprised. "Did they keep up? Maybe if I reached out—"

"No, no." David sadly shook his head. "Don't think so. Sammy was so busy with school and work, he let a lot of his friendships slide. All but one—for the longest while. Then eventually, he dropped that one, too."

"Oh?" Angie asked, her curiosity piqued. "Who was that?"

"Why, Ken Larsen. He and Sammy worked summers together at the nursery."

"The Holly and the Ivy?"

"That's the one." David tapped his chin. "Ken owns it now."

After they all had coffee in the living room, David showed Sam and Angie around the rest of the house, lingering an extra while in Sam's old bedroom so he could pick up and explore things, like the old high school yearbooks and photo albums he flipped through. But nothing really seemed to spur Sam's memory. He generally recognized the room, but not a lot of its contents. David said that was likely because those were things he'd added as decorations when he was older, like the lava lamp on his student desk and the dog-eared band posters lining the walls.

"I'm sorry we bothered you," Sam said to David, feeling defeated.

"Why, don't be sorry at all." His dad viewed him with compassion. "I want to help, Sammy. All that I can."

"Thanks, Dad," Sam's tongue tripping awkwardly on the word.

"It will probably take time," Angie said in an encouraging manner. "Time for things to come back to you. The more you're around what you know, the better you'll get."

"She sounds awfully sure about that," David told Sam with a twinkle, and Sam knew the two of them were trying to bolster his spirits.

"Yeah. She's in my corner, and I appreciate that." He beheld Angie warmly, and she blushed under his perusal.

"David," she said. "Thanks a ton for having us over."

"Anytime," David replied. "I hope you'll come by again."

"Of course we will," Angie stated, giving him an impromptu hug.

Sam unsurely hugged David as well. "I'll be in touch."

"Please do." David's eyes misted over. "I've really missed having you around."

Sam's gut clenched and his chest constricted. How long had it been, he wondered, since he'd paid a cordial visit to his dad? Come over just to chat? Or, for goodness sakes, help David pick up his messy house? "I can probably come back by this weekend. Maybe help with a few things around here?" Sam glanced at Angie, and she nodded.

David appeared surprised, yet touched. "I can't bother you by putting you to work, Sammy. Not when you're needing to recover."

"It might *help* him recover," Angie said sweetly.

"She's right," Sam agreed. "I noticed a few light bulbs that need changing. The knob on the kitchen pantry door's come loose, too. And the air filters in here probably should be replaced."

Angie appeared impressed. "You can do all that?"

"And more." Sam grinned confidently, somehow knowing he could. The thought of visiting a hardware store made him feel oddly empowered.

"Sammy always was the handy type," David told Angie.

"Harris Hardware," Sam mused. Then he met David's eyes, some barely perceptible memories surfacing—the scent of sawdust and hay, and an image of his dad wearing a dark red apron and standing at a cash register... "You worked there, right?"

"That's right, my boy." David patted Sam's shoulder. "Used to take you into work with me on Saturdays sometimes."

"Yeah..." Sam drew out the word. "It will be good to go back there and see it."

"I can go with you if you'd like?" There was a hopeful note in David's voice.

"I think that's a great idea," Angie said, addressing David. "Sam's seeing a specialist tomorrow. We'll ask the doctor what he thinks about Sam driving. If there's a concern, then I'm happy to chauffeur you. I have Saturday off."

Sam considered her thoughtfully. "Maybe we could bring Pepe?"

Angie's eyes lit up. "He'd *love* that."

When David glanced at Angie, she explained. "Pepe's my little boy. He's six."

"What a nice age," David said. "For sure, bring him along."

Chapter Ten

"I CLEARED OUT SOME SPACE IN the coat closet for your hanging bag," Angie said once they returned to her apartment. "You can set your suitcase in that corner until I can figure out a place for you to unpack it."

The rest of the family was in the kitchen. Pepe colored at the kitchen table, while Lita worked beside him writing letters to her friends and family in Puerto Rico. Elena stood at the stove cooking something that smelled delicious.

"It always smells so good in here," Sam said to Angie, setting his suitcase aside and hanging up his clothes.

"We're having adobo pork chops for dinner," Elena announced merrily from the kitchen, apparently having overheard him.

Sam raised his eyebrows at Angie, and she giggled. "I'm afraid there's not much privacy around here."

"Black beans and rice, and fried *plátanos*, too!" Elena shouted.

"*Plátanos*?"

Angie smiled at Sam. "You call them plantains. Ma cooks them in butter, vanilla, and sugar. They get all caramelized and sticky."

"And *yum*," Pepe said, skipping into the living room.

"Thanks for cooking tonight, Ma!" Angie called into the kitchen.

"No problem," Elena answered. "You and Sam have had a very busy day."

Pepe gazed happily at Sam and handed him a piece of paper. "I drew you a picture."

Sam stared down at the little boy's rendering of what looked like an igloo with a couple of stick figures standing outside it. "It's a snow fort," Pepe proclaimed proudly. "Just like we're going to build."

Sam admired the drawing at length and then said to Pepe, "It's a masterpiece! Thank you. Can I keep it?"

"Will you put it on your refrigerator when you get home?"

Sam thought of his spick and span condo with its lack of personal adornments. "Sure, I will," he said, brightening at the boy. "It's just what I need."

"Sam doesn't have much on his refrigerator," Angie told Pepe from behind the back of her hand.

"*Ay, no*?" Lita said sadly, gliding in from the next room in her wheelchair. She had one hand on the controls and another held a piece of sketchpad paper. "You can have this one, too," she said gently in heavily accented English.

Sam's neck flushed at the embarrassment of riches as he accepted Lita's gift. It was a gorgeous colored pencil drawing of a pair of cardinals: a male and a female perched together on the bow of a pine tree before a snowy background.

"Lovebirds," she told Sam.

Angie laughed indulgently. “I think those are cardinals, Lita.”

Lita raised her finger and waggled it from side to side. “Lovebirds,” she stated again, this time with conviction. Her gaze darted from Angie to Sam then back again.

Angie’s cheeks colored and she ducked her chin. “Anyway,” she said, setting her hand on her grandmother’s shoulder. “They’re beautiful.”

Sam’s voice grew husky. “Extra lovely. Thank you, Lita.” He met her gaze and her brown eyes sparkled. “Thank you for the generous gift.”

“Sam and I are going to build a snow fort,” Pepe informed Angie.

“Oh, gosh...Pepe,” she carefully addressed her son. “Today might not be the *best* time. Sam still has to see the doctor tomorrow, and—”

“But he promised,” Pepe protested, and Sam agreed.

“It’s true,” he said, nodding at Angie. “I did.”

Angie checked her watch, seeing it was nearly four o’clock. “But it’s getting late, and it will be dark soon.” She glanced toward the kitchen as Lita observed the goings on with interest. “Ma’s already started dinner.”

“Dinner can wait!” Elena exclaimed loudly, and Sam couldn’t help but chuckle.

“I think you’re outnumbered,” he whispered to Angie.

She folded her arms in front of her. “I don’t think it’s a very good idea. Not until you’ve seen the doctor.”

“But I’m fine.”

She arched an eyebrow.

“I mean, physically fine.”

Pepe bounced up and down on his heels and tugged at Angie's hand. "Oh, boy! Oh, boy! Can we, puh-leeze?"

Sam lifted his forehead in a petitioning manner, and Angie's heart caved. Pepe wanted this so badly, and Sam was being extra kind to indulge him. It probably wouldn't hurt *that much* to let Sam play in the snow with her son, and the fresh air might even do Sam good. Sam's heart was certainly in the right place. The fact that he was being so kind to Pepe warmed her through and through.

Angie glanced at Lita who was grinning. "*Déjales jugar en la nieve*," Lita told Angie in sing-songy tones, and Pepe beamed up at his mom.

"Yes, Angela." Elena stood on the threshold to the kitchen and leaned a shoulder against the doorframe. "We're in no hurry. Schools have already been closed for tomorrow."

At this announcement, Pepe let out a "Woo-hoo!"

Angie huffed, feeling cornered. "All right already." She set her hands on her hips and stared Pepe down. "But you don't overtire him." Next, she sternly addressed Sam. "You feel anything at all. Any sign of weakness. You come back indoors."

"Aye-aye," he said with a grin. Sam studied her curiously. "Anything else?"

"Yeah," Angie said, grabbing her coat from the closet. "I'm coming with you."

Forty minutes later, Angie, Sam, and Pepe were in the snowy field behind Angie's apartment building, and their fort was nearly done. Angie had been working on bended knee stacking "bricks" made from snow along the front side of their structure, while Sam and Pepe toiled purposefully together, completing the rear wall. The two sidewalls were finished, and they stood about three feet high. It wasn't a huge fort, and it didn't have a roof on it, but Pepe appeared extremely pleased with it anyhow.

"I think that just about does it," Sam said, standing and dusting off his gloves. Sam's face was red from the cold, making his blue eyes seem to shine brighter beneath his dark woolen cap, which was speckled with white.

Fluttering snow cascaded down all around them, but Angie didn't feel cold. It warmed her heart to see Pepe having so much fun. She could see by the way he stuck close by Sam's side how much her son looked up to him. No matter how hard she tried to be a great parent to Pepe, she couldn't be both mother and father. It made her sad that Pepe didn't have someone like Sam in his life. At the same time, Angie was happy, too. Happy for Pepe to experience this little bit of joy right now, even if it was fleeting.

She got to her feet and wiped the icy cold snow from her knees. "I think it's marvelous," she said, admiring their handiwork.

Pepe skipped around the front of the fort and danced through the opening they'd left as a door. "Woo-hoo! I'm the Snow King!"

Sam walked around to stand by Angie. "Yes, you are."

"You're probably more like a prince, Pepecito. My little prince," Angie said warmly.

Pepe glowered at this, but he was only kidding. "Well, if *I'm* the prince," he said resolutely, "then, you're the queen." He pointed at his mother and grinned, pointing next at Sam. "And, Sam's the king."

Angie nervously avoided Sam's gaze. It was just childhood play. She understood that. Pepe wasn't trying to insinuate anything. "Ha-ha!" she said brightly. "My kingdom for a kiss." Then she bent down as Pepe raced toward her, planting a big kiss on her cheek.

"Will you knight me?" Pepe asked happily, glancing at Sam.

"Of course I will, fine sir. Just let me grab my saber." Sam strode toward the woods' edge and scooped an errant branch off the snowy ground, striking a regal pose. He returned to Pepe, who squared his little shoulders.

"I, King Sam, of Snowy Land Kingdom, hereby knight you, Sir Pepe!"

"Jose," Pepe informed him. "I want to be Sir Jose." He beamed up at his mother. "That's more grown-up sounding."

Angie smiled at her son, her heart melting. "It most certainly is."

Sam lightly tapped each of the boy's shoulders with the stick, knighting him Sir Jose. Then Pepe took the stick and scurried around to the back of the fort, defending it from imaginary dragons invading from the forest.

"He's having such a great time," Angie said to Sam. "Thank you."

"Thank you, too." He gazed down at her longingly. "For this. For everything."

"Are you feeling okay?" she asked, still holding his gaze as Pepe yelped joyfully in the background.

"Better than okay, actually. Angie, I..." Sam cleared his clogged throat. "Can't remember having this much fun."

"That's just because you can't remember," she said sassily, in part to deflect the rapid pounding in her veins.

"I'll always remember this." His tone was warm, caressing.

Angie's pulse quickened. "How do you know?"

"Because I've never seen you looking so beautiful." Sam's eyes sparkled, and Angie caught her breath.

"Sam...I... We..." Heat flooded her face.

"It was just an innocent compliment." But the way his eyes danced said that it wasn't. Sam liked her, and liked being around her—and Pepe. Probably even their whole family. The thought that Sam could fall for her made Angie's heart flutter. The idea that he might eventually come to care for all of them was almost too much to hope for. It was an impossible dream. An unattainable wish. A secret prayer that Angie realized she was starting to hold in her heart.

She licked her suddenly too-dry lips, still awash in Sam's gaze. "Thank you." *Thank you for so many things*, she ached to say. *For helping me feel happy and hopeful, and for being so kind to my son.*

Sam grinned handsomely, and she had to will her knees not to buckle.

"You're welcome."

Angie stared up at the living room window to her third-floor apartment spying Lita and Elena watching them, their faces practically pressed to the glass, and she covered her face with her gloves. "I think we have an audience," she said, peeking at Sam through her splayed fingers.

Sam chuckled and gave Lita and Elena a cheery wave. Then, he thoughtfully perused Angie. "*Lovebirds, hmm,*" he murmured under his breath. Next, he seemed to collect himself, as if he hadn't realized he'd spoken out loud. "It's getting dark," he said, rubbing his palms together. "And the temperature's dropping. Maybe we should get Pepe back inside?"

"Great idea," Angie agreed, acting like she hadn't heard him earlier. But she had, and her heart was racing like a runaway train.

Chapter Eleven

ANGIE WAS GLAD SAM HAD his doctor's appointment the next morning. The sooner they got him back to normal, the better, and she was optimistic the specialist could help. Sam had only been there two days, and already things were getting complicated between them. The old Sam would never have looked at Angie the way *this Sam* had beheld her in the snow. Like she was some sort of woodland goddess who'd entranced him. Angie hadn't had a man look at her that way in so long, she'd almost forgotten what it felt like. Almost, but not quite. Sam's warm perusal had brought it all back to her—in spades.

Angie got ready for bed, brushing out her long brown hair in the bathroom mirror. She'd already washed her face and scrubbed off her makeup, so why were her cheeks glowing brightly? It had to be Sam and his effect on her. All through dinner, he'd barely taken his eyes off her, and—from the private looks they'd exchanged—Lita and Elena had definitely noticed. Pepe, for his part, was in his happy little boy bubble. He'd worn himself out playing in the snow and had gone to bed shortly after supper. Angie swore he was asleep the second his head had hit the pillow.

Angie set down her brush and switched off the

bathroom light, preparing for bed by pulling back the covers. She'd already dressed in her cute flannel pajamas, which were powder blue and dotted with snowflakes and snowmen. Each year for Christmas, Lita gave her another pair of winter pajamas, and Angie always loved them. She started to climb into bed but hesitated. She should probably say goodnight to Sam and thank him again for building that snow fort for Pepe. While she and Pepe had helped with the finishing touches, Sam had really done the brunt of the work.

She strode to her door and crept out into the hall, padding toward the living room barefoot. The door to Lita and her mom's room was cracked open, and Angie spied the warm glow of a nightlight beaming inside it. Lita was sound asleep in her twin bed, and Elena had left for work a couple of hours ago. As Angie approached the living room, she saw a light was still on. She also heard the low hum of conversation on the television. She'd told Sam to help himself by watching it whenever he wanted, so she guessed he was up late taking in a show.

But when Angie entered the living room, she found Sam propped up on his pillows on the sofa bed, head bowed forward and totally asleep. *Gosh.* He must have been just as exhausted as Pepe. Maybe more, considering the psychological toll of the day. He had been by his condo, and he'd spent time at his childhood home speaking with David, as well. She could tell that the visit had been difficult for him, and frustrating, creating more questions than answers about things he couldn't remember. Angie gingerly approached, deciding not to wake him. If she could get him to lie down, she could cover him with a blanket and he'd be fine for the night.

Angie neared the sofa bed, noting that Sam wore a long-sleeved, navy blue T-shirt, and gray sweatpants with a University of Virginia emblem on one of the legs. As she stepped closer, he let out a startling snore, and she jumped. Then, he seemed to settle down again, his chin dropped toward his chest and one arm slung over the back of the sofa. She inched toward him, then held out her hands, unsure about how to proceed. He was certainly a lot bigger and heavier than Pepe. Trying to maneuver him wouldn't be nearly as easy. She attempted to slip one hand under his knee while placing the other on his shoulder. Then, Sam stirred—and Angie froze.

"Sam," she whispered to him. "Sam..."

He mumbled something but still didn't awaken.

"It's time to...lie...down." She gently patted his arm as she said this, but the action didn't elicit any results. Then the show playing on the television broke for a commercial, and the volume seemed to increase exponentially. Angie glanced at the screen, spying a familiar scene. A man was proposing to a woman on a chair lift at a ski resort. It was one of Sam's commercials.

Sam, meanwhile, had begun sinking deeper into his bed. *Good! He's nearly horizontal. If I can just ease him down the rest of the way.* Angie inched toward Sam and steadied her hand on his arm, coaxing him to scoot down further and place his head on the pillow that now rested between them. The moment she touched him, a voice on the television blared:

"When your love is written in the stars, a Singleton's Signature Diamond says—"

"*Forever,*" Sam groaned groggily, reaching for her when Angie tried to cover him with a blanket. She hovered over him, paralyzed, as he wrapped his arms around her in a bear hug. She dropped the blanket with alarm, and it fluttered over him, but he still didn't let her go.

"Um...er...Sam?"

This only made him hold her tighter, his beard stubble brushing her cheek. Sweat broke out on Angie's hairline and her face burned hot.

Sam smacked his lips and muttered beside her ear, "Single best deal in town."

His warm breath tickled her neck, and Angie's heart beat harder. "Sam, uh...*oh...oh....*" She pried his grasp from around her shoulders, and he sleepily released her, grabbing onto his second pillow and rolling onto his side.

Angie stared down at him agog, her pulse racing. That had been so weird. So intimate. And yet, tomorrow, Sam wouldn't remember anything about it. *Thank goodness.* She lifted the remote and switched off the TV and turned off the light beside the sofa. Then, she scuttled down the hall as quickly as she could without tripping over her own two feet.

"Good morning, Sam. How did you sleep?"

He'd just awakened and set his feet on the floor beside the sofa bed as Elena peered into the living room from the kitchen. Her pink nurse's scrubs were decorated with little brown teddy bears beneath her overcoat, which was dusted with snow. She carried a shopping bag from the grocery store in her arms. The rest of the apartment was quiet, with only the light pinging of snow against the windowpanes.

"Uh, good," he told her, keeping his voice down. "Good morning."

"The others still sleeping?"

"Think so."

"Yesterday was a busy day," Elena said. She set her grocery bag on the counter and walked toward the coffee pot.

Sam stood and walked her way. "Maybe I can help?"

She smiled warmly. "If you'd like."

Elena directed Sam where to find the coffee filters and the coffee. Sam picked up and studied the yellow and red coffee canister in his hand. "This is really good stuff," he said, reading its label. "Strong."

"That's why we drink it *con leche*," Elena said with a wink. "With milk."

"It's different from what I... What I mean is, I like the taste of it *con leche* very much."

Elena laughed then instructed him on how much water and how many scoops of grounds to add to the coffee maker.

Once Sam set it to brew, he excused himself to go freshen up. "You know," he said, turning on the threshold, "I was thinking I could make breakfast for everyone this morning."

Elena's eyebrows rose in surprise. "You cook?"

"I have a hunch I can flip a flapjack or two," he said, grinning.

She grinned back and swept her arm across the kitchen. “Then, by all means.”

Angie woke to the delectable smell of frying bacon. Then, she spied the time on her alarm clock and sat up with a jolt. It was almost eight a.m., and Sam’s doctor’s appointment was at nine. She couldn’t recall sleeping this late in forever. Yesterday’s full day of activity must have worn her out. She peered through her blinds and saw that it was still snowing outside, deciding she’d better wear snow boots and carry her heels in her bag. Angie also selected slacks in lieu of a skirt. She had the perfect pair of black pants to go with a white turtleneck top. Her gray plaid jacket had a thin sliver of cherry red in its design, which would go with Angie’s cranberry-colored shoes and purse, and—of course—her adorable Santa Claus pin.

Angie showered quickly and dressed for work, since she planned to go in after taking Sam to the doctor. It was Sam’s intention to go into the jewelers, as well. He was anxious to check on his shop and also see George and Pam. Angie brushed through her hair and added her jewelry, studying her reflection in the mirror. She might have put on a few pounds since having Pepe, but the extra bit of curviness didn’t embarrass her. It made her feel feminine, confident. She didn’t look bad for a thirty-two-year-old woman and single mom. In fact, she’d looked really good. Excellent. Better than she had in ages.

Angie caught herself smiling at the prospect of spending another day with Sam. Then, she told herself not to be silly. She'd spent plenty of days with him since September. The difference was Sam seemed interested in her now. But was she interested in him?

When Angie entered the kitchen, her heart skipped a beat, giving her a ready answer. Sam stood at the stove in charcoal slacks and dress shoes. His azure button-down shirt was cuffed at the sleeves, and his red-and-navy-blue tie sat slightly askew as he expertly flipped pancakes on the griddle. "*Buenos días,*" he said, flashing Angie a grin.

"*Buenos días,*" she said, totally gobsmacked. When had Sam learned to cook, and how had he commandeered her kitchen? Angie glanced around, spotting Lita and Elena sitting at the kitchen table with their coffees watching Sam admiringly like they were viewing a stage play on Broadway.

Pepe was beside him, standing on a stool and eagerly stirring water from a measuring cup into a bowl full of batter.

"I'm the Second Mate," the child said with a toothy grin.

"What?"

"Sam's the First Mate," Pepe said, continuing to work. "And you're the Captain!"

Sam winked at Angie when Pepe said this and her belly warmed. "Is that so?" she asked, leaning her shoulder against the doorjamb. She hoped her face wasn't as red as it felt, but from the sparkle in Lita's eyes, Angie guessed that it was.

"Aye-aye," Sam quipped, his eyes dancing.

"*Ay, que lindo,*" Lita said to Elena.

"I didn't know you were making breakfast today?" Angie said, trying to ignore her mom and Lita's curious stares. They clearly sensed the chemistry between her and Sam. And Pepe just seemed joyful having him around.

"I didn't know it myself," Sam said, chuckling. "Not until I woke up and got the idea." He shot Angie an apologetic frown. "Sorry about last night. I guess I fell asleep in front of the television."

"That's all right," Angie said. "I...er...turned it off for you."

"I was talking with your mom and Lita," he said, removing four pancakes from the griddle and setting them on the top of a stack on a plate. Then, Pepe proudly handed him more batter and a ladle. "About those television commercials."

"Oh?"

"For Singleton's Signature Diamonds," Sam went on. "They seem to be running an awful lot of them."

"That's because it 'pays to advertise.' That's what you always said."

Sam beamed her way before adding more batter to the griddle. It sizzled on impact. "I've got to say, that slogan's stellar. Not just the 'single best deal in town' one. *When your love is written in the stars...*"

Angie walked into the kitchen, deciding to fix herself some coffee. "You came up with that one, too."

"Did I?" She could almost hear him mentally patting himself on the back. "Nice."

"Those TV spots have proven profitable," Angie told him.

"Yeah, apparently so." When the group eyed Sam curiously, he went on to explain. "I checked the store accounts on my laptop yesterday evening. I had a lot of work tabs bookmarked and my security details saved."

"Well, that's good, so you can access things," Angie said.

"Exactly." He finished the last batch of pancakes and cut off the burner. Angie noticed he was wearing her reindeer apron, the one with a big red pompom on Rudolph's nose, and she suppressed a giggle. "Hungry?" he asked, meeting her eyes.

She fell into his deep blue gaze, thinking of all the things she'd been missing by not having a man in her life. The warmth...the companionship...the affection. "Starved." Angie pressed her lips together when that came out a little breathy.

Lita hid her grin behind her hand, and Elena's brow shot up.

"That's great," Sam said huskily. "I made plenty."

Angie's heart thumped and her temperature soared. What was she—crazy? Standing here in the center of her kitchen crushing on some guy who'd lost his memory? But this wasn't just *any* guy. This was Sam. The Sam Angie knew and had always believed in. The person deep inside him who was so full of goodness, happiness, and light. She wondered why he had kept this part of his personality sequestered for so long. Had something happened in those intervening years between boyhood and now that had caused him to become such a driven individual? With his amnesia still in full force, it was impossible to know. Just like it was impossible to not find herself falling for him.

Sam must have been thinking favorable things about Angie, too, because he took a step closer, and the coffee mug slipped in Angie's hand.

"They're pecan pancakes," Pepe announced, jumping down off the stool and breaking the spell.

"How awesome!" Angie took a giant step backward and casually gripped the counter. She had to hold onto something to keep from falling down. The look in Sam's eyes had knocked her socks off and caused her knees to totally melt. *Oh boy, am I in trouble. Oh, boy. Oh, boy, Oh, boy.*

Sam's neck reddened beneath his slightly open collar and he turned away. "I'll just set the platter on the table," he said confidently. Still, his voice came out a little rough.

Elena stood to help Sam by setting the kitchen table, as Pepe went to the refrigerator to grab the juice and milk. "The snow plows were out this morning," she said to no one in particular. "I suspect school will be back on again tomorrow."

Pepe gave a whiny pout. "Noooo..."

"It's just as well, Pepe," Elena said as they all took their seats at the table. "Tomorrow's Lita's art class day, and I'll be driving her to the Senior Center."

"You're taking an art class?" Sam asked Lita. "That's wonderful."

Lita held up her hand. "I'm *teaching* one."

"Wow," Sam said, obviously impressed. "That's very cool." He glanced at Lita's wheelchair and then toward the door that led into the stairwell. "But how do you—"

"Very slowly," Lita said with a twinkle.

"We get out with Lita a few times a week, at least," Angie explained. "The stairs are always the most challenging part."

"I'll bet," Sam said sympathetically

"Someday we're going to get a real house," Pepe piped in. "One with no stairs and a big yard so I can get a *dog*."

Sam smiled at the boy. "That sounds like a great plan, little buddy."

When Sam looked up, Angie held out her hand. "Shall we?"

The group joined hands, but this time when Sam held Angie's, something was different. There was a warm connection between them, and Sam's touch felt comfortable and right. Angie's pulse fluttered and her face warmed when she realized what she was secretly wishing. She was wishing she'd never have to let Sam go.

"May the Lord make us truly grateful," they all said, bowing their heads, "for what we're about to receive. Amen."

Chapter Twelve

When Sam and Angie reached the door to his condo, Sam was surprised to find a bag of laundry hanging from the handle of the doorknocker. Through the thin plastic bag marked with an emblem from the cleaners, Sam spied a couple of suits, several pressed dress shirts, a few Polos, and—*yes*—two pairs of jeans. He gripped the collection of hangers in one hand, chuckling at Angie. "I knew I couldn't have been that much of a geek."

She spotted the blue jeans as well and giggled. "So you *do* send them out to be laundered. Have you ever used that washer and dryer in there?" Angie's eyebrows arched, and heat warmed the back of Sam's neck.

"Possibly once or twice," he said, inserting his key into the lock. The appointment with Dr. Sullivan had gone exceptionally well, and Sam was in good spirits. He had no lasting neurological damage, and Dr. Sullivan was encouraged by Sam's slight memory jog regarding his mother when he'd been visiting his dad at home. All Sam needed to do now was step back into his regular routine, and hopefully the rest of his lost memories would be spurred into returning. That morning, Angie planned to leave her SUV parked at

Sam's condo and accompany him into work along his regular pedestrian route. Then, she would help him get settled into his former role at the jewelers to the extent possible.

Sam pushed the door to his condo open and waited for Angie to enter the living area ahead of him. He had so much to be grateful for. Unlike with some amnesia cases, he was surrounded by people who already knew who he was and cared for him. At least, he hoped Angie cared for him because he was certainly beginning to care for her. It was impossible not to be drawn in by her generosity of spirit and those warm, dark eyes that took his breath away.

He'd nearly tripped up in the kitchen and made a fool of himself by taking her in his arms, right there in front of Lita and Elena, not to mention little Pepe. Sam hadn't felt like a visitor in Angie's home at that moment; he'd been a *part* of it. And that rare sense of belonging had helped him understand what it meant to be a family. It meant doing for each other and being there for each other—like everyone tended to sprightly Lita, and she watched over them. Elena, as a role model, was loving yet strong. And Angie was... all of it put together.

She blushed when she caught Sam looking at her. "Want me to help hang that in your closet?"

"No, that's all right," he uttered hoarsely. "I've got it."

Angie waited in the living area near the bar by the kitchen, rather than following Sam into his bedroom, which was just as well. Sam needed a moment to collect himself and put these silly romantic notions out of his head. With all Angie was doing to help him, he didn't need to repay her by making a move on her. What if she were shocked—or offended? Sam wasn't even in full command of his identity, so how much sense did it make for him to tinker with the notion of starting a relationship with someone who was likely just being kind to him out of human goodness?

Angie *was* a good person, too. So genuine. Sam wasn't sure what he'd ever done to deserve her friendship, but it must have been something pretty spectacular. He found himself wanting to make a gesture, something to say thank you, but which didn't appear overly forward, like he was trying to make a play for her. Perhaps in time, the right idea would come to him. Maybe he could even ask his dad about it. They were going to see David on Saturday for their trip to the hardware store, and Sam was already thinking about going back over by himself on Sunday to help his father with some things around the house.

When Sam returned to the living room, he found Angie standing before the big, plate-glass window overlooking the snowy rear lawn and forest, with the purple-and-blue outline of the mountains in the background. It had mostly stopped snowing, with the air being dotted by just the occasional swirling snowflake.

"It's gorgeous," she said in a whisper.

He walked up next to her. The view really was breathtaking, but not nearly as beautiful as the woman beside him. "Yeah."

She turned to face him, and he fell into her gaze, tumbling down, down, down into that dark-brown warmth that made his soul yearn and his heart ache to know her better. Had he ever known love? Real love? The all-consuming, life-changing kind?

"It's a shame I didn't spend much time here," Sam said, reflecting on how pristine his condo appeared. From their gleaming state, it was fairly obvious that he'd scarcely used his appliances, and the furniture still appeared brand new.

"It's true, you were pretty much married to your work." Angie bit her lip as if she regretted her choice of words. But they resonated with Sam in a special way, making him wonder if he'd ever considered settling down with someone. Creating a different sort of life.

"Married," he muttered thoughtfully. "Hmm."

She shyly hung her head. "It's just a figure of speech."

Sam reached out and righted her chin in his hand. "I know," he said gently.

Angie covered his hand with hers, pressing his fingers to her cheek, and it heated beneath his touch. Sam longed to slide his hand into Angie's silken hair and tenderly bring his lips to hers. One gentle kiss was all he'd need to die a happy man.

"I was a crazy kind of guy, wasn't I?"

"What do you mean?"

"Crazy not to notice how exceptional you are."

Angie's skin took on a rosy hue and her chin tilted up toward his as Sam found himself moving nearer.

"Was I seriously that self-absorbed? All about work?"

"You were successful."

"What does success mean?"

"You'll see when we get to the store."

"Something tells me I couldn't have done it without

you." *What's more, I wouldn't have wanted to.* His heart stilled at the startling déjà vu. He was certain he'd said that to Angie before. Or, at least, that he'd intended to.

"Sam."

"You helped me, didn't you?" he asked her. "Pushed me to be a better man. Kind of like you're doing now."

"No. I didn't push." She drew in a breath. "I just suggested..."

"Improvements?" he asked huskily.

There was a flicker of light in her eyes. "You remember?"

"You mentioned it that first night at your apartment. Back when you said you were always right."

"Well, I was wrong."

Angie licked her lips, and Sam's heart pounded. "About?"

"So many things." Her voice was feathery light, less than a whisper.

"And now?"

They were standing so close he could draw her into his arms in one swift move. But would Angie want that? Or would Sam be overstepping his bounds?

"Now, I..." Angie stepped back self-consciously, answering him in tone and deed, as his hand slipped from her cheek. "Think we'd better get going."

"Of course. Angie, I'm sorry—"

"No, please. Don't apologize." Her generous forgiveness made Sam yearn for her even more. "You didn't do anything wrong. It was just—the moment."

"The moment, yeah."

"I'm glad the doctor was encouraging. You might have your memory back soon."

"I hope that's a good thing," he said with self-effacing humor.

"I think it will be." She grinned and nudged him with her elbow, setting things firmly on friendly terms again. "Now, come on! Let's walk to work. I have a hunch the fresh air will do both of us good."

A short time later, Angie and Sam strode down Main Street together through the chilly morning air. The sidewalks had been shoveled and the streets had been cleared, allowing the lazy pace of routine traffic to reensue. There wasn't even a stoplight on Main Street. Hopedale was that small a town. Cheerfully lit-up shops lined the main thoroughfare, and Singleton's Jewelers was just three blocks down, after crossing Broad Street and Water Street.

Angie stole a peek at Sam, walking purposefully along, and she couldn't help but think about how much he'd changed. Or, perhaps, the man she'd gotten to know these past few days was the authentic Sam, and the other guy had merely been an imposter who'd covered up the true nature of the real Sam underneath. What had caused him to bury himself so deep, and for so long? Angie had long ago admitted to herself—and to Elena—that she saw Sam as a handsome man. But that was externally. Now that she was getting to know him on the inside, she found him attractive all the more. Way attractive. So attractive she'd nearly forgotten herself back at his condo and fallen into his kiss.

Angie knew she couldn't do that. It wouldn't be

right to muddy the waters for Sam with an emotional attachment that might confuse him further about his former life. Yet, from her view, his old life hadn't been that fantastic. Nobody who spent nearly all their time at work, without maintaining friendships or family ties, could actually be happy, could they? Or maybe that was just her projecting how she might have felt about the situation.

When they reached Broad Street and the corner near Harris Hardware, Sam held up his hand. "Wait. I think we need to cross the street here."

"Here?" Angie gazed at Sam. Singleton's was on this side of the road. So, why cross over to the other side?

He read her puzzled look. "This is the way I always do it. I'm sure."

A woman and her daughter scurried down the sidewalk past them as Angie and Sam paused at the crosswalk. Angie recognized the pair as Mrs. Stewart and her daughter, Elizabeth. "Good morning," Angie said, greeting them pleasantly.

Mrs. Stewart turned Angie's way. "Oh, hi, there! Thanks for your help the other day. Elizabeth and I are very excited about our bracelets." She nodded at Sam and said cordially, "Mr. Singleton."

"Oh. Uh, hi...hello."

Once the mother-daughter pair had hustled past, Sam leaned toward Angie. "Customers?"

"You bet." She smiled at Hannah Harris Smith, who was on her way back to the hardware store she ran. The friendly woman in her thirties had light brown skin and darker freckles, and her natural, ebony-colored hair formed ringlets beneath her knitted cap.

She held a carryout cup of coffee from the Main Street Market in one gloved hand.

"Good morning, Angie!" Hannah angled her cup toward Sam. "Sam."

"Um...hi?" he said uncertainly, and Hannah scrunched up her brow, halting in her tracks. Hannah clearly could tell that Sam didn't recognize her, and she gaped at him in surprise.

"We've known each other since the fourth grade."

"Sam's having a few memory issues," Angie confided quietly. "He had a minor mishap on Monday."

Hannah's face hung in a frown. "I saw the ambulance down at the jewelers..." Her eyes lit in recognition. "Oh, no, that was Sam?"

"Yeah," Angie said in a whisper. "His memory's temporarily shot, but the docs think it'll return."

Hannah eyed Sam with compassion. "Goodness. Is there something I can do?"

"Actually," Angie said, "we were planning to visit your store on Saturday with Sam's dad, David. The doctors said Sam immersing himself in familiar surroundings could help to spur his memory."

"Then, absolutely," Hannah said. "Please, come on by."

When traffic stopped to allow them passage, Angie and Sam exchanged pleasant goodbyes with Hannah then made their way across Main Street. After walking merely a block, Sam's hand shot up again.

"Hang on," he said, halting before reaching the next corner. The library was just past Water Street on this side of Main. He glanced at Angie, confusion marring his features. "I think we need to cross back again."

"What? Why?" She eyed the library ahead of them on their side of the sidewalk and wondered if that was what Sam was avoiding. She turned and peered over her shoulder at the distance they'd covered so far, noting that Sam had wanted to cross to this side of Main Street prior to reaching Harris Hardware. Could it be he'd deliberately been avoiding walking by that, as well? "Sam," Angie said as they traversed Main Street a second time, putting them back on the same side as Singleton's. "This is a really convoluted way to walk to work."

"I know." He blinked in agreement then shook his head. "Sorry, I really don't remember why I do it this way, I just know that I do."

Angie perused the expanse of Main Street once again. "Could it be you didn't feel comfortable walking past the hardware store and the library?"

"That sounds a bit psychoanalytic, Angie."

She had to agree Sam had a point. Still, what else explained his weird trajectory to work? It was a straight shot from his condo to the jewelry store. "Yeah, I guess," she said. "It just seems a little strange."

"Well, my dad did work at Harris Hardware for many years," Sam answered.

"And the library?"

Sam shook his head, and then they heard a rumbling sound. It was the noise of a freight train clickety-clacking down the tracks on the far side of the library and the other buildings fronting that side of Main Street. Sam squinted in thought, turning toward the commotion. "Yes, that's it!" His face lit up like a ray of sunshine that had broken through storm clouds. "The *train*."

"What about it?" Angie prodded gently. They continued toward the jewelry shop, making conversation as they went and issuing an occasional hello or good morning to passersby. All of them apparently knew Sam, although he didn't seem to recognize anyone in more than a vague fashion.

"My dad, he... I mean..." Sam spun on her, excitement in his eyes as they paused outside the post office. "My dad used to take me there! To the library." His gaze traveled toward the refurbished former train depot. "We'd pick out books and read a story or two. Watch the trains roll along." He grinned at the memories that seemed to resurface in his mind. "Boy, did I love those times."

"When was this?" Angie asked, starting to piece something together. "How old were you?"

"I'm not sure." he shrugged. "Little. Six? Seven? Maybe—"

"Eight," she finished for him, something clicking in her brain. Sam's mom had passed when he was nine, and David had sent Sam off to boarding school shortly afterward. Was that sad part of Sam's past what he didn't want to face? Could that possibly be impacting his recovery?

"Yeah, maybe." he scanned her eyes. "Angie," he said just as they reached Singleton's Jewelers. "What are you thinking?"

Angie decided her hypothesis was too much to lay on him now. Her speculation was very personal. They needed a quiet space to discuss it, which didn't included standing in the middle of Main Street. And, anyway, what if she was wrong? "I'm thinking we can talk about it later."

Sam started to protest, but she stopped him, pointing to the marquee above his store. "Right now, I think it would be good for you to see your shop and get reacquainted with George and Pam."

Sam stared up at the stylized lettering of Singleton's Jewelers, and emotion filled his eyes. "Wow, cool," he said, taking in the whole front of the shop, including the gorgeous holiday jewelry display. "That's all mine?"

"Yep." Angie shot him a smile. "Come on. Let's go inside."

Chapter Thirteen

"SAM!" A SHORTER GUY WITH amber skin, dark hair, and brown eyes made for Sam in brisk strides. The man, who wore round rimless glasses, wrapped his arms around Sam in a bear hug. "Welcome back."

"You, too, George," Sam returned, patting George's back.

George released him, viewing Sam with happy surprise. "You mean, you remember?" George sounded borderline emotional about it, and Sam hated bursting his bubble. Even if George was violating the dress code by wearing a tweed jacket with patches on the elbows over a forest-green sweater and brown corduroy slacks.

"I'm sorry, no," Sam answered, stewing over the knowledge that he insisted his employees dress in business suits in a strict color palette, pertaining to blacks, grays, and dark blues. Sam glanced over at Angie, who was removing her snow boots and stepping into bright-red high heels. The shoes looked great on her and were such a festive color, too. Sam got that he'd probably been too hard on his employees in dictating their dress. Professional attire was one thing. Insisting on dressing drab was something else.

It was a stuffy and unnecessary regulation, which he intended to ease up on entirely.

An attractive redhead called out, "Sam, you're back!" Unlike George, she didn't race to hug him, but she did wear a welcoming smile beneath her twinkling pale blue eyes. The woman, in light gray slacks and a blazer, held out her hand. "I'm—"

"Pam," Sam answered in understanding. He took her hand and shook it warmly.

"Why, yes." She sounded pleased. "That's right."

"You just missed the Stewarts," Pam informed Sam and Angie together.

"Yes," Angie said, stepping into her second shoe. "We passed them on the street." Sam wondered how she managed to walk in heels that high, and supposed she'd gotten used to it. Their vibrant color did nicely accent her dark pants suit ensemble, which included that cute Santa pin. He had noticed her wearing the pin again that morning in the kitchen and guessed it might become one of her regular pieces of jewelry between now and Christmas. "Several other folks, too."

"Mr. Jeffries was here asking about you," George said to Angie before he turned to Sam. "Mr. Jeffries is the older gentleman who often window shops but never buys."

"He was here this morning?" Angie inquired.

George nodded. "I told him you'd be in later, so he said he'd drop by this afternoon."

"All right. Thanks, George." She held her snow boots in one hand and had her workbag slung over the opposite shoulder. She'd already undone her coat but hadn't removed it. "Why don't you come with me?"

she said to Sam. "I'll show you around the back area and our office."

He paused in thought, studying George and Pam. "Thank you both for running the shop."

"It's been no problem," George said, and Pam agreed.

"Our pleasure." Oddly, Pam blushed when she said that, and Sam wondered why. "What I mean is, George and I got along just fine on our own."

It was George's turn to redden now, and Sam became convinced there was something going on between the two of them. He also had the hunch it was something personal, like some kind of romantic attraction.

George straightened his tie—which Sam saw was dotted with reindeer. "Yes, well! I think I'd better go check on that fitting I was working on in back."

"Would you like me to—" Pam attempted to follow George, and he appeared more embarrassed than ever.

"Nope! No, thank you." George put on his most professional tone, and Sam had to keep the corners of his mouth from twitching. "I've got it."

"Right." Pam's cheeks brightened then she demurely addressed Sam. "And I'll just go and check the receipts."

"You know," Sam said loudly, stopping both George and Pam from retreating. George was nearly to the back room entrance while Pam had barely reached the register. They each turned to stare at him. "I've been thinking you've both put in a lot of extra hours these past few days." George and Pam waited, with rapt attention. "So, why don't you two go on and take the afternoon off?"

Pam gave a happy gasp. "Seriously?"

"Sure."

"Well, I suppose I could stand to do a bit of early Christmas shopping," George said, stridently avoiding Pam's gaze.

"Uh, er...yes. Me, too." Sam noted Pam was trying awfully hard not to look at George, and he repressed a chuckle. There was really nothing wrong with two coworkers becoming involved. It wasn't like one of them was the boss, and the other his employee. Sam's gaze roved involuntarily toward Angie, and his heart beat harder.

"That's a fine idea," Angie said, emerging from the back room after depositing her coat. Next, she addressed George and Pam. "You're both due an afternoon off, and Sam I will be fine here."

"You're sure?" Pam asked, but Sam saw she'd already begun collecting her things.

"Absolutely," Sam answered with a laugh.

George grabbed his coat off a hook in the break room and joined Pam by the front door. As they slipped out together with Pam ahead of George, Sam heard him whisper, "He's really not himself right now, is he?"

The moment George and Pam departed, Angie covered her mouth and giggled. "Oh. My. Goodness," she said to Sam. "Did you just see what I saw?"

Sam chuckled and recalled Lita's labeling of the cardinal pair. "Lovebirds," he whispered, still smiling.

"Who knew?" Angie's musical laughter filled the shop, which Sam saw was glittering with an elegant selection of jewelry and an entire case of Singleton's Signature Diamonds. He approached the case, marveling at the intricate design of each diamond solitaire. They were all individualized and incredibly striking. And directly behind the case, hanging prettily on the wall, was an enormous Christmas wreath made from mistletoe and crowned with a big gold bow.

"Nice touch, that mistletoe wreath," he told her. "Was that your idea?"

Angie's cheeks colored slightly. "It was."

"Looks good there," he said, surveying the entire showroom once again. "Everything around here looks great. Really holiday-like."

"Thank you."

He glanced out toward the street then asked her, "What do you suppose is really going on between Pam and George?"

Angie shrugged. "Some kind of early flirtation? They very clearly like each other."

"Clearly."

"There's no hiding an attraction like that."

"I suppose not," he said, holding her gaze.

The moments ticked by, and Angie's blush deepened. "Anyway," she said, drawing in a breath. "Now that you've seen the sales floor, let me show you around the rest of your place."

"My place." A grin warmed Sam's face. "I like that."

"Nothing yet? On the memory?"

"No, but George and Pam seem awfully nice."

"I'm glad you gave them the afternoon off. Do you think they're going for coffee at Lit and Latte?"

"I wouldn't be surprised."

Angie shared a mischievous grin. "They're kind of cute together, if you ask me."

"Yeah, they are." Sam agreed and considered his surroundings. The store was very well organized. It even had a seating area with white bucket swivel leather chairs and a low glass coffee table, which at the moment held a red poinsettia plant in its center. *It's so cheery in here*, he thought, picking up strains of upbeat holiday music playing in the background. "Angie?"

"Yes?"

For the second time today, Sam found himself wanting to thank her. For taking him in, for being a friend...for so obviously having played such an important role in the success of his shop. But Sam didn't want to overdo it. Especially not after his display in the kitchen this morning, and the totally obvious way he'd mooned over her at his condo earlier. So, he settled on something much more mundane, which was why he'd come here anyway. "Why don't you show me around?"

It didn't take long for certain things to come back to him, leaving both Sam and Angie surprised at his facility for stepping back into the technical aspects of his job. When she started to instruct him on logging onto the cash register, he was two steps ahead of her and apparently already knew. He displayed the same acumen in accessing their books, although she had to help him make sense of some of the financial data. She showed him the vaulted room, which held their extra inventory, and explained how their stock numbers were automatically updated with each new purchase or order logged at the register using the store's accounting software. It was all making sense, and his brain was eager for the information, like a coin machine readily accepting quarters, dimes, nickels, and pennies into their appointed slots.

Sam grew increasingly confident as he banked "new" knowledge. Though it was exhausting absorbing so much information so quickly, he was eager to obtain it. The more he learned, or re-learned in a way, the closer he became to the man he used to be: the competent and thriving owner of Singleton's Jewelers. Who apparently was also a bit of a grouch, and extremely stern with his employees. Why did it matter what folks wore on the job, as long as they looked professional and worked hard? Sam saw now that he must have been an uptight, stuffy guy. At least he owned blue jeans, and he intended to wear them this weekend.

Sam heard the door chime sound at the front entrance and leaned back in his chair a tad to see an elderly gentleman with silvery hair enter the showroom. When you exited the sales floor, there was a break room beyond that, which held a long lunch table and a coffee machine in a pint-size kitchen, containing a small sink, a microwave, and a refrigerator. The break room also held wall hooks along a back hall leading to the parking area, on which people hung their coats. George's separate workspace was situated through a right-hand door, off the break room, and the vaulted inventory safe was beside it. Sam shared a large office with Angie that was directly behind the break room. When the door to their office was open, he could stare straight through it and all the way into the showroom, assuming the door between that and the break room was propped open, like it was right then.

Sam had his feet on his desk and rested his laptop on his thighs, while Angie worked to restock inventory out front. He'd been extremely pleased by the results of their last two sales, which had apparently made Singleton's Jewelers a tidy bundle. Even when deducting the cost of advertising—which had a huge price tag unto itself—this year's profits had been astounding. He understood there'd been a brief slowdown in store traffic these past few days due to the weather, but Sam wasn't worried one bit. Things would pick back up again soon. And even if they didn't, the business was set financially for well into the coming year. Sam heard the customer's good-humored laughter and angled his chair back further, tipping it back on its two rear legs.

"Why, Angie," the older gentleman said. "How good of you to remember." He and Angie sat in two of those leather chairs, each holding a cup of that fancy-brew coffee from the break room. When Angie had brewed some for herself and the fellow, the toasty aroma of roasted coffee had filled the air, wafting toward Sam in the office. Angie had offered Sam a cup, but he'd declined.

"So, they'll all be home for Christmas?" Angie queried. "Your two boys and their families?"

The older man nodded. “It will be a full house. My wife, Madeline, and I can’t wait.”

Sam wondered how she knew so much about this shopper’s family. She addressed him as Mr. Jeffries, and Sam struggled with a hazy memory. *That’s why we employ the hard-sell,* Sam recalled himself saying to someone. *Lead the customer to what he or she needs.*

And yet, Angie didn’t appear to be leading anything other than a conversation. Although she’d told Sam she had a ton of catch-up work to do, she gave Mr. Jeffries the impression that she had all the time in the world.

“I want to make this Christmas extra special,” Mr. Jeffries said, meeting Angie’s eyes. “For the girls as well as the boys.” He set his cup down on the coffee table. “For my sons, I was thinking vintage pocket watches.”

“Ooh! Those would be nice,” Angie agreed, following Mr. Jeffries’s gaze to the corner of the room that housed the Singleton’s Classic Choice offerings.

“And for the girls...” He stopped himself, chuckling soundly. “I only have granddaughters, you know.”

Angie smiled in understanding. “Tony and Peg have three girls, and Jack and Terry have four.”

His face lit up in a grin. “How kind of you to remember.”

Sam marveled at her adroitness in handling this customer with such compassion and caring. Amazingly, it appeared Angie’s good manners were resulting in purchases.

She swiveled her chair toward Mr. Jeffries, and Sam briefly lost sight of her.

"And for the girls?"

"Jewelry!" Mr. Jeffries proclaimed decidedly. "Something elegant and Christmassy." Then he added, "I saw some very nice items displayed in your store's front window."

The rubies and emeralds? Sam's heart thumped harder as he leaned back in his chair a fraction more. Angie was making this incredible sale—and she was doing so with such class. Pride surged through him, and the feeling resonated in his soul. Maybe he didn't remember running this business, but this sense of accomplishment was deeply familiar. And he liked it. He liked it a lot. Sam had obviously enjoyed being successful before. That was how he'd built his business. With drive. Although Angie seemed to be exhibiting a softer sort of sales tactic that involved more congeniality than push.

"How old is Jennifer now?" Angie asked. "Jack's youngest."

"She's just turned thirteen." Jefferies beamed. "And is starting to become interested in grown-up jewelry."

"I'm sure she has excellent taste," Angie said. "Just like her grandpa."

Sam caught a glimpse of her, but just a sliver, as she crossed one leg over the other, those smart red shoes contrasting with her dark pants legs.

"I'll need several sets of gifts," Mr. Jeffries said. "Ensembles of earrings and necklaces, or bracelets perhaps, for the younger girls, and something a bit more worldly for their mothers—my daughters-in-law."

"I'm sure we'll find just the right gifts for all the women in your family. The men, too." Angie leaned forward, preparing to stand, and that was when she spotted Sam, through the open doors to the break room and the office, leaning way—way—back in his chair. The instant her eyebrows knitted, Sam knew he'd been spotted. The next thing he knew, he'd tumbled backward with a startled cry, lifting his head just in time to keep it from smacking the carpet.

Angie leaped to her feet, addressing Mr. Jeffries. "If you'll excuse me just one second—"

Sam clutched the laptop that had flipped shut across his chest, suddenly mortified. He'd been spying on Angie, and now she'd caught him.

"Sam," she whispered, powering toward him in those spiky red heels. "Oh, my gosh, are you okay?"

"I...um, yep. Uh-huh." He stared up at her from his prone position, and then scrambled sideways and got to his feet, righting the chair. "Think so."

She set her hands on her hips. "What on earth were you doing?"

"I honestly can't remember."

Angie smirked, but she didn't look seriously mad. "Well, cut out the monkey business, all right? I'm about to make a very big sale."

"I know. Great going."

"Thanks," her brow creased with worry. "But, *please*, be careful. You've already had one bad fall. We don't want you having another." Sam knew she was talking about his fall on the ice, but instinct told him he was falling in another way. Romantically—for her. He rubbed the back of his neck, trying to make sense of these overwhelming emotions Angie brought out in him. "You're sure you're okay?"

"Oh, yeah." His heart beat harder when her dark

eyes met his. "Fine." But inside, Sam knew he wasn't. He was dangerously close to losing his heart to this woman. He didn't need his twenty-six years of missing memories to tell him that.

Chapter Fourteen

PEPE SKIPPED DOWN AN AISLE at Harris Hardware, excitedly dragging Sam along by the hand. "I want to show you what I found!" the child exclaimed. "It's the coolest stuff."

Sam had no clue what Pepe considered so interesting, but he was about to find out. They'd left David and Angie chatting near the register with Hannah, who was happy to see David again after such a while.

Sam had his own short list of items to purchase while he was here. Things he wanted to pick up for the work he planned to do at his dad's place, like a few packages of light bulbs and new air filters. Sam already had what he needed to make the other basic repairs in his toolbox. He'd located it on a shelf in his condo's laundry room, and none of the tools looked like they'd been touched in years. They were still serviceable, though. And Sam had plenty of nails, screws, hinges, and such for basic handyman work around David's house. If it turned out he needed something more, he could always return to the hardware store later.

Sam enjoyed its earthy smell and the scent of hay and sawdust lingering in the air. It took him back to a place disguised in a hazy memory bubble. It was a happy place, though. Sam could feel that in his heart. What's more, he felt relaxed being here. Relaxed and comfortable, wearing blue jeans and a sweatshirt under his parka like any other ordinary weekend guy.

"It's right over here," Pepe said as they rounded the corner. Sam couldn't help but be infected by the kid's enthusiasm. The child looked at the world wide-eyed, taken in by its endless possibilities. Sam remembered feeling like that when he was Pepe's age.

Pepe gaped happily, goggling up at a wall. "Look at all the *dog* stuff," he said, as if he were viewing a shrine. The display really was quite fantastic. Apart from the typical assortment of dog collars and leashes, there were tons of doggie sweaters and booties, too. There were specialty toys and numerous treat dispensers, as well as games meant to improve your canine friend's IQ. Sam certainly didn't recall the pet section of the store being stocked like this when he was a kid. Sam guessed that Hannah was a dog person.

Sam peered to the right, spying an equally lavish display of cat accoutrements. And a cat person...

"There's bird and gerbil stuff down there," Pepe announced, apparently having taken a complete inventory of the pet section earlier when the adults were talking.

"Wow," Sam said, eying the stacks of extra cushy dog beds that came in four sizes: small, medium, large, and extra-large. "That's quite a selection."

"I know which one I'm getting." Pepe grinned picking out a medium-size dog bed and wriggling it free from its sandwiched position between two others. Sam saw it was covered with red-and-brown checked fabric, which was accented with black doggie paw prints.

Sam recalled his conversation with Angie where she'd shared about Pepe wanting a dog, and his heart hurt for Pepe. It was terrible to be a child and wish for something with all your might only to... Sam reached out and gripped a nearby shelf holding dog dishes. All of a sudden he felt dizzy.

Pepe's dark eyes rounded as Sam felt the blood drain from his face. "I'm going to get my mom."

"No, wait." Sam inhaled deeply and then exhaled. "It's okay, little buddy. I'm fine."

Pepe scrunched up his lips. "You don't look fine."

"I am. I'm just..." Sam leaned forward, gripping his gut as his stomach clenched. "Catching my breath."

Pepe surveyed him worriedly, and then said. "Bobby has asthma, too."

"No, no." Sam worked to reassure the child, gesturing with his palm toward the floor. "It's nothing like that." Sam marshaled his reserves and straightened, but his stomach was sour and there was an odd metallic taste on his tongue. He stared down into Pepe's big innocent eyes, and then he got it. He'd been only a few years older than Pepe when he'd lost his mom. Sam had wanted more than anything to bring her back, but he couldn't. Then, the very next year Sam was sent away.

But why was he being maudlin? He'd toughened himself up as a kid, hadn't he? A vague image of a wrought iron gate set on stone pillars came back to him, and a big metal placard on one of the pillars read Ashton Academy. Sam had gone there as a boy and gotten a great education. He'd even made a couple of friends. He just couldn't recall their names or faces.

Pepe tugged at Sam's hand, and Sam realized he'd drifted away. "Are you feeling better?"

"Why, yes!" he smiled at the child. "Yeah, Pepe, I am." Sam saw that Pepe still held the medium-sized dog bed, which he'd tucked beneath his arms. "Why don't we put this one back, shall we?"

Pepe shrugged and then frowned when Sam returned the dog bed to its place in the stack. "I won't be getting a puppy till Christmas anyway."

Sam wasn't sure how much he should say about that. This was Angie's territory, not his. Still, he hated seeing the kid get his hopes up so high for something impossible. "Pepe, about that..." Sam began tenderly.

"I am getting a dog. I asked for one."

"From Santa?"

"Uh-huh."

"Well, you know, sometimes Santa's sleigh is awfully—"

"That's okay if he can't bring it." Pepe's eyes sparkled tellingly. "I have a backup plan."

Sam chuckled at the little boy's self-assurance. "You do?"

Pepe nodded seriously. "Melchor, Gaspar, and Baltasar."

"Who?"

"The Three Kings, Sam. You know." Pepe rolled his eyes. "The wise guys on camels?"

Sam chortled a laugh. "Wise men, you mean?"

"Uh-huh. The ones who came to baby *Jesus*. But now they come to kids."

"Like you?" Sam guessed, surmising this was a Puerto Rican tradition.

"Every year we fill up boxes with lots and lots of grass! The camels come and eat it, and the wise guys leave their gifts."

"How cool. At Christmas?"

"On January sixth."

"Ahh," Sam said, getting it. "Your backup plan."

"One year, I wanted a Lego Super Hero kit, but Santa didn't bring it."

"Let me guess—"

Pepe nodded smugly. "Those guys are *really* wise."

"There you are," Angie chirped. "We've been hunting all over the store for you."

David accompanied her. "Have you had time to look around?" he asked Sam.

"Yeah," Sam answered. "Thanks." He shot a look at the boy. "Pepe was giving me a tour."

Angie surveyed her son who, to her knowledge, had never been in the store. "But how did he—"

Pepe's left eyebrow quirked and he held a finger up to his lips in an "it's our secret" sign.

Sam winked in reply then turned to Angie. "Pepe scampered ahead. Did some advance recognizance."

David chuckled at this. "What do you think, little man? Isn't this place awesome?"

"Yeah," Pepe agreed. "It's super cool."

Angie questioningly met Sam's eyes, while Pepe chattered with David. "Well?" she asked in a whisper. "Anything?"

"A little," Sam confided quietly. "Maybe we can talk about it later."

"Later sounds good." Her dark eyes sparkled, and

Sam's load felt lightened. As if he wasn't in this totally alone. Of course he had his dad, but those memories he'd had surface today weren't things he was ready to discuss with David. He wanted to share them with Angie, though, as a friend. Sam trusted Angie's judgment and valued her opinion.

As they walked toward the front of the store, David asked them, "Are you all ready to go, or do you want to look around some more?"

"I just need to pick up a thing or two for Sunday," Sam told him. "Then, I'll be ready. It won't take a minute."

"What's happening on Sunday?" David asked, looking hopeful.

"I was thinking I'd drop by," Sam told him. "Maybe make a repair or two around the old homestead."

David's eyes misted over. "That would be very nice of you, Sammy. Very nice indeed."

Later that night, Angie knocked on the hallway wall by the living room as Sam prepared for bed. He'd already change into his Virginia sweatpants and long-sleeved T and was about to open the pullout sofa. She wore her pajamas and a bathrobe and was about ready to turn in, too.

"I just wanted to say goodnight," she said. "And thank you. Taking Pepe to the hardware store was a great idea. He had the best time. He really hit it off with your dad, too."

"Yeah." Sam smiled thoughtfully. "David and Pepe definitely seemed to get along."

“I’m sure it was good for David,” she said. Angie shyly lifted a shoulder. “Getting out. You know.”

“I agree.”

“I know it’s late, and you may not want to talk about it now, but there was so much going on earlier, with Lita and Elena, and dinner, and—”

“Pepe. I know.” Sam beheld her warmly. “You have such a great family, Angie. You really do.”

“Thanks. David’s pretty special, too. I could see how much it touched him when you volunteered to come over.”

Sam’s face took on a ruddy hue. “I guess I didn’t do a lot of that in the old days, huh?”

“It’s never too late to make a new beginning.”

“No?” Sam’s gaze washed over her, and Angie’s heart stilled.

“You’re already starting over, can’t you see? And Sam,” she murmured gently. “Once you get back your memory…”

Sam’s Adam’s apple rose and fell. “What a happy day that will be,” he said, not sounding at all like he meant it. There was a bitterness in his voice that surprised her.

“We’ll still be friends, and colleagues.”

“But things will be different.”

She tried to read his eyes and the mysteries they sheltered. “Some things will be, of course.”

Sam laughed hoarsely. “I’m sure the four of you will be glad to get me out of your hair.”

“I doubt that,” she said, mistakenly speaking out loud.

It was Angie’s turn to blush. After a beat, Sam said, “I had a memory today about my mom. Well, not actually about her, but about what happened after... after my dad and I lost her, I mean."

"Oh, Sam." She walked toward him and sat on the edge of the sofa, motioning for him to join her.

Sam hesitated before sitting. "It's late. We should probably—"

"Why don't we talk first?" Angie patted the sofa cushion beside her, and Sam settled in.

"It wasn't a huge memory," he told her. "No big breakthroughs or anything. But I did remember something about Ashton Academy. The way it looked. How I felt when I went there."

She stared at him imploringly, and he hung his head with the admission.

"Pretty lonely, actually."

Without thinking, she took his hand. He didn't resist or pull away. Instead, he held her hand firmly, clenching his fingers around hers at the painful memory.

"I wasn't a whole lot older than Pepe when I lost my mom, and then my dad he sent me—"

"Sam," she said softly. When he looked at her, she continued. "Your dad was at a loss, just like you were. His heart was broken, too, and he didn't know how to cope."

"Who told you that?" Sam asked doubtfully.

"He did."

Sam's forehead furrowed in confusion. "When?"

"At his house the other day." Angie gently squeezed Sam's hand. "I'm sure it was a hard time for the two of you. Your dad was hurting also. Plus, he was a single dad when not many men were filling that role. He only wanted what was best for you."

A single tear glistened in the corner of Sam's eye. "How can you be so kind when life has been so rough on you?"

"It's hard on everyone at times." A smile trembled across her lips. "It's an equal-opportunity world, you know."

"And yet, you never lost your faith?"

"Oh, I might have lost it a time or two," she answered honestly. "But it never really abandoned me in my times of need. It was waiting there all along for me to come back to it. Sort of like David's been waiting on you."

"I see." The honesty in his tone gave him away. Sam really was starting to see a lot of things with brand-new eyes. But he wasn't the only one who was changing. Angie found herself changing, too. She was starting to believe in love again, and that new beginnings were possible, even for her.

"When we were walking to work on Wednesday, there was something that you started to tell me, and then you didn't."

She squeezed his hand. "It was about the hardware store and the library. Maybe you didn't used to like walking past them because they made you remember."

"The sad times," he said thoughtfully.

"Yes."

Sam met her eyes with new understanding. "But those were happy times too. Good memories of me and my dad being together."

"Maybe you mixed in the good with the bad. You didn't much like thinking about those days, so you found ways to avoid any triggers."

"Yeah. Then, what am I avoiding now?"

He appeared so sincere that Angie's heart ached. How she wished she had the answers. "Honestly," she said, "I don't know. It may not even be that. It's a physiological thing, your memory loss. And already..." She smiled encouragingly. "It's getting better."

He held her hand tighter. "Thanks to you."

"Thanks to the doctors' advice," she said, "and everything we've been doing."

"Well, I—for one—don't think we're doing nearly enough."

"Why, what do you mean?" she asked, taken aback.

Sam released her hand and stood, motioning around the room. "Look at this place. It's not even decorated for Christmas."

"Yeah, right," she said, chuckling. "Like, when have we had the time?"

"We can make time tomorrow evening."

"Tomorrow?"

"I can stop by the Holly and the Ivy when I'm done at David's," Sam said, appearing delighted with the idea. "Pick up a gigantic Christmas tree!"

Angie consider this, deciding tomorrow might actually be the perfect time. A work friend of Elena's had needed to swap shifts tonight, so Elena would be home tomorrow.

Sam glanced around the living room. "I'm actually surprised you haven't decorated already. I thought you'd be all decked out the day after Thanksgiving. Just like you outfitted the shop."

"It's different here because we leave our decorations out until after the Epiphany."

Sam scrutinized her like he wondered what she was hiding, but Angie wouldn't dare tell him she would've decorated last Saturday had he not called her into work. Or that she'd been so preoccupied since then with his care that she hadn't had a moment to consider decking the halls. She also declined to mention that she and her family typically used an old artificial Christmas tree she'd bought secondhand at a thrift store because the live ones were too expensive. "So?"

"So, that's a long time of holiday cheer."

"Says the lady with the Santa Claus pin?"

Angie's heart fluttered because this sounded a little flirty.

She giggled, taken in by his persistence. "I do love to decorate."

"Is tomorrow too soon?" Sam asked, and Angie knew she couldn't disappoint him.

"No."

"Well then, good. I'll make sure that it gets done. Picking up the tree, that is." He twinkled in her direction. "You'll be responsible for digging out the decorations."

"I think I can handle that part. With Pepe and the others here to help me."

"Then, great," Sam said with a chipper air. "It's settled."

"Yeah." She stood as Sam walked toward her and was accidentally nearly in his arms. "Oops! Oh! Sorry."

He stared down at her, not appearing the least bit regretful himself. He inched closer, and Angie's heart thundered. He was so handsome, and so thoughtful and kind. And the soulful look in his eyes completely swept her away.

"I hope you know you're making this awfully tough."

"What's that?" In spite of herself, her voice was a breathy whisper.

He caressed her cheek and rasped warmly. "Not crushing on you."

It took Angie a full five seconds to believe she'd heard him correctly. Then, her heart swelled with happiness when she understood she had. Angie knew what her rational self should say. She should tell Sam that now wasn't the time for the two of them to become involved, not yet. Not when he was already making such great strides in his recovery. But instead, her impish self gave him a saucy stare and said, "What's stopping you?"

Sam laughed and pulled her into his arms, his eyes dancing with affection. "You are just too adorable. You know that?"

Angie's spirit soared. "Oh, yeah? So are you."

His gaze washed over her and then he said, "I know this sounds crazy, but I feel like I've just been on the best six-day date of my life."

"I know what you mean." She grinned up at him, her heart light. "Because I feel that way too."

Angie's pulse pounded and her knees went all wobbly. The scent of his cologne was heady and masculine, and there was a longing in his eyes that spoke of romantic desire. If Sam kissed her now, she didn't know what she'd do. Faint, probably.

"Lovebirds," came a little chirp, and Sam and Angie backed apart. It was Lita—toddling her way into the kitchen with her walker.

"Ooof!" Angie cupped a hand to her mouth, and Sam pursed his lips.

"Maybe not the best spot for our first kiss," Sam whispered, and Angie's cheeks heated.

Our first kiss. She'd loved the way he'd said that. It made her feel all warm and tingly inside. What's more, he'd indicated that it might happen later.

"Lita!" she called after her grandmother. "What are you doing up this late?"

"Just going to the kitchen for some water," Lita answered with a lilt.

Chapter Fifteen

THE FOLLOWING MORNING, SAM ACCOMPANIED Angie and her family to church. They started out early, as was their custom, to allow enough time for transporting dear Lita down the stairs. Sam marveled at the production the group typically undertook. First, Sam helped Angie load Lita's hand-push, travel wheelchair into the trunk of her SUV. Next, Angie attempted to carry the foldable walker down the steps, but Sam rushed forward to help her, taking it all the way to the bottom. Afterward, he returned to the third floor landing where Angie and Elena were preparing to steady Lita by her elbows, as Lita firmly gripped the railing and cautiously descended one step at a time.

Pepe was right behind the women, walking slowly, his small arms burdened with the ladies' purses.

The entire operation looked very precarious to Sam and more than a little dangerous. "Here, allow me," he said, sidling up beside Lita and taking Elena's place in the stairwell. Lita continued to grasp the railing with Angie on her other side to assist her. "*Un caballero.* A true gentleman."

Sam hooked his arm under Lita's, but the next riser was too much of a challenge for her weakened legs, and she stumbled.

"Whoa, there!" Sam caught her surely, shoring her up in his embrace. He stared warmly into the old woman's eyes. "I've got a better idea," Sam said with a twinkle.

The group stared at him expectantly, and then he addressed Lita. "How about if I carry you the rest of the way?"

"Carry?" Lita giggled like a schoolgirl, yet she seemed intrigued.

"I don't know, Sam," Angie said worriedly. "What if you drop her?"

"I've never dropped a woman in my life." Sam winked at Lita, and she nodded. Sam bent forward and gingerly scooped Lita into his strong arms. "We'll be down before you know it," he said as Lita swatted his shoulder and merrily kicked her heels, giving another titter.

"*Que fuerte.*" Lita chuckled.

"You're light as a feather," Sam returned with a grin.

A short time later, they arrived at the red brick church with tall white columns and a high steeple. The pathway leading up to it from the parking area had been shoveled, and light snow continued drifting from the sky. Sam pushed Lita's wheelchair, while Angie carried in the walker. Today was communion Sunday, and proud Lita wanted to walk herself to the altar, although Elena and Angie would stay close by to help her. By prior arrangement, Sam decided to stay in the pew with Pepe, who was too young to partake of communion, anyway. Sam was certainly old enough, and the kindly middle-aged pastor had welcomed everyone who'd been baptized to the Lord's table, but Sam didn't feel quite right joining in the ritual this time.

Something he thoroughly enjoyed engaging in was the singing before and afterward. Several of the songs were seasonal, and Sam detected familiar chords and verses in the lovely holiday hymns. He didn't think it was his imagination that Lita kept shooting him knowing grins each time Angie glanced down at her hymnal. Despite—or perhaps because of—her advanced age, Lita was an astute observer of people, and she clearly guessed there was romance brewing between them

Sam was delighted to believe that, too. He felt so lucky to have a woman like Angie interested in him. He didn't know what she saw in him; he was just glad it was something. He'd dressed nicely in a work suit for church today, and the rest of the family had dressed up, too. Pepe even wore a coat and tie. Sam considered the substantial obstacles presented in getting Lita here. This arrangement was no good for Angie and her family. They were making things work at present, but logistics would become even more difficult as Lita got older.

Angie had said she was saving for a house, and Sam could see how badly she and the others needed one. And what about Pepe wanting that puppy and a yard? When it came time for the Passing of the Peace, another church member reached out to cordially shake Sam's hand.

"I don't believe we've met before," the elderly

woman wearing a floral corsage pin said. "You must be Mr. Lopez."

Angie flushed brightly, and Sam felt his neck heat. "It's Sam," he said, shaking the woman's hand. "Sam Singleton."

"Sam's a family friend," Angie said quietly as the congregation settled back down. "Just visiting today."

Then, as they all took their seats, Lita leaned forward from where she sat on the far side of Pepe and winked at Sam.

After the service, the group stopped for soup and sandwiches at Lit and Latte on Main Street. Elena suggested it, and the others readily agreed. Lita loved the cozy atmosphere of the bookshop and café combo. One of the owners, Fred Etheridge, was especially kind to her, often making an effort to address her in Spanish. "*Buenos días, señora.*" Fred bowed deferentially toward Lita as Sam wheeled her into the shop.

Lita grinned at the slender man in his early sixties with wavy blond hair and tortoiseshell glasses. A red-checked Christmas scarf wrapped around his neck above his forest-green sweater and chinos. "*Buenos días*, Fred."

Fred smiled cordially at the family. "Party of five for lunch?"

"That would be great," Angie answered. "Thanks!"

"Why don't we take a moment to look around first?" Elena suggested.

Angie glanced at Sam. "If everyone's not too hungry..."

"I'm fine," Sam told her, then Fred gave him a sympathetic nod.

"I heard about your fall from Hannah. I'm really sorry, Sam. If there's anything Daniela or I can do—"

"Did I hear my name?" Daniela asked, emerging from the crowded café area into the book section of the store, which fronted the street. Daniela was on the shorter side and slimly built with short, curly brown hair, light brown eyes, and a generous smile. She'd dressed in jeans and a Christmas sweater, and she wore candy cane holiday earrings to match.

Angie had heard the pair moved here from Georgia not more than three years ago, after Fred had retired from his job in engineering. Daniela had managed a ladies' retail shop there, and they'd made a raging success of this new business, which was popular with the locals and the ski resort tourists who ventured into Hopedale, when taking a break from the slopes.

"Angie," Daniela said warmly, "so good to see you again."

Angie smiled and took Daniela's outstretched hand.

Then Daniela circled around, shaking hands with the other adults. When she reached Sam, Daniela said, "I'm sorry about your accident. I hope you'll be feeling better soon."

"I already am," Sam replied, looking like he meant it.

Daniela glanced down at Pepe. "I have some news," she uttered temptingly. "We got some new kids books in featuring vintage comics."

"You mean—"

"*Batman*," Daniela supplied with a merry grin.

Pepe glanced desperately at Angie.

"Yeah, sure," she said, chuckling. "Go on. Take a look."

"They're over there," Daniela told Pepe, indicating an area near the front of the store. "On the table by the window with the elf display." Her smile sparkled at the child, and then she said, "Come on. I'll show you."

As Pepe scampered along behind Daniela, Fred addressed Lita. "You should check out the periodicals section. We got some new magazines in, including Spanish versions of the ones you like."

"Oh, thank you." Lita smiled graciously and glanced over her shoulder.

Elena took the handlebars on her wheelchair. "Let's go take a look."

"I'll just put in a reservation to hold your spot," Fred told Angie. "What do you say? Another fifteen minutes?"

"Fifteen minutes would be great." She smiled at Sam. "What do you think? Want to look around?"

"Yeah." Sam scanned his surroundings, taking in the store's brimming shelves of books on myriad topics as the sound of clattering dishes and happy chatter spilled forth from the café area. "I'll just browse around and see if anything jumps out at me."

Angie wished she could ask Sam which sort of books he liked to read, but she decided the question would be futile. She'd spotted some classic literature on his bookshelves back at his condo, as well as a few contemporary thrillers. Angie grinned when she saw him gravitating toward the suspense area of the store.

"This one looks good," he said, picking up a heavy tome and flipping it over to examine its jacket copy.

"Maybe you should buy it?"

Sam smiled, holding the book in his hands. "What do you like to read?"

"Well..." Angie shrugged shyly. "You've seen my apartment."

"Paperback romances?"

"Sweet romances," she corrected. "The lighter sort that focus on the sunnier aspects in life and happily ever afters."

"I can see why those would be appealing."

His gaze washed over her, and she blushed. "It's nice to believe there's hope out there."

"There's always hope," Sam said. "As long as you don't give up believing."

Angie's heart hammered as Sam stared down at her with warmth and affection in his eyes. "Yes," she murmured, transfixed by his gaze.

"Table for five!" a waitress called, and they glanced toward the end of the aisle at a pretty college-age brunette wearing a server's apron. "Lopez?"

"Yeah." Angie backed away from Sam and straightened her coat. "That's us!"

Chapter Sixteen

After lunch, Angie dropped Sam at his condo so he could grab his toolbox and handyman supplies and pick up his SUV. Dr. Sullivan had cleared Sam to drive now that he was getting back into his routine and had re-familiarized himself with Hopedale. Riding around with Angie this past week had helped tremendously in that regard.

Sam planned to spend the rest of the afternoon at his dad's while the others had obligations back at Angie's place. Elena had a knitting project she was working on for the premature babies at the hospital nursery, and Lita needed to prepare her next art lesson. Angie had finally arranged that play date for Pepe with his best bud, Bobby, who was coming over. Apart from supervising the boys, she promised to dig out those Christmas decorations. Sam was tasked with picking up a Christmas tree after helping out his dad.

Sam didn't know when he'd ever felt so happy or included. Perhaps the answer was never, which was why these sentiments resonated so strongly with him now. He couldn't wait to get to David's house and start working. There was a lot of fixing up to do, and Sam was the perfect guy to do it.

Three hours later, Sam returned his screwdriver to his dusted-off toolbox and clamped down the lid. He'd made a number of repairs to his dad's house, including fixing the faulty knob on the kitchen pantry door, the chore he'd tackled last.

"Thanks for all the help, Sammy," David said, bringing Sam another mug of coffee after just having poured it at the counter. Sam stood and accepted it, gratefully, taking a sip of the steaming-hot liquid that warmed his throat and tongue. David didn't drink the fancy dark roast Sam was used to. He purchased the store brand coffee and made it so weak, it almost tasted like hot tea. Particularly when compared to the extra strong *café con leche* Sam enjoyed at Angie's place. But none of that mattered to Sam, who was just happy to be here making a difference in his dad's life for the first time in a while, from what he had gathered.

"Thanks for the coffee," Sam said, taking another sip. "It's delicious."

"You've grown up to be a very fine man." David studied his son admiringly and then his eyes glistened. "I only wish..."

Sam's soul ached because he understood. "I know I haven't been around much." He met his dad's sad gaze. "But all of that's going to change now."

"Yeah?" David sounded hopeful, yet a hint of doubt underscored his optimism.

Sam sat at the kitchen table, beckoning for David to join him. When he did, Sam said, "I know I haven't been the best son—"

"That's not true," David cut in. "You have been the best. The very best son. It's me who let you down." David hung his head in confession. "When Jocelyn died."

"Dad—"

David slowly looked up. "You were sad about your mom too. Don't think I didn't know that then. I just felt so lost, like a shell of a man. I worried I had nothing left to give you."

"That wasn't true."

"Perhaps it wasn't." David furrowed his wrinkled brow. "But that's what I believed back then. Ashton Academy seemed like the right choice." Remorse was written in his eyes. "But, if it was the wrong one..."

Sam stoically pursed his lips. After a beat, he said, "I got a great education at Ashton, and that helped me get where I am today."

"And where is that, Sammy?"

He laughed warmly. "I suppose sitting here with you."

A grin graced David's face. "That's a good thing, yeah?"

Sam smiled softly in return. "Yeah."

An awkward moment passed. Then David asked suddenly, "Can I make you a sandwich? Something to eat?"

"I appreciate it, but no, thanks. I'm eating with Angie later, back at her apartment."

"She's a nice gal, that Angie Lopez."

"Yeah, she is."

"Very pretty too."

"Dad."

"Her boy is really great, as well."

"Yeah. Pepe's awesome."

"Some things you can't put a value on," David continued. "Love. Home. Family. Those things are priceless. Wouldn't you say?"

"Um, sure," Sam answered, uncertain about where his dad was going with this.

"You know those television commercials you run?" David asked. "Where you promise customers 'the single best deal in town'?"

"Yeah?"

"The single best deal is here, Sammy." David placed his hand on the table and patted its smooth surface. "Home is where the heart is, don't you know?"

Sam took a minute to process, and then he chuckled in understanding. "I do know that, Dad. Yeah. I can sense that here, with you." Heat welled in his eyes, but he pushed ahead. "I've also experienced it at Angie's, which is why..." Sam gathered his nerve. "I wanted to ask you a question."

"Go on."

"It's about a recipe, actually. Something that's hopefully very easy to make."

David's eyebrows arched in surprise. "You're going to be doing some cooking?"

"I'm planning on it."

"That's great!" David rubbed his chin. "Let me think on what I've got that's big enough to feed a family."

Sam fumbled with his coffee mug. "I was actually thinking more about dinner for two."

"I see." David's eyes twinkled merrily. "Well, then! Let me just take a look." He rose unsteadily from the table. Then, leaning on his cane, he ambled across the room and nabbed an old wooden recipe box off the countertop. It was nestled tightly between an assortment of plants, and David nearly toppled the pot holding the aloe plant when he reached for it.

While Sam had made several repairs to the house this afternoon, and had tried to streamline and organize the clutter, one thing he hadn't been able to work his way around was David's enormous collection of houseplants. That was when a light bulb went on in Sam's brain and he had the most stellar idea for a birthday gift for David. He couldn't wait to run the concept by Angie to see what she thought.

David thumbed through the index cards in his recipe box, and then pulled one out, handing it to Sam. "Your old man's not much of a cook," he said humbly, "but your mom was. This was one of her favorites to make for us when we were first married. I really loved this recipe a lot."

Sam took the recipe card from David's outstretched hand and scanned it. A wave of melancholy washed over him when he recognized his mom's perfectly crafted, big-looped script. All at once, Sam could almost see Jocelyn's sweet, motherly smile and hear her warm, encouraging voice telling him to *swim fast*, which was what she always said when she urged Sam to do his best. Sam's heart filled with happiness, and a warm buzz hummed through him. He'd wanted to do something special for Angie, and a very specific plan was formulating in his mind. "This is perfect," Sam told David. "Thanks. Thanks so much."

Angie stood at her kitchen sink cleaning up the

baking dishes as colorful Christmas cookies cooled on oven racks on the countertops and kitchen table. Two platters were stacked with more cookies, and one of them was covered with cellophane.

She'd helped Pepe and his friend Bobby make a festive array of Christmas cookies. They'd had the best time cutting the sugar cookie dough into holiday shapes and decorating the cookies with egg-yolk paint made from food coloring. The brightly colored cookies baked into a shiny glaze, and the dough batter included a hint of orange rind, lending the entire apartment a sweet and tangy aroma. The cookies were mildly sweet, but not overpowering, and because they were smaller in size, she'd let each boy devour four of them, along with a cold glass of milk. This had all been after a raucous bout of play in the snow fort between Pepe and Bobby, with Angie watching happily from nearby.

It was nearly five o'clock, time for Bobby's folks to come get him. Bobby Ramirez was a cute little boy with short black hair, big dark eyes, and exceptionally good manners. It had been a pleasure having him over, and Angie was going to let his parents know how well behaved he'd been.

The bell rang, and Angie turned for the door, her hands still covered in soapsuds up to her wrists, as she cleaned the electric beaters.

"I'll get it!" Elena said, breezing through the kitchen with a bright smile. She'd been knitting on the sofa and keeping Lita company, the two of them chatting occasionally as Lita sat at the card table and worked on her newest art project—a spring garden full of butterflies, drawn from her imagination.

Pepe and Bobby were playing with Legos in Pepe's

room, so Angie figured she'd need to go and get them. "Thanks, Ma." Angie dried her hands on her apron. "Don't let me forget," she said to Elena, "we made a plate of cookies for Bobby to take home."

Elena nodded and opened the door.

"Good evening," an older gentleman's smooth voice said. He spoke in lightly accented English with clear Spanish undertones. "You must be Bobby's mother?"

Elena tittered a laugh. "No, no."

"Aunt?"

"Grandmother," Elena said, blushing.

"Amazing." The suave man in his fifties with graying hair, a moustache, and a beard entered the kitchen and smiled at Elena. "You don't look a day over twenty-nine."

Angie caught her breath, stalling before leaving the room. Was this man actually flirting with her mom?

Elena batted her eyelashes, apparently thinking he was. "And you are?"

"Ernesto Ramirez." He held out his hand. "Bobby's grandfather."

Angie saw her mom sneakily scan Ernesto's left hand, spotting no wedding band. Seconds later, she answered, "Charmed, I'm sure."

Elena shut the door behind Ernesto, and Angie waved. "Hi! I'm Angie, Pepe's mom." She grinned tightly at Ernesto then shot a quizzical stare at Elena, who simply widened her eyes. Angie's gaze swept over Ernesto and Elena one more time before leaving the room. Since losing her husband six years ago, Elena hadn't looked at another man. Then again, Angie hadn't done much looking, either. It seemed times were changing. And not just for Angie. "I'll just g-go and grab the boys."

When Angie returned with Pepe and Bobby in tow a couple of minutes later, Elena had the covered cookie plate in her hands and was passing it to Ernesto.

"I'm so sorry about your late wife," she said with utmost sincerity.

Ernesto gave a solemn bow. "My condolences on your loss, as well."

Bobby rushed to his grandfather, grabbing onto his legs. He'd already dressed in his snow boots and coat. "Papacito! We played in a snow fort and built a snowman!"

"My!"

"*And* we baked cookies."

Ernesto's brow rose in delighted surprise. "That's what I heard." Then, he added pseudo-confidentially to the women, "It's very important for men to develop culinary skills."

"I think that too," Angie said.

Elena simply pursed her lips and blinked. And Angie knew why. Elena had never let Angie's dad set foot in the kitchen to prepare anything. Angie was surprised Elena had even allowed Sam to cook breakfast. Then again, Elena had told her daughter that with Sam, things were different. Angie and Sam were the younger generation. When she'd said this, Angie had ribbed Elena, telling her that she really wasn't that old.

"My mom's a big advocate of men in the kitchen too," Angie joked, to which Lita lifted a hand in the next room and called out *mentira*, which means fib.

Ernesto chuckled deeply and peered into the living

room, nodding at Lita. "Who have we here? Another sister?"

Lita scoffed and waved her hand, but Angie saw her face take on a pink hue.

"Ernesto Ramirez," he said, politely addressing the older woman. "*Mucho gusto.*"

Lita twinkled his way. "*Igualmente.*"

"Such a beautiful family," Ernesto told Angie, by way of leaving. "It's been so nice meeting you all." He glanced down at Bobby. "What do you say?"

"Thank you for having me over!" Bobby crowed with so much enthusiasm the room broke out in grins.

Angie leaned down to address the small child. "You're welcome here any time." Next, she smiled at Ernesto. "Your abuelo too."

Elena shut her eyes briefly and appeared to be praying as Ernesto and Bobby headed for the door. Suddenly Ernesto stopped and stared down at the cookie plate, realizing it wasn't a throw-away. It was regular ceramic dinner dish. "Thanks for the cookies," he said to Angie. Then, with a telling look he glanced at Elena, whose cheeks were as rosy as a schoolgirl's. "We'll be sure to get you back the dish."

Sam entered the Holly and the Ivy Nursery and a welcoming sensation took hold. It was the same feeling he'd experienced when walking through David's front door last week with Angie, and also while he was at Harris Hardware. Familiar scents and sights surrounded him, from the earthy warm smell to the pretty holiday displays of door wreaths on the walls and evergreen garlands layered in bins. Cheery sprigs of mistletoe, tied up with silky white ribbon, heaped in a wooden tray by the register, and numerous poinsettia plants filled the shelves. The majority of the poinsettias were red or white, with some having a combination of red and white patterned leaves. Various-sized fir trees lined the entrance to the building, and additional ones stood on stands under the open-air, covered side of the building, sheltered by a slanted, shingled roof.

A tall man wearing jeans and a flannel shirt walked toward Sam. "Sam Singleton," he said, extending a hand. "It's been a while." The guy seemed around Sam's age and was nearly his build, just a bit taller. Sam wasn't sure why, but his expression seemed a little melancholy.

Sam shook hands with the stranger, sensing an odd connection. "I'm sorry. You're...?"

The nursery worker blanched then shot Sam a disbelieving look. "Honestly, man. It hasn't been that long."

"I'm...um..." Sam glanced around the nursery once more, seeing a family had entered behind him. The mom and dad were sorting through greenery in one bin, while the kids excitedly ran circles around an elaborate Christmas decoration showcasing a miniature Santa's village, complete with a small wooden workshop and eight miniature reindeer, positioned as if they were prancing before a toy-laden sleigh.

"Where's Rudolph?" the little boy asked his sister. He couldn't be more than Pepe's age—likely a couple of years younger.

"Rudolf came later," the little girl in pigtails said with authority.

What is it about that village and all that fake snow?

"Took us a whole week to put that together," the man he'd been conversing with said, noting Sam's eyes on the Christmas village.

"You mean, I... I'm sorry, you and I—?"

The fellow set his hand on Sam's shoulder. "Hey man, are you all right?"

Sam blinked, remembering something. Him and Ken building a table to house the Christmas village display. "You're Ken?"

Ken cocked his chin. "Ken Larsen, sure." He squinted his eyes at Sam. "Want to tell me what's going on?"

The room went tilt-a-whirled around him. Sam's dad had said he'd worked at the nursery during summers and on school breaks from Ashton. Ken had apparently worked here with him and was now in some sort of managerial position.

"I had a bit of an accident," Sam confided quietly. "Took a knock to my noggin." his shoulders sagged. "Now, I can't remember much at all."

"Oh, gee. That rots."

"Yeah."

"Is it...permanent?"

"Don't think so." Sam met Ken's kind brown eyes, intuiting something. "We were friends, weren't we? Buddies."

"*Were* is the operative word." Ken said matter-of-factly, but Sam detected the note of hurt in his voice.

"Wow, Ken. I'm sorry."

"It's all right," Ken stated with bluster. "Takes a

lot of time offering the 'single best deal in town.'" He said this last part with his fingers raised in quotation marks, and Sam knew now that he'd really hurt Ken's feelings by neglecting their friendship.

"When's the last time we got together?" Sam asked him, sincerely wanting to know.

"Sometime in college." Ken shrugged. "Water under the bridge. You know."

Sam did the mental math— that had been years ago. That was a whole lot of water, and Ken seemed like a truly nice guy. Sam was sorry he'd let their friendship slide. This made him wonder about the other missteps he'd made, like falling out of touch with his dad. He had the uncomfortable feeling that he'd been bad with personal connections in the past. He'd placed a priority on his business, clearly. But what about his dealings with people?

Sam surveyed the nursery anew, assessing the upgraded shelving and the fancy skylights that had been installed in the front area. The back section was fashioned like a greenhouse, which reminded Sam of his other goal.

"You're the manager here?"

Ken smiled proudly. "Manager—slash—owner."

"Well, good for you. Congratulations."

"Business seems good at Singleton's."

"It is. Only, it would be nice to know how I *built* the business."

"How much time have you lost?" Ken asked in mild shock.

"Twenty-six years."

"Whoa."

"At first, it was that long," Sam corrected. "Some

things are starting to fill in. The doctors say the rest will come along eventually."

"Good. That's good. Glad to hear it."

Sam hung his head. "I'm sorry, Ken. Really I am. The more I learn about my past, the more I start to wonder what kind of person I was."

"Successful. Rich. Eligible," Ken teased, nudging his shoulder. "Every bachelor's dream!"

Sam looked up, not feeling so sure about that. "Ha-ha, yeah. Maybe."

Neither one spoke for a minute, then Ken bridged the awkward silence between them. "Is there something I can help you with today?"

"Oh, right! Right." Sam chuckled and shook his head, recalling his mission. "I'm here with a very important task: to pick up a Christmas tree."

"Glad to help with that," Ken said jovially. "How high are the ceilings at your place?"

"It's not for my place." Sam shifted on his feet. "I'm actually staying with a friend."

"Ah."

"The doctors didn't think it would be a good idea. I mean, not until I've fully recovered my memory."

"Gotcha," Ken said with a wink. "So how high are the ceilings in your friend's place?"

"Well, Angie's in an apartment, so I'd say—"

"Angie? Wait a minute? Are you talking about that pretty Angie Lopez who just moved to town?"

"That's the one."

"She works with you, yeah?"

"As my accountant."

"Single?"

Sam wondered whether Ken was asking out of

curiosity or on behalf of himself. He bristled at the thought that Angie would probably consider Ken attractive. Ken was a nice-looking guy and apparently single. "What does that matter?"

The corners of Ken's mouth twitched. "You like her that much, huh?"

"I didn't say—"

"Didn't have to." Ken's grin brightened.

"It's not like that," Sam said defensively. "It's not just me and Angie. She lives with her mom, and grandmother. She'd got a kid, too."

"Ready-made family," Ken razzed, and Sam felt the old familiar burn of friendly teasing.

"Cut it out, Ken."

"Fine by me." Ken held up his hands. "How tall did you say those ceilings were again?"

"Not more than eight feet."

"Great. Come with me. I've got several trees that might suit you."

Sam shoved his hands in his coat pockets and trudged along behind Ken. When they exited the door and stepped out into the drifting snow, Sam ventured, "As long as I'm here, I'd like to ask you one more thing."

"Shoot."

"It's about greenhouses..." he began as winter winds whistled around them.

Chapter Seventeen

A HALF HOUR LATER, SAM ELBOWED his way in the front door to Angie's apartment, a six-foot Frasier fir in tow. He wore a cheerful Santa hat on his head. "Ho-ho-ho!" he boomed. "Merry Christmas!"

Lita looked up from her art project with delighted surprise, and Elena dropped her knitting in her lap. "Why, Sam," she said, standing to greet him. "It's marvelous!"

Pepe scampered out of his bedroom wearing his Batman pajamas. Angie was close behind. "A Christmas tree! Woo-hoo!" the little guy yelped.

"What a beautiful tree." Angie's pretty brown eyes lit up as Sam righted the tree in the kitchen, setting its trunk on the floor. "It's even taller than you are."

Sam chuckled and cut a sideways glance at his specimen. "Just barely, but yeah."

"We're all ready to get started decorating after dinner," Angie told Sam. "Pepe had his bath early." Sam noted two cardboard boxes stacked together beside the television, and a long plastic storage bin resting beside them on the floor. Per usual, the aromas in the air smelled delicious.

"What's cooking tonight?" he asked with a grin.

"A homemade turkey chili," Angie replied. "It's

been in the crockpot all day." She motioned toward the kitchen. "We've been a little busy."

Sam surveyed the tidy kitchen, spotting a brimming plate of Christmas cookies covered with plastic wrap on the counter. "I thought I smelled something sweet."

"Could also be the cinnamon in the chili," Elena commented.

"I can't wait," Sam told her before turning his attention to Angie. "You got a Christmas tree stand in one of those boxes over there?" he asked, steadying the tree in his gloved hand.

Pepe scampered over and patted one of the branches.

"It's soft," the kid said. "Not scratchy like the fake tree we had last year."

"Smells better, too," Elena added, and everybody laughed.

Angie walked to the long plastic box and removed its lid, pulling out a Christmas tree stand. "This one should do."

"Where would you like this?" Sam asked her.

Angie uncertainly glanced around. "We don't want to block the window. Lita and her birds..."

Lita waved a hand as if telling them not to worry, but Sam saw Angie had a point. There was only one window in the living room, and apart from providing Lita with a view, it served as a source of natural light.

Sam spied a vacant space to the left of the TV. "How about in that far corner on the other side of the bookshelves?"

Angie glanced at Elena and Lita, and both women nodded. "Perfect," she said to Sam with a heartwarming grin.

After a nice dinner, during which Pepe filled Sam in on the exploits of his day with his new best friend Bobby, the family joyfully discussed decorating the tree. But first, there were a few things to pick up in the kitchen. Sam insisted on cleaning up, and—after a bit of back and forth between him and the ladies—the women relented.

"Besides," Sam said, "I've got my Second Mate to assist me."

Sam tossed Pepe a dry dishtowel, and the boy caught it gleefully.

"What do you say, little buddy? Want to help out?"

"Uh-huh," Pepe said with an enormous smile, and Angie's heart pinged. Pepe liked Sam so, so much. It was clear her son enjoyed having a man around, and Pepe was starting to follow Sam everywhere. To the point that Angie worried the boy might be becoming a nuisance.

"You're sure?" Angie asked Sam for about the billionth time.

"One hundred percent positive." He sent her a meaningful look, and warm tingles resonated to Angie's core. "You go on in there with your mom and Lita and start setting up."

Sam's relaxed air gave the impression of a guy who did the dishes all the time, with the equal aplomb of bringing home Christmas trees—or carrying octogenarians down the stairs. Angie tried to make sense of this new Sam, but every time she did her heart tripped over itself and only beat harder.

"You really can trust me with a scrub brush,"

Sam said, displaying the soapy implement, and Angie realized she'd been standing there goggling at him.

"Oh...er...yeah. Of course!"

Pepe giggled. "Sam's a great First Mate."

"Aye-aye," Angie blubbered nervously, stumbling toward the living room.

Sam watched her keenly as she backed away. "I think I'm supposed to say that to you."

"Yeah, right! Go to it, then. K.P. away!"

Pepe cackled, gripping the dishtowel to his side. "*Mo-om.*"

"I think the Second Mate and I can take it from here," Sam said in mock-solemn tones.

Pepe beamed reverently up at Sam, then surprised Angie with a salute. "Aye-aye, Captain."

Happiness bubbled up inside her. Pepe wasn't the only one liking Sam. Angie was liking him, too. *A lot, a lot, a lot...* And, not just as a friend, either. The very thought made Angie's face hot. "Well, " she said, inhaling sharply, "I can see the kitchen is in good hands."

Then, she went to join Elena and Lita, who were already unpacking decorations in the living room and exclaiming excitedly over each newly uncovered item.

Later that evening, Lita scooted forward in her wheelchair to hang the last ornament on the tree. It was a special-order eggshell white Christmas tree ball with a purple crown on it and the words *Puerto Rican Princess* scrawled across it in fancy lilac lettering.

"Pepe gave me this one," Lita proudly informed Sam, and Pepe glowed.

Sam perused the tree, noting it lacked a finishing touch. "Do you have an angel or star to go on top?" he asked the group.

Elena smiled softly. "An angel for *Anh-gel-la*, of course." She reached into a box and gingerly unwrapped a beautiful dark-haired, fair-skinned angel with big brown eyes. With her long curly hair beneath her halo, Sam had to agree the ornament did favor his very attractive accountant. "My husband, Jose, and I got this when Angie was little. It was always her favorite part of the tree."

"Still is." Angie grinned and took the angel in her hands, turning it this way and that to examine the fine details on its sparkly wings. "She really has held up pretty well."

"We pack her very carefully," Elena explained.

Angie passed the angel to Pepe, who eagerly stood nearby. "Would you like to do the honors?"

"Yay!"

"Better get the ladder," Elena instructed Angie.

"Not necessary," Sam said, tucking his hands beneath Pepe's arms. Then he hoisted the grinning boy onto his shoulders. "What do you think, little buddy?" Sam asked, glancing up at the child. "Can you reach it from here?"

Pepe leaned toward the tree. "A little closer..."

Sam scooted over, steadying Pepe on his shoulders by holding his legs, and heat warmed Angie's eyes. If her husband had lived, he might have been doing something similar with Pepe now. *But, he didn't.* Angie gave a light sniff, and Sam peered in her direction with a questioning look.

"I'm okay." Angie dabbed her nose with a tissue. "Just so happy, that's all."

Sam's smile warmed her through and through. "All right! Let's top this tree."

Pepe leaned forward and wiggled the angel into place on the very top branch of the tree.

"Perfect!" Angie cried.

"Very nice," Elena agreed.

Lita smiled softly, first at the tree and then at the trio of Angie, Sam, and Pepe standing in front of it. "*Ay que lindo.*" *Oh, how beautiful*, she said.

The tops of Sam's ears turned red as he lifted Pepe up in the air and then set him down on the ground in one smooth move. "The tree does look great," he said, standing back to admire it fully.

Had they been married, and Sam Angie's husband, he might have placed his arms around her shoulders right now. It would seem natural and feel so right. Angie felt a raw ache in her soul when she realized that was what she longed for with Sam. A deeper and more intimate connection. And yet, how could she entertain such thoughts? Sam wasn't even himself again. When the old Sam returned, would these vestiges of the new Sam remain, or would they simply disappear like dissipating smoke above an extinguished candle?

"Let's turn out the lights," Pepe crowed happily.

"*Sí, sí,*" Lita agreed.

"Well, go on, Pepecito," Elena nudged the boy, and he scampered around the room killing light switches and turning off lamps. At last, it was just the family, Sam, and their gloriously adorned Christmas tree.

"It's lovely." Sam's voice sounded rough, and all at once hope bloomed in Angie's heart. When he set his eyes on hers, her cheeks grew hot and her pulse fluttered.

"Thanks for picking up the tree," she said. "You'll have to tell me how much it was, so I can—"

"Nuh-uh," Sam said firmly. His eyes twinkled. "My treat."

"But I can't let—"

"After all you've done for me?" Sam asked hoarsely. "Are you kidding?"

"Thank you, Sam," Elena said decisively, as if closing the subject, and Lita added her *gracias*.

"Yes, thanks," Angie said, still awash in his gaze.

"Anytime."

Elena checked her watch. "It's almost time for a certain someone to go to bed," she said, glancing at Pepe.

"Aww, Grandma."

Angie addressed Pepe in a firm yet loving tone. "You've had a very full day, and school's in session tomorrow."

Pepe stared up at Sam, hoping for a reprieve.

"Your mom and grandmother are right," he said kindly. "There'll be plenty more time for play tomorrow."

"Will you play Legos with me?"

Sam blinked, apparently caught off guard.

"I've got a new set. They turn into cars!"

"Now, Pepe—" Angie started, but Sam finished first.

"I'd love to," he told the boy. "But it will have to be after work."

"After work's okay," Pepe chirped cheerfully.

"*And* after homework," Angie amended.

Pepe huffed a little breath, but he honestly didn't look disappointed. He appeared thrilled at the prospect of playing Legos with Sam. "O-kay."

Angie laid a hand on Pepe's shoulder. "Now, go brush your teeth and get ready for bed. I'll be there in a bit." She glanced over at Lita, who was grinning merrily.

"*Un coquito?*" the elderly woman asked.

"What's that?" Sam wanted to know.

"A very excellent Puerto Rican eggnog," Elena supplied. "Made with rum and coconut milk."

Angie couldn't think of a better way to end the evening than indulging in this tropical treat with her mom, grandmother, and Sam. "Would you like to try one?" she asked him. "I can fix it?"

"That would be great. But only one." Sam shot her a handsome grin, and Angie's stomach flipped. "I've got to work tomorrow."

She grinned back, her spirit feeling happy and light. "Yeah, me too."

Pepe dashed out of the bathroom, holding his toothbrush in one hand. "Did I hear *coquito*?"

Angie laughed indulgently and twinkled at her child. "Okay, you. I'll make one for you, as well." She cast a sidelong glance at Sam. "Without the rum." Next, she sent Sam a flirty look. "Want to come and help me?"

"I'd love to," he said.

Angie stood by the blender in the kitchen while issuing orders to Pepe and Sam to bring her ingredients. She'd already reached into the spice cabinet and set cinnamon, nutmeg and cloves, and a small bottle of Vanilla extract on the counter.

"Coconut milk," she said to Pepe, and he scampered to the pantry. "Two cans!"

Pepe grinned and retrieved two cans of light coconut milk, bringing them to his mother.

She told Sam, "We have to be careful with Lita and dairy these days, so this vegan recipe is perfect."

Angie next instructed Pepe, "And get the almond milk from the fridge, please."

As Pepe went to do that, Sam's forehead rose. "What can I do?"

"Grab the rum." Angie grinned. "It's in the high cabinet over the refrigerator."

Sam waited until Pepe had gotten the almond milk and closed the refrigerator door before nabbing the bottle of white rum from the cabinet.

Angie winked when Sam handed her the bottle. "This is just for the adult drinks."

Sam chuckled in reply. "Of course."

"Angie," Sam said before she turned on the blender. "I think you should let me help with things."

"You do help," she answered, thinking of his efforts in the kitchen.

"I mean financially."

"Sam, no—"

"You know, I'm feeling much better. Maybe I shouldn't even be—"

Angie shot him a silencing look, and Sam noticed what she'd seen. Pepe observing them with wide eyes. "We'll talk later." She kept her tone light to keep Pepe from worrying. "All right?"

Sam rubbed his cheek, apparently realizing he shouldn't have brought this up in front of her son, who was growing so attached to him. "Yeah, sure."

Angie focused on her task, trying not to fret over the topic Sam had nearly broached. He *was* doing better in many ways and functioning just fine on the job. Theoretically, he could get by on his own at his condo. Angie was sure that was what he was about to tell her when she stopped him because of Pepe. She prepared herself for the conversation she knew would be coming later. But oh, how it made her heart ache.

Angie whipped up her concoction, blending it at low speed. Then she filled two of the glasses with the frothy mixture. "These are for Pepe and Lita," she explained. "I'll add the rum to the others. Lita loves it but can't have any this late at night due to her medications." She finished making the drinks and dropped a whole cinnamon stick into each glass.

Sam's gaze snagged on the snowman-patterned napkins on the counter. "Napkins all around?"

"Excellent thought." Angie smiled. "The glasses will be chilly."

They carried the drinks into the living room with Sam handing Lita hers and Angie delivering a glass to Elena. Once they were all supplied with *coquitos*,

Lita raised her glass at the Christmas tree and then toward the others. "*Feliz navidad!*"

"*Feliz navidad,*" they chorused together.

A short time later, Elena and Lita excused themselves to go get ready for bed. Angie had tucked Pepe in soon after he'd wolfed down his tasty coconut drink and brushed his teeth for the second time. Angie and Sam were still savoring the last bit of their mixed drinks when they overheard Lita whisper to Elena in the hall. "Lovebirds," she said authoritatively, and Angie's cheeks burned hot.

"Oh, gosh, Sam. I… I mean, Lita…she—"

"Didn't hear a thing," he said, smiling over the rim of his glass.

Sam perused Angie thoughtfully under the gentle glow of Christmas tree lights. Only one lamp was on in the room: the one beside the sofa, and it was turned down low. "Besides," he added huskily. "It's Lita's prerogative to think what she wants to."

"Think, yes." Angie gave an embarrassed laugh. "But saying is a little different."

Sam shrugged easily. "Doesn't bother me. I think your family is great."

"Sam, about Pepe—"

"What about him?"

"You're being so kind, but please. I don't want you to feel like you have to—"

"I don't." He gazed at her earnestly, and she knew he was telling the truth. It flustered her to think about how seamlessly Sam was blending into her family.

It concerned her all the more because Angie was starting to entertain notions of wanting him to stay. She decided to change the subject to more neutral territory.

"How did things go at your dad's today?"

"Really great." Sam eyed her thoughtfully. "Better than I expected, actually."

"I'm so glad." she heaved a contented sigh. "For you and David both."

"I came up with an idea for Dad's birthday." His face lit up. "I wanted to run it by you to see what you think."

"Sure," Angie said, privately flattered Sam was seeking her opinion, rather than trying to pawn off the idea of getting his dad a gift on her. Sam had changed so much since his accident, and she was liking this new Sam very much. More than liking him. Angie was feeling her heart start to open like a new bud under the springtime sun. It was a wonderful feeling, but scary too. And yet, she couldn't stop it, any more than winter can help yielding to spring.

Sam set his empty glass on the coffee table. "Well, you know my dad is a plant man."

"Gosh, is he ever! I've never seen anyone with such a green thumb."

"Or such a supply of houseplants, it's true."

"You gave him a lot of those, you know."

"Did I?" Sam appeared mildly surprised. "Well, good for me. But I apparently didn't think things through."

"What do you mean?"

"My dad's house is small. That third bedroom's so tiny it almost doesn't count as a bedroom. It's more like an office, really, and it's packed to the gills with plants."

"Just like the rest of the place," Angie agreed, chuckling.

"Precisely why it would be nice for my dad to have somewhere else to keep them."

"What do you mean?"

"I was thinking of an addition," Sam said. "Something pretty simple, like a solarium—or a greenhouse type arrangement. It could be free-standing, or attached to the back of the house. I was thinking we might even enclose the back porch and convert it to a sun room."

"That sounds great." Angie frowned pensively. "But also like a lot of work."

"It's not, really," Sam informed her. "Not when you know what you're doing. I talked to Ken about it." Sam angled forward resting his elbows in his knees, clearly enthused about the idea. "Apparently, he and I built quite a few greenhouses for folks back when I was in high school, and we worked together at the nursery."

"Is that right?" Angie grinned.

"Money for materials isn't a problem," he told her. "I've got that covered, and Ken's offered to help me with the labor."

"I can help, too," Angie volunteered impulsively, and Sam viewed her askance.

"I think you've got enough on your plate as it is, Ms. Lopez."

She grinned at his use of the formal title. Perhaps it was true, but this was such a great plan, Angie wanted to do something to contribute. "How long do you suspect it will take to complete it?"

Sam gave it some thought. "A real construction project would require permits and be a bit more involved, but greenhouses can be purchased in kits. The kind Ken and I used to set up for customers can be assembled in a weekend."

"Will it be safe? Sturdy enough to withstand the elements?"

"I wouldn't purchase anything but the best."

"And it will be done by David's birthday?"

"If Ken and I get busy ordering things now, yes."

Sam's excitement was contagious. "Then maybe that's what you should do." A brilliant thought occurred to her. "Sam," Angie said, growing animated. "We could plan a surprise party for your dad in the greenhouse. With balloons, party decorations, and everything."

Sam grinned gratefully. "How about if I put you in charge of that part?"

"It would be my pleasure," Angie said, envisioning how touched and pleased David was going to be. "I'll bake a cake too."

"I hope Elena and Lita can be there. Pepe too, of course."

"They wouldn't miss it," she replied, grinning.

"Great. I'll go over to the nursery at lunchtime tomorrow and set things in motion."

"David's going to be so thrilled," Angie said happily.

"Yeah." Sam appeared wistful a moment and then his smile brightened. "Hope so."

Since Sam hadn't brought it up yet, Angie decided she ought to. It was better for them to talk about things now when they had a rare moment of privacy. "Sam, about what you said in the kitchen..."

"I'm glad you mentioned that. I was just sitting here thinking about that myself." He peered into her eyes. "You and your family, you've all done so much for me."

"It's been our pleasure."

Sam raised his hand. "Thanks. I do appreciate it. But you know, I'm the kind of guy who likes to carry my own weight. I understood in the beginning why I needed to be here, and all of you were very generous to take me in."

Angie's heart plummeted because she knew where he was going with this. "You still don't have your memory back."

"No, that's true. But the fact is I can pretty much take care of myself."

Oh, but can't you see, Sam. I want to take care of you. "I get that." Her lips trembled and she pressed them together. After a beat, she said, "I was just hoping we could give things a little more time."

"I'm not sure what good that'll do."

She reached out and clasped his arm. "It might give you a chance. A chance to remember."

"Maybe that would happen more easily with me back at my condo?"

When he said it out loud, it made so much sense that Angie wanted to cry. Heat burned in her eyes. "You're saying you want to go?"

"No, not at all." Sam's voice grew raspy. "Angie, seriously. Any guy would have to be crazy to want to leave you."

Her heart pounded at the implication, then Sam seemed to backtrack.

"What I mean is, I don't want to be a burden."

"You're not."

"Then there's no reason."

"Pepe!" she blurted out. "He adores having you around." She swallowed past the lump in her throat. "The rest of us do too."

Sam spoke tenderly. "You know I can't stay here forever."

"How about until Christmas? It would be so nice for Pepe. He really loves having you around." She lifted a shoulder, embarrassed by how much she loved having him here, too. Nothing changed the fact that Sam was her boss, which made everything extra complicated. If they became involved and then things didn't work out, that could compromise things for Angie at the jewelers. Could she really risk putting both her heart and her job on the line with him?

Sam appeared lost in his own thoughts for a moment, and then he said, "You're sure that won't put you out?"

Relief flooded through her. "No, not at all. It will be great having you here on Christmas morning. Pepe will be so happy. That'll give us a chance to transition, as well. I can explain to him that you're doing better and will be moving out after the holiday."

"All right." Sam smiled handsomely. "But under two conditions."

"Two?"

"First, you let me start helping with the grocery bill." When she started to protest, he stopped her. "It's only reasonable, Angie."

"All right," she agreed. "What's number two?"

"It's about later in the week. Friday."

"Yes? What about it?"

"I was hoping I could ask you out."

Angie flushed, so, so flattered. "Sam."

"Nothing fancy," he continued. "Just dinner at my place." There was a mysterious gleam in his eye. "It's the least I can do to say thank you."

Angie wanted to leap at this chance to spend an evening alone with Sam, an evening that might even turn romantic. But what about their status at work and her fears about a personal relationship between them complicating things? Angie gave herself a stern mental nudge, given that things already *were* complicated between them. They'd been complicated ever since Sam had woken up on that hospital bed and asked whether they were personally involved. They may not have been then, but it certainly felt like they were now. And oh, how Angie's heart yearned to explore these feelings to see where they might lead.

"Are you sure that's the right idea?" she began shyly. "The two of us being alone?"

"I have really good manners," he said in all seriousness. "I'm a gentleman too."

"Oh, yes. I'm sure."

"I'd really like to do this for you, Angie. Treat you special. Please give me the chance."

It was pretty hard to refuse an invitation like that.

"All right," she agreed. "It's a deal, but I get to do the dishes."

Sam grinned, and Angie's heart warmed. "Aye-aye."

Chapter Eighteen

"SOMEONE WAS LOOKING AWFULLY COZY last night," Elena said as she poured her morning coffee. "Two someones, actually."

"Shhh," Angie hissed quietly, grabbing her own mug from the cabinet. "He'll hear you."

"Sam's in the shower," Elena said, nodding in that direction. Lita was already dressed prettily for the day and parked at her card table by the window with her sketchpad in front of her and a mug of coffee at her elbow.

Angie rolled her eyes. "Gosh, Ma. You and Lita—"

"Are two very keen women with eyes. Eyes that see what's going on between you and Sam."

"Oh, yeah? And what's that?"

"Don't play coy with me, *mija*. The two of you are developing feelings for each other."

Angie's mouth dropped open.

Elena arched an eyebrow. "I wouldn't be surprised if Sam became more of a permanent fixture around here."

"Ma! *Shush.*" Angie warned sternly, her cheeks burning. "That's not how it is, okay? Sam's a sick man—"

"His mind seems to be working fine." Elena sipped from her mug. "His heart, too."

"He has *amnesia*. Gosh. Sam can't even say where the last twenty-six years have gone."

"Well, maybe they weren't so important."

"That's crazy."

"I mean it," Elena persisted in her bullheaded fashion. "What matters is now. The here and now. Have you thought about it, Angie? What if Sam never gets his memory back? What if he stays like this forever?"

"But the doctors said—"

"Doctors can be wrong."

"And *right*," Angie argued.

"Okay. So, say they're right." Elena eyed her carefully. "You still don't know what the timeline might be."

"That's true. Some things are out of our hands."

"Well, if you love him—"

Angie choked on her coffee. "Ma," she said, sputtering and grabbing a napkin from the holder on the table to wipe her lips and dribbled chin. "Just stop."

Elena set a hand on her hip. "Well, I like Sam. Lita does, too. And anyone can see that Pepe adores him."

Angie stared at her agape. "So what?"

"So, what's a minor memory issue? Your father couldn't remember things half the time. I'd send him to the store for milk, he'd come back with butter."

Angie held her mom in her steely gaze, and Elena threw up one hand. "Fine, I'll back off. I just haven't seen you like this in years." Her expression softened. "Happy."

"Of course I'm happy. It's the holidays."

"It's more than the holidays, Angie. So much more."

"Good morning!" Sam boomed from the living area, walking toward them. He'd dressed in his work slacks and dress shirt but still was barefoot as he strode toward them, toweling off his hair. "Just coming to grab some cof—"

He stared quizzically at Angie, who'd frozen in place, and next at Elena, who appeared equally culpable. "Hey, um...is something going on?"

"Nope!" Angie supplied readily.

"Nothing at all," Elena concurred.

"We were just discussing the weather," Angie fibbed.

"Weather? Hmm." Sam peeked into the living room and smiled at Lita, staring past her and out the window. "It looks like the snow has stopped. At least momentarily."

"Yeah, and I'd better get dressed," Angie said, scurrying out of the kitchen with her coffee. "I need to wake Pepe and get him ready for his bus soon."

As Angie slipped away, she heard Sam ask Elena, "Is Angie okay this morning?"

"Oh, yes," Elena replied in a sing-songy way. "Fine."

Sam was in great spirits the whole rest of the morning, probably because he was contemplating the fun surprise he was planning for David. Pam and George were in a pretty good mood too. They both were only scheduled to work half a day, since they'd manned the store on Saturday. With the streets cleared and weather conditions improving, business picked up at the shop. A steady stream of holiday shoppers came in to make purchases, and Angie learned that a number of them were staying at the nearby ski resort for the holidays. She tucked a gift-wrapped package into a pretty silver store bag that with the white-scripted Singleton's Jewelers logo. The dot over the "i" in Singleton's was shaped like a diamond, of course.

"Merry Christmas!" Angie told the customer, who was a heavy-set woman in her sixties. "I hope your husband enjoys the cufflinks."

"He's going to love them," the buyer responded cheerfully. "He needed a new set to go with his tuxedo." The lady winked. "Holiday parties, you know."

Angie said she did, but naturally she didn't. She had never been to a Christmas party requiring tuxedos, and she didn't envision attending any soirees like that soon. But that didn't matter to her. She was happiest just hanging out at her apartment, especially when Sam was around. Angie was sad about him moving out after Christmas, and she knew her family would be disappointed about it too, particularly Pepe. She planned to tell them later this week when she had an opportunity. Even with Sam returning to his condo, Angie was hopeful that all of them would stay connected and keep in touch, in a personal sense and not simply relating to her job. Sam's invitation for Friday had sounded a lot like a date to Angie, and in her heart she wanted it to be. She was becoming so incredibly attracted to him, and she couldn't help but hope that the feeling was mutual. That something special might develop between them. A different and romantic sort of relationship.

Angie waved goodbye to the cufflinks-buying customer as a cute couple entered through the front door and Pam went to greet them.

"Good morning," Pam said pleasantly to a young blond man and a brunette who appeared to be in their late twenties. "Welcome to Singleton's Jewelers."

It really hadn't taken Pam any time at all to learn the routine around here, and she demonstrated skill in working with their customers. Angie wondered about Pam's coffee date with George and how that had gone. Angie had only seen George today briefly, as he'd been busy in his workshop in back making jewelry repairs and adjustments.

Pam made small talk with the couple then asked what she could help them with today.

"We wanted to take a look at your Signature Diamond Collection," the fellow said.

"Of course." Pam's smile sparkled. "Congratulations are in order, I suppose?"

The young woman ducked her chin with a shy smile. "We got engaged on Saturday. Connor asked me while we were on the ski lift—just like in your television commercial."

"Only, I didn't have the ring yet." Connor chuckled abashedly. "My bad."

"That's o-*kay*." His pretty fiancée nudged him. "You're going to make it up to me now."

Pam chuckled along with them then inserted her key into the lock on the jewelry case. "Which ones would you like to see?"

Sam breezed in from the break room, wearing his overcoat and a scarf. He held his hat in one hand. "Do you mind if I step out?" he asked Angie, who was at the register, reviewing some numbers on their software program. "I thought I'd run up to the Holly and the Ivy and have a chat with Ken."

"No, no," Angie told him. "That's great. No problem."

"I should be back before Pam and George leave for the afternoon."

Angie smiled, so proud of Sam for doing such a kind thing for his father. "Take your time. I'll handle things here."

An hour later, Pam and George emerged from the break room ready to leave.

"Well, I guess we're off," Pam said brightly, slipping on her gloves.

"Nice job on that sale," Angie said, congratulating her. "Claire and Conner seemed very pleased with their purchase."

"I'll have the ring fitted for her by Wednesday," George supplied, holding the front door open for Pam.

"Bye, you two," Angie called after them. "Have a great afternoon!"

When the door shut behind them, Angie couldn't help but notice George's arm slide around Pam's waist as they strolled away. Next, Pam leaned toward George with a sunny grin and tousled his hair. *So there is something going on between the two of them. Love is in the air.*

Angie's gaze flitted to the mistletoe wreath mounted on the wall behind the Singleton's Signature Diamond Collection, and her heart thumped. Sam had been so annoyed with her when she'd wanted to remove that bear painting, and yet the holiday wreath fit in with the Christmassy décor perfectly. She thought back to Cyber Monday when she'd first brought that wreath in after purchasing it at the Holly and the Ivy Nursery. She'd assumed Ken and Sam were acquainted, but she hadn't known about their former friendship then. Could it be this new project would bring the two of them back together?

Sam's accident certainly had inspired unexpected consequences. He was reconciling with his dad and had formed a completely different sort of relationship with Angie. He had never even met Angie's family before his fall, and now they were completely taken with him. Angie recalled her morning conversation in the kitchen with Elena, wondering how her mom always saw through her. The truth was Angie *was* developing feelings for Sam. He was so kind and caring, it was impossible not to like him. The fact that he tried so hard with Pepe scored him bonus points too. Plus, he was handsome and swoony...and when he gazed at her with those deep blue eyes, he frankly took her breath away.

Angie thought of the young couple who'd been in here buying that diamond solitaire. What a fun and hopeful stage that was for a relationship, the point where you were just setting out on your journey together. A marital journey as husband and wife. She remembered those feelings from her first marriage of course, but they seemed so long ago and far away that the sentiments had grown fuzzy. What registered clearly with her at present was her incredible attraction to Sam.

A Singleton's Signature Diamond says forever.

Angie recalled the first time Sam had uttered that phrase. He'd been sitting in the office with his feet up on his desk and sketching away on a legal pad in his lap. He'd said he was brainstorming for a new slogan. When he hit upon it, Sam held a glimmer of inspiration in his eyes. "What do you think of this?" he asked excitedly, and Angie looked up from her computer. "I mean it," he persisted. "I think I'm onto something."

She flipped shut her laptop, giving him her full attention.

He gave a dramatic pause before sweeping his hand through the air. "*When your love is written in the stars...*" he gave a self-congratulatory grin, "*a Singleton's Signature Diamond says forever.*"

Sam waited expectantly until Angie grinned. "I have to admit," she said cagily, "it's got a ring to it."

"Har-har."

"No pun!"

"It's good, right?" his smile sparkled. "I mean, really, really good."

"It's great, Sam," she said surely. "Absolutely. What woman could resist that?"

Sam smirked playfully. "Probably you."

"Probably me," she agreed with a nod.

Angie pulled herself out of her reverie, eying the jewelry case in front of her. She'd absentmindedly walked toward it and set both her palms on its smooth glass surface. There was one ring in particular she'd always liked. The white gold setting looked antique but wasn't. It was a brand-new style featuring a tiny collection of sculpted rosebuds around its base. They worked together to serve as a mount for a generous one and a half carat diamond, and each silver-colored rosebud had a tiny ruby set in its center. It was exquisite, unusual. Angie had never seen anything like it. She'd always been tempted to try the ring on but had never worked up the nerve. Perhaps now that she was alone in the shop, this would be a good time.

She stole a glance at the street and then, seeing that no one was coming, slid behind the jewelry case. Within minutes she'd unlocked it and removed the tray housing her coveted piece. She stretched out her hand, examining her empty ring finger. It was a silly fantasy. Ridiculous. But it certainly wouldn't hurt to see how it looked.

Angie plucked the ring from its satiny resting spot and slid it easily past her first knuckle. The ring caught a bit at the center of her finger, but she was able to shove it on. *There.*

She extended her fingers, admiring the gorgeous ring as its gems glimmered in the shop's light. Cheery Christmas music played in the background, and Angie felt herself getting swept away—into Sam's arms and under the spell of his kiss. She sighed heavily, and the front door chime tinkled. Her head jerked up, and Angie's heart thundered. *Sam.*

"Well, hey...there?"

Angie lowered her hand behind the counter and fiddled with the ring, trying to get it off. "Oh...er... hey!"

Sam's eyebrows knitted together. "What are you doing?"

"Just...um..." She twisted the ring and tugged harder. *Gosh, no. It's stuck!*

Sam strode her way, and perspiration swept Angie's hairline.

"No! Stop!"

Sam halted abruptly. "What? Why?"

"It's, er...the carpet!"

"The carpet?"

"I...I mean, she dropped a contact!"

"Who?" Sam whipped his head around in surprise, seeing no one else in the store. "Angie." His forehead rose. "What on earth are you talking about?"

"The...the woman who was in here earlier."

"Claire?"

"Yes! That's the one." Angie's pulse pounded in her ears and her cheeks burned with the fire of deceit. "She...she called to say..." Angie drew in a deep breath, mildly queasy. Her middle knuckle was starting to swell and the ring pinched tighter. The more she wrestled with it, the worse things got. "To say that she'd lost a contact, and she thought it happened in the store."

"That's weird." Sam scratched his head and studied the jewelry tray in front of her. She quickly reached up and splayed out her right hand over the vacant spot where the ring on her finger belonged. "What's that tray doing out?"

"I...er...thought maybe the contact had fallen out in here."

"In there?"

Angie's voice came out a squeak. "Just checking."

Sam took another step in her direction.

"Watch your step!" Angie warned frantically.

"Oh, right. Right. Of course." Sam removed his hat wearing a concerned expression and set it down by the register. Next he unbuttoned his coat and got down on his knees.

"Uh, Sam?" Angie asked as he ran his hands over the carpet. "What are you doing?"

He looked up. "Helping you search. Of course."

"Of course." Angie's heart hammered as she sidestepped her way toward the back of the store.

Sam shot her a stare from where he perched on all fours. "Wait. Where are you going?"

"Just...to the bathroom," Angie spouted lamely, concealing her left hand behind her back.

Then, she dashed through the break room and into the small restroom where she scrubbed her hands with soapy water until she was able to slide the stubborn ring off her aching finger. Angie dried the ring and slipped it in her pocket, massaging her aching knuckles as panic spiked through her.

While Angie was gone, Sam got to his feet and carefully walked to the case containing his Singleton's Signature Diamond Collection. He took care to skirt along the edges of the room, circumventing the area directly in front of it. He couldn't help but feel Angie was acting awfully strange. Sam stared down at the jeweler's tray holding a selection of his most precious rings. *Hang on! Two of them are missing.* There was the one that had been purchased today. George probably had that in back. But where was the second one? Sam narrowed his eyes in thought, surveying the remaining rings. *Ah-ha. It's the one with the roses that's—*

"Here it is," Angie said pertly, appearing from out of nowhere. She held the rose ring in her hand and slipped it back into its designated spot with practiced finesse.

"Where did that come from?" Sam asked her.

"Oh! Er..." Angie bit her bottom lip. "I asked George to clean it. When Claire tried it on, she'd just put lotion on her hands, and it got a little grimy."

Sam studied Angie like this was a pretty odd story, because—well—it was.

"In any case," Angie said with a relieved smile, "we don't have to worry about that contact any longer."

"No?"

"Claire texted when I was in back to say that she'd found it."

"Claire? But, how did she—? Never mind." Sam shook his head, deciding he didn't even want to know. "Well, good. Good that's good. Crisis averted."

"Crisis averted." Angie's cheeks bloomed red. "Yep."

Chapter Nineteen

"OH, ANGIE, YOU LOOK BEAUTIFUL." Elena said as Angie entered the living room.

"You look so pretty, Mom," Pepe crooned.

Lita eagerly agreed. "Yes."

Angie fretted that she'd overdone it by wearing the fitted red sweater dress and knee-high boots. It was far more casual than anything she ever wore to work, but then, these weren't exactly play clothes, either. She was dressed up as if she were going on a date. Which she *was*. Sort of. The very thought knotted her stomach and made her feel like a bundle of nerves. Happy nerves. But still.

She slightly gritted her teeth. "Do you think it's too much?" she asked Elena and Lita.

Both women shook their heads.

Elena's assurance was warm and motherly. "You look perfect."

The doorbell rang, and Angie jumped. That couldn't be Sam already. She hadn't had time to curl her hair and apply that spritz of perfume. Angie checked her watch, seeing it wasn't quite seven. After work, Sam had stayed at his place to get things ready, while Angie had driven her SUV back home. These past few weeks they'd adhered to the routine of her driving him in to his condo and parking there each morning. Afterward, they walked to the jewelers together, taking Sam's usual route.

These past few nights, however, Sam had lingered a little extra at his condo while Angie had gone on ahead. He said he was trying to step back into his exercise regime, and Angie couldn't blame him for wanting to resume one more regular activity. Not that she thought his buff body needed any extra working out, she found herself reflecting with a blush.

While Sam was doing well with his job and retaining his new memories, most of his past still alluded him. Other than the few recollections that had come back to him, there'd been no new stunning revelations. Angie was starting to wonder if her mom had been correct in thinking Sam might never totally regain his memory. She could only guess at how sad and confusing that must feel, even if he was busy building happy memories now.

This past week had probably been the happiest. Angie and Sam had reestablished their routine at the shop, and she relished the extra time she got to spend visiting with him during their daily walks to and from work. It was nice having Sam around her apartment in the evening, too. He was kind and often played with Pepe, indulging the child in a game or two while maintaining some boundaries for himself and for adult time. Angie guessed it had to be tough on him, having absolutely no privacy while camping out in the living room.

In any case, Sam seemed very adept at tuning out the household commotion when he wanted to. He could put in his earbuds and listen to music while working on his laptop or reading. After he'd devoured the new thriller novel he'd purchased from Lit and Latte, Sam had started revisiting a lot of classics he'd found back at his apartment, both for his enlightenment and in hopes of jogging his memory. So far, Sam had enjoyed the literature but hadn't experienced any revelations regarding his past.

The doorbell rang again, and Angie walked toward it, thinking she could ask Sam to sit for a minute while she grabbed her purse and coat—and secretly touched up her makeup and hair. Though she wasn't going to mention the primping. Yet, when Angie opened the door, it wasn't Sam standing there at all.

"Ernesto," she said, smiling up at the older gentleman. "What a nice surprise."

"I hope I'm not intruding," Ernesto said. He held up an empty plate in his hands. "We wanted to return your dish before too much time went by. My daughter-in-law, Carla, and her whole family thank you. The cookies were very delicious." He smiled handsomely and peered past Angie's shoulder. "Is your mother home?"

"Why, yes," Angie said, grinning. Then she stepped back out of the way, allowing Ernesto passage inside. "Ma!" she called into the living room. "Visitor for you."

Elena scuttled into the kitchen, nervously clutching her hands together. "Ernesto," she said, her cheeks flushed. "Good to see you."

Ernesto bowed reverently. "You, as well." He glanced around the kitchen, noticing the saucepans simmering on the stove. "I'm not interrupting dinner?"

"Oh, no," Elena demurred. "We haven't eaten."

"Why don't you *stay*?" Angie warmly patted Ernesto's coat sleeve. "I'm sure Ma made enough."

"Angie!" Elena blurted before she could stop herself. She covered her mouth with her hands. Next, she sighed resignedly at Ernesto. "My daughter."

He winked good-naturedly. "I understand. I've got one of those, too." Next, Ernesto surprised them by unbuttoning his coat. "If there's really enough...?"

"*Muchisimo*," Lita called from the living room, and Ernesto chuckled warmly.

"*Buenas tardes*, Lita."

"*Buenas tardes*," she said, her face glowing delightedly.

Angie clapped her hands together. "Well! I guess that's settled."

Pepe darted into the kitchen and tugged at Ernesto's hand. "Will you play Legos with me?"

"Of course." Ernesto's dark eyes danced. "But first, I'd like to visit with your grandmother." He glanced around. "And maybe help out in the kitchen?"

"Oh, no—" Elena protested.

The doorbell rang again, and Angie's pulse raced. This had to be Sam for real. "Can you get it?" she asked Elena. "I just need to grab a few things from my room."

"Ernesto seems pleasant enough," Sam said as he and Angie exited the elevator on the fifth floor of his building.

"He's a very nice guy," Angie agreed. She grinned at Sam. "I also think he's sweet on Ma."

"Seriously?" Sam grinned from ear to ear. "Wow, that's great." He led them to his unit, then laid his hand on the doorknob and paused. "What does Elena think of him?"

"Oh...I'd say it's mutual," Angie replied, and Sam chuckled.

"I hope you like the dinner tonight," he said, holding the door open. "I got the recipe from my dad. It's one my mom used to make him, and one of his favorites."

"Oh, how sweet!"

When Angie entered Sam's condo, she felt like she'd been transported into a magical realm. Strings of twinkling white lights hung around the perimeter of the room and framed the large glass window overlooking the darkened forest. Snow still crowned the trees, their shadowy outlines wavering in the chilly blackness. But that wasn't all that was Christmassy about this place. Sam had decorated. In style. A pretty fir tree stood at one end of the plate-glass window. Its blue shimmering lights reflected in the glass beyond it. Nearly every item on the tree was blue—from the blue-tinged Christmas balls to the shiny blue tinsel adorning the branches, and ornamental snowflakes and stars, sprinkled with glitter. "It's so...manly!" Angie said, laughing.

Sam laughed right along with her. "Yeah. That's what I thought too."

"Seriously, Sam." Angie eyed him appreciatively. "Your tree looks great." She surveyed the room again, noticing a few more holiday touches here and there. A wooden prancing reindeer on the mantel, and some snowman coasters on the coffee table... "Everything else does too." Her gaze snagged on a red-and-white Christmas stocking dangling by the blazing hearth. "You even got a Christmas stocking?"

"Not for me," Sam informed her, helping Angie out of her coat. "For Pepe."

Angie couldn't believe he had done something so kind for her son. His thoughtfulness touched her to the core. Sam really was such a nice man. So kind and giving, too. It was impossible not to be attracted to him, or moved by this gesture.

"Oh, Sam. That's so sweet of you! But Pepe has a stocking at home."

"Where do you hang it? I didn't see one?"

"Well, since we don't have a fireplace, we lay it out with the milk and cookies for Santa the night before."

"Ah."

"But that's all right. No reason he can't have two." she beamed up at him. "I'm sure Pepe will be thrilled. Thank you."

Sam laid Angie's coat over his arm. "Let me just go and hang this up. I'll be right back."

Angie grinned, surveying the beautifully decorated space anew. Candles flickered on end tables and soft jazz music played over Sam's high-end sound system. Angie hadn't overdone it with the dress. This definitely felt like a date. She observed the elegantly set dining room table. Two place settings were at the end of the table closest to the kitchen. One was at the head of the table facing the sweeping window wall, while the other was to the left of that and situated so that person had a full view of the fireplace, and the window as well. A single red taper stood in a squat brass candlestick holder near the place settings, but it hadn't been lit.

Angie turned toward the kitchen, spying a bottle of red wine on the counter with two empty wine goblets beside it. Something was baking in the oven, and a small saucepan sat covered on the stove. Delectable smells wafted toward her. Some kind of poultry, she thought, maybe with rosemary and a multitude of other herbal scents that reminded her of fresh produce from a farmer's market.

"What's cooking?" she asked when Sam re-entered the room.

"Two Cornish hens roasted with rosemary, wild rice, and braised asparagus."

Angie's mouth watered just from the description. "Sounds yummy!"

"There's a special dessert." Sam winked, and tiny tingles raced down her spine.

"You're being so good to me," she uttered warmly.

"You deserve it," he said, walking toward the island. "Wine?" Sam displayed the label on a fine Virginia vintage, and then offered an alternative. "I've also got a bottle of white chilling in the fridge."

"You've thought of everything." Angie laughed warmly, and then decided. Even though white probably went better with poultry, she much preferred a full-bodied cabernet franc. "I'll take the red, thanks."

As Sam opened the bottle and poured, she said, "I can't believe you pulled all this together in one evening."

"I didn't." he twinkled her way, and Angie's heart fluttered. "I've been working on it all week."

"What? You mean...?" Her jaw dropped with the

realization. "I thought you were staying here to exercise?"

"I was." Sam grinned. "Exercising my decorating acumen."

Angie laughed heartily. "Oh, Sam!"

"When I went to the Holly and Ivy on Monday," he further explained, "I consulted with Ken and he helped set me up. The blue decorations are actually extras he had on hand from a former display at the nursery." Sam indicated the tree, and Angie chuckled.

"I see."

"I tried to buy them from him, but he insisted on making them a gift."

"What a good guy."

"Yeah." Sam grinned and poured her some wine. "He let me pay for my tree, though, and all those little lights you see around."

"Man has to stay in business somehow," Angie said, accepting the wineglass Sam handed her.

"Most certainly."

Sam filled his glass as well, then raised it in a toast. "Here's to..."

When he hesitated, Angie chimed in. "Christmas!"

"To Christmas it is." He clinked her glass, and they both took a small sip of wine.

"Oh my, this is *good*."

"It's one of my favorites—I think," Sam said with a self-deprecating laugh. "At least, I'm guessing it is. There were three bottles of it in my wine rack." He thumbed over his shoulder, and Angie saw that the wine rack attached to the cabinetry and to the right of the refrigerator held a half dozen bottles.

"This is all very nice," Angie said, immeasurably

impressed. "I had no clue you could cook. Remember all those takeout menus?"

One half of Sam's mouth tipped up in a grin. "Yeah. It's pretty crazy, all right." He swirled the wine in his glass. "I must have cooked at some point in the past. When I was in your kitchen, making flapjacks came back to me."

Angie's face warmed as she remembered how close they'd stood that morning and how hard her heart had jackhammered when Sam's eyes had met hers. Like it was doing right now.

"It was the same way tonight," he continued. "I seemed to find my way around the kitchen okay." He chuckled and shook his head. "But you want to know a secret?"

"Yeah?"

"I don't believe I've cooked much in this place before. Some of my cookware still had the original price stickers on it."

"*Noooo...*" Angie said, snickering.

"It's true." Sam held up his hand in a pledge, and this only made Angie laugh harder.

"Hey, where are my manners?" he said, remembering himself. "Would you like to have a seat?"

"Do you need help with anything in the kitchen?"

"Nope. Everything's coming right along."

"Well, then, sure! In that case." Angie took a seat on the sofa in front of the low-burning gas hearth. Despite the austere chrome-and-glass furnishings, Sam's condo felt homey and warm outfitted for Christmas. Or maybe it was Sam's sheer proximity causing Angie's temperature to soar. He sat beside her on the sofa, cradling his wine.

"So, tell me about Ernesto?"

Angie sighed happily. "He's Bobby's grandpa."

"Pepe's friend, Bobby?"

"Yeah." Angie smiled at the recollection. "He came to pick up Bobby from his play date last Sunday, and I guess he and my mom hit it off."

"But, you didn't say anyth—"

"I wasn't sure there was anything to talk about until tonight." Angie giggled. "Now, I'm certain Ernesto's interested."

"That's nice, don't you think?" he asked warmly. "Nice for Elena."

"I guess. But it's kind of a shock."

"What do you mean?"

"She hasn't dated since my dad and... Well, you know, since then." Angie felt a painful tug at her heartstrings, and she wondered what she was doing here. She'd gotten all dressed up and had wanted to look pretty for Sam. And she'd been so pleased when she'd seen all the trouble he'd gone to on her behalf. Sam had really worked hard to make this evening special. And yet, Angie wasn't sure if she was ready to move on.

Sam gazed at her compassionately, and Angie knew what he was thinking. He was wondering if she was the same as her mom. "How about you?" he asked her kindly. "Has there been any—"

"No one," Angie said, taking a quick swallow of wine to soothe her nerves. This was silly, ridiculous. She probably shouldn't even be here.

"Angie..." Sam gently removed her wineglass from her grasp and set it on the coffee table with his. "What you went through was awful. Really heart-wrenching. Probably the worst time of your life."

"It was," she said, hearing the warble in her voice.

"But you came out of it."

"No, I—"

Sam took both of her hands in his and held them firmly. "Look at me." When she did, he whispered huskily. "You came out of it, Angie. You're here. And Angie?" He squeezed her hands. "I'm here with you."

Heat prickled the backs of her eyes and her cheeks suddenly felt moist. How could she dare to hope for something so wonderful when it might get taken away?

Sam reached up and stroked back her tears with his thumbs. "I've never known a stronger woman. Or a more talented, or beautiful one."

"Sam, I..."

His gaze poured over her, and her heart stilled.

"I mean it," he said surely. "You, Angie Lopez, are a force to be reckoned with."

This brought a smile, albeit a shaky one. "You're pretty formidable, too."

"Oh?"

"You're strong, Sam. Strong enough to conquer lots of things, even a past you can't remember."

"How exactly am I doing that?"

"Pretty excellently, from what I can see."

He cradled her face in his hands. "I don't know why this thing happened to me, but it did. And honestly?" he rasped softly. "I can't say that I'm sorry."

His face drew nearer, and Angie caught her breath as her head spun and her heart yearned so badly for Sam's kiss.

Then, the kitchen timer went off, beeping steadily.

"Wow. Sorry." Sam laughed awkwardly. "Bad timing."

An hour and a half later, Sam sat with Angie at his dining room table. They'd both finished their dinners, and she'd thanked him profusely for the meal which, fortunately, turned out fairly tasty. Sam poured them each a second glass of wine and set the bottle down beside the red taper, which had burnt three quarters of the way down.

They'd had a nice conversation about their childhoods. The more Sam talked about his, the more he seemed to recall things. It was like articulating the memories out loud helped drag them to the surface and make them clearer. He'd been a good kid overall and had only gotten into mischief occasionally.

Angie claimed she'd always been an angel, and Sam didn't have to wonder about that. It certainly seemed like she'd come straight out of heaven to him. He admired her greatly—for her courage and her kindness, as well as her sharp intellect on the job. He must have been an idiot not to have seen all that before and fallen head over heels in love with her. Sam's heart pounded when he realized that it was happening now.

It had pained him badly to see Angie so upset before dinner. He'd wanted nothing more than to take her in his arms and promise her everything would be all right. Or, at least that he'd do his very best to help make things better, for Angie, for Pepe, for everyone.

"What do you say?" Sam asked, standing to clear their plates. "Are you ready for dessert?"

"Oh, no. I couldn't." Angie gripped her belly. "Dinner was delicious and—" She stopped talking when she saw his play pout.

"Okay," she said with a lilt. "I'll bite. What is it?"

"A dark chocolate mousse with an orange Grenache."

Angie gaped in delighted surprise. "You didn't."

Sam's mouth twitched at the corners, and then he chuckled. "All right. You've got me. I didn't. I picked it up special order from Baron's Bistro," he said. It was the most upscale restaurant in town.

Angie grinned in amusement. "Oh, Sam. That's so sweet."

"No pun," he said with a wink, and Angie hooted.

"Okay, I'll take a tiny portion."

"Should we have it here? Or would you like to sit by the fire?"

Angie glanced at the comfy seating area. "On the sofa would be nice." She got to her feet. "But first, let me help you carry these dishes to the kitchen."

"I'm not letting you clean."

"But Sam," she scolded lightly. "That was our deal."

"That was *your* deal," he answered, teasing.

"At least let me put these plates in the dishwasher," Angie persisted.

"You can do that while I serve the dessert," Sam agreed, compromising. "Let's leave the rest for a while."

"Are you sure?"

"The pots and pans can wait." Sam locked on her

gaze, and Angie's breath quickened. When he didn't look away, her cheeks burned hot. And then they burned hotter, until Angie feared her whole body was going to burst into flames.

"All right," she said a bit breathlessly. Angie picked up her water glass and took a long swallow as Sam pivoted toward the kitchen. "Coming right behind you!" she reported, following in his footsteps.

Angie savored her last bite of delectable chocolate mousse, thinking that she'd never felt so pampered. Sam had planned the ideal romantic evening, and she was falling for him hard. And yet, there were so many complications. Sam's memory loss...their status at work...

"What are you thinking?" he asked, sipping from his wine. Sam had already finished his dessert and set down the bowl.

Angie placed her bowl beside his on the coffee table.

"I was thinking that's about the best chocolate mousse I've ever had in my life."

Sam smirked knowingly. "Liar."

Angie gasped. "Now, that's unfair."

"What? I always tell you what I'm thinking."

Angie's forehead crinkled. "That's so *not* true."

"Sure it is. I've told you everything that I remember. All that I can about my past. I've told you what a great mom you are and what a wonderful family you have. I even recall standing right over there..." Sam pointed to the window wall reflecting the cheery Christmas tree and room lights, as well as the flickering glow from the candles. He cocked his chin. "And telling you how pretty you are."

"Exceptional," she said, correcting him.

Sam's eyebrows arched. "Ah, so the lady remembers."

Angie felt herself flush. "Certain things, yes."

"So then," Sam challenged warmly. "You admit I'm telling the truth."

She stared up into his deep blue eyes and was utterly swept away.

"You always know what I'm thinking."

Angie's lips trembled and her head felt light. "I don't know what you're thinking now," she said weakly.

"I'm thinking..." Sam leaned nearer, and Angie's heart thumped. "I'd like to dance with you."

"Now?" Angie asked, totally thrown.

Sam lifted the remote from beside the sofa and flipped to a different song on his sound system before asking huskily, "Will you do me the honor?"

"But, you and I... I don't know." Angie worriedly bit her lip. "What about work?"

"Work?"

"You're the boss."

"Maybe that's where we've got it wrong," he said good-humoredly. "You're the one who's so good at ordering me around." He took her hands in his and tugged Angie to her feet. "If you don't want to, just say the word."

How could she refuse a dance with Sam? All she'd dreamed about these past few weeks was being close to him. She gazed into his eyes, revealing the truth. "I want to."

Sam cupped her chin in his hand and his eyes twinkled. "I'm glad." He pulled her into his arms in such a practiced maneuver Angie had to tell herself not to be jealous because he must have done this before. Sam was a good-looking man, and accomplished. He also had a great job and was single. He'd surely dated before. Probably a lot, if his smooth moves were any indication of experience.

Sam led her toward the center of the room where they were clear of the furniture. He held her closer then as the music finished its introduction and a soft crooning voice began to sing.

Unforgettable...

That's what you are

"I know this song," Angie said, thinking she recognized the lyrics but not the artist, who sounded like a contemporary male jazz singer.

"It's nice." She laid her head on Sam's shoulder, feeling sheltered in his strong embrace as he guided her expertly around the floor. Her arms were linked around Sam's neck as he wrapped his arm around her waist, and they swayed to the romantic tune. "What made you choose this one?"

"I found it on my playlist," he whispered in her ear, "and it just seemed—right."

Warm tingles raced down Angie's spine as she sighed against him.

"I know I'm not right in the head. I mean, not completely." Angie peered up at him, and Sam pulled back to gaze at her. "But these new memories that we're making, they're ours to keep."

Sam cradled her face in his hands, and Angie licked her lips.

"We've stopped dancing," she murmured, her heart pounding like a drum.

He quirked a subtle grin and shot a glance skyward. "That's because we're standing under the mistletoe."

Angie gasped and looked up, seeing it was true. A dainty sprig of waxy white berries on green stems was tied up with a silky white ribbon and tacked to the broad doorframe dividing the living area from the kitchen. "Oh," she said, her cheeks burning hot.

"Angie," Sam said. "May I kiss you?" He tenderly stroked her cheek, and she pressed her face against his palm, delighting in the feel of him. His steadiness. His warmth. Then she closed her eyes, tilting her mouth up toward his.

"Yes," she whispered as the music played on.

Sam's lips brushed over hers, and Angie felt faint, deliriously dizzy with sensation. "Sam…I'm…falling…"

"I know, darling," he said, kissing her again. "Me too."

"No, I mean…" Angie huffed out a breath. Her knees shook and her lips trembled. But not out of fear, out of longing. "My legs are going to cave."

Sam shored her up and held her tighter. "Not on my watch, they won't."

Then he kissed her again, and Angie's worries melted away.

"I've got you," he said between feathery-light kisses, each one as silky and lovely as the tiny wisp of a butterfly's wings.

"Just don't let me go."

"I won't."

He gave her one more lasting kiss, and this one was

firmer and deeper than all the others. Angie caught her breath, clinging to him. "Sam."

She opened her eyes to find him beholding her with tenderness. Adoration. And yes, love. Emotion rocketed through her, bursting through all her defenses like fireworks on the Fourth of July. Everything she felt for Sam was genuine and real.

"I may not remember much," he rasped hoarsely. "But I'll never forget this."

"Neither will I."

Sam smiled gently and kissed her again.

"It's getting late," she muttered quietly, her arms still looped around his neck. "We should probably finish up in the kitchen."

"Yeah," he agreed, but neither one moved.

Angie's heart brimmed with happiness, and yet she had those niggling doubts. Things could never be perfect between them. Not this way. Not with Sam unable to recall his whole past... But, for tonight, and during this magical moment, Angie didn't want to think about what might come. She merely longed to enjoy the glorious present.

"Angie?"

Her heart beat harder because she intuited this was it. Sam was about to say I love you. But instead, he said, "You're the best."

"Thanks, Sam," she said softly. "So are you."

Chapter Twenty

ANGIE WAS SO EXCITED FOR David's party on Sunday. Everyone else was too. Everyone but David, that was, because the event was still a total surprise. Sam and Ken planned to assemble as much of the greenhouse as possible in advance, and then transport portions on Ken's flatbed truck. Angie's job was keeping David away from his house for most of Saturday during the daylight hours. Sam didn't guess David would go out back at night. Just to cover his bases, Sam set up a large tarp concealing the screening on the back porch, telling his dad he was "making repairs."

"What kind of repairs?" David asked Sam as Angie herded him into the house.

"Let's get back indoors," Angie urged David. "Brr! It's cold out there. You'll need to grab your coat so we're not late for Pepe's basketball game."

Pepe waited in Angie's SUV with Lita and Elena. The plan was for Angie to take David along to watch Pepe play on his rec league team. Then, the five of them would go out for pizza at Pepe's favorite spot. David had been delighted to say yes, particularly as little Pepe himself had asked David to come along. Nobody mentioned David's upcoming birthday, and he was too polite to hint at it himself. David just appeared jovial that he was included in the busy goings-on in Angie's family.

"David," Angie said as she escorted David into the passenger seat of her SUV. "This is my Ma, Elena."

"Nice to meet you," Elena said, and David nodded.

"And my grandmother, Alma. But we call her 'Lita.'"

"Lita," David said pleasantly. "How do you do?"

"Cold." She smiled, hugging her arms around herself.

"Lita moved here not too long ago from Miami," Angie explained. "She hasn't been in Virginia long."

"Welcome to the sunny south!" David said in an effort at light humor, and Lita chuckled in understanding.

Pepe leaned forward in his middle seat. He was sandwiched in back between Elena and Lita and wearing his basketball uniform beneath his parka. "We're getting more snow next week," Pepe said excitedly.

"That's what I hear." David buckled his seatbelt and peered at the child. "Might even have a white Christmas."

"I'm getting a *dog*," Pepe crooned brightly, and Lita and Elena exchanged worried glances.

"Now, Pepe," Angie said, studying him in her rearview mirror. "We've been through that."

"Santa can't bring everything," Elena added. "There are many children in the world. Lots of obligations."

Pepe grinned at David, who still had his eye on the child. "I've got a backup plan."

David pursed his lips, and Angie cocked her chin.

"The Three Kings," she said smartly. "As *if* they can carry a dog on their camels."

Pepe crossed his little arms and harrumphed. "*Of course* they can."

"This is the celebration of the Epiphany?" David asked the group.

"Yes," Elena said. "On January sixth. But the Wise Men generally bring small gifts." She pointedly eyed Pepe. "Whatever they can fit in the boxes left for the camels."

"Filled with *grass*," Pepe informed David.

"Sounds like a delightful tradition," David said, then he glanced at the child. "I should think those Wise Men know what they're doing. Santa Claus too. I'm sure they'll bring just the right things for you, Pepe."

"Pepe's pretty lucky this year," Angie said, thinking placating her son with this information might take his mind off the impossible. "He's getting *two* Christmas stockings."

"Woo-hoo!" Pepe squealed, bouncing up and down on the seat until Lita patted his leg, and Elena told him to cut it out. "Why two?"

Angie glanced in the rearview mirror, before she pulled out of David's drive. "Sam put one up for you at his condo."

"That was nice of Sammy," David said, evidently pleased.

A few hours later, Sam and Ken loaded big segments of the partially constructed greenhouse onto the flatbed truck Ken used to transport bulky nursery items. They both wore parkas, hats and gloves, jeans, and sturdy boots, as wintry winds nipped at their cheeks and noses. The lightly drifting snow didn't halt their progress, though. If anything, it made Sam feel more cheerful about the entire ordeal. This wasn't just about his dad's birthday; Christmas was coming, and Sam's heart felt so light.

He'd had the best time helping Angie and her family set up their Christmas tree, and his date with Angie last night couldn't have been more perfect. Sam was falling for Angie and falling hard. She was wonderful, sweet, and kind, and her tender kisses had made his heart soar while filling him with warm crackling electricity all over. Even if he could remember his past, Sam was certain that no other person could hold a candle to Angie. She was the kind of gal who made a guy forget every other woman who'd come before.

Ken finished covering a portion of the greenhouse with a tarp and secured the broad strap that held it in place. "So?" he asked merrily. "How did everything go with the dinner last night?"

"Pretty perfect." Sam tried to downplay it but a grin crept up on his lips nonetheless.

Ken's forehead rose in understanding. "I might have guessed that from your chipper mood."

Sam gave the holding strap on his side of the truck one final tug then walked toward the passenger side of the cab. "I'm 'chipper' because of this surprise for my dad."

"Uh-huh," Ken said knowingly, climbing into the driver's seat. "I'm sure that's all it is."

When Ken cranked the ignition, Sam asked, "How about you?"

Ken turned to him. "How 'bout me?"

"Is there a special woman in your life?"

Ken shook his head. "Not anymore there's not."

"I'm sorry, man."

"Don't be," Ken said jokingly, but Sam could read the hurt between the lines. "Trust me on this. I'm far better off without her."

Sam buckled his seatbelt, and Ken did the same. "Well, you know what they say," Sam told him. "It's better to be with no one than the wrong one."

Ken chuckled. "I'm hearing that loud and clear."

Sam was so glad to be reconnecting with Ken. At the same time, he couldn't help but feel a bit down for him. The holidays were times for being around loved ones. Sam had learned that more than ever this year. And Sam had heard that Ken's parents had both passed away during Sam's memory-lapse years.

"So," Sam said a bit more brightly. "What are your plans for Christmas?" If Ken was flying solo, Sam was going to find a way to include him in his own celebration. He reasoned he'd be spending Christmas with his dad, and perhaps also with Angie and her kin.

"Going to spend it with my sister, Julie, and her family in Colorado. I'm shutting the nursery down between Christmas and New Year's."

"Sounds like you're due for a break."

"And for some good skiing," Ken added with a grin.

"There's lots of great skiing here."

"That's true." Ken's brown eyes twinkled. "But the powder's *mighty fine* out there."

Sam chuckled at Ken's enthusiasm. "I'm sure."

As they began rolling along, Sam said, "Thanks a lot for doing this, man. Helping me with the greenhouse and all."

"I'm glad to do it." Ken shot him a sincere look, and all at once Sam knew that everything was forgiven. "Anything for a friend."

Angie texted Sam from the pizza parlor, but he said to stall David longer. Maybe they could go out for ice cream.

"Ice cream in winter?" Elena asked.

Lita firmly replied, "*No.*"

"How about coffee and cocoa then?" Angie suggested with a hopeful grin. "We can drop by Lit and Latte."

David checked his watch. "I don't want to take up too much of your time."

"Oh, it's no bother," Angie said.

After the coffee and cocoa at the book café, Angie suggested a movie.

"A movie?" David shook his head, and Lita yawned. "I think not. Thank you for the thought, though."

Angie's phone buzzed, and she spied the reply from Sam.

Not yet.

Maybe one more hour...

Angie gulped and glanced at David. "I've got it! Why don't you come back to our place?"

"What?"

"We'd love for you to see it." She spun toward

the back seat for reinforcements. "Wouldn't we, everybody?"

"Oh, yes," Elena said.

"*Si, si,*" Lita chimed in.

Pepe peered up at David with hopeful eyes. "Can we play Legos?"

A short time later, Angie showed David around her apartment—for the fourth time. "And this is the living room where we all hang out, and Sam stays—"

David leaned wearily on his cane. "It's all very lovely, dear." He furrowed his wrinkled brow. "But do you think I could sit down?"

"Oh, yes. Yes! Of course."

"I'll go work on dinner," Elena said. "We're just having hamburgers." She shot David a kind look. "Would you like to stay?"

"Why, no. No, thank you." David shook his head. "Where has Sam been all afternoon?"

Pepe bounced on his heels, tugging at David's hand. "He's been building a—"

Angie cupped her hand over Pepe's mouth. "*—eem. Ouss.*"

David leaned toward the boy. "Pardon?"

"Field mouse!" Angie said, tugging Pepe in toward her side. When David wasn't watching, she shot Pepe a sly look, drawing her finger to her lips in a quiet sign.

David sat weightily on the sofa, steadying his cane. "I've got rodents? In my house?" He appeared aghast, so Angie quickly backtracked.

"Not *in* your house. No, no. *Outside.* On the porch. They, er, nibbled through the screen."

"Oh, dear," David said with concern. "I didn't know they were capable of that."

"Sam says it will all be fine," Angie assured him. "He's taking care of everything and can share the details with you in the morning."

"In the morning," David said, still appearing befuddled. "Well. All right."

Angie's phone buzzed, and she checked it. It was a new text from Sam.

Clear.

"Are you sure you won't stay for dinner?" Angie asked David. "That was Sam, texting to say he's on his way here."

Pepe puffed out his lower lip, addressing David. "We haven't played Legos yet."

"That's true," David acknowledged kindly. "I did make that promise."

"So, you'll stay?" Angie asked with a hopeful smile.

"Yes, indeed." David grinned. "I'd be delighted."

Chapter Twenty-One

ANGIE WALKED BESIDE SAM AS he led David along by the elbow, and Pepe scampered ahead of them. Sunday had finally come, and Sam had managed to keep his dad from going into the backyard on Saturday evening by keeping the screened porch covered with tarps. He'd kept his dad away from the windows facing the backyard, too, and had stayed with David until he was exhausted from the day and ready to turn in for bed.

"I really don't understand what all the fuss is about," David said. "What's more, why do I have to wear this blindfold?"

"It's just a little surprise, Dad," Sam said warmly.

"Well, I don't like not being able to see," David retorted. Pepe darted forward and opened the door to the back porch.

"Cold!" David complained.

"That's why we had you put your coat on," Sam explained.

"What about those mice?" David questioned. "Did you fix the screen?"

"Everything's all patched up," Sam said. Pepe covered his mouth in a giggle and opened the second door, leading out to the snowy lawn.

"Watch your step here," Angie cautioned David. "We're going down the two short stairs to the backyard."

"Yes, yes. I guessed that," David barked, his irritation clear. Angie fretfully glanced at Sam, but he shook his head, indicating she shouldn't worry.

"Almost there," Angie promised as David's shoes crunched through the snow.

"Let's hope so," David grumbled.

Pepe pulled back the greenhouse door, and Angie ushered David inside it. Lita and Elena were waiting to surprise him, and a number of gorgeous new plants were, as well. Sam had enlisted Ken's help in suggesting new offerings and planned to move some of the plants from David's crowded house out here with his father's permission.

"Ah," David said, noting the change in temperature. He rubbed his palms together, savoring the heated space. "This is better. Where are we?"

Angie winked at Sam, and he addressed David. "Are you ready?"

"For what?" David replied in cranky tones.

Sam slipped off the blindfold, and David's eyes widened. A lush array of ferns and flowering plants greeted him. And they were inside a gorgeous greenhouse, teeming with crepe paper streamers, a cheery Happy Birthday sign, and colorful helium balloons.

David rubbed his eyes in apparent disbelief. "What's all this?"

The group began the first chorus of "Happy Birthday" as David's gaze fell on the decorated card table holding a beautiful birthday cake. The lettering on the cake read Happy Birthday, David!

Tears misted the old man's eyes. "This can't possibly be..."

"It is, Dad." Sam set a hand on his shoulder. "Happy birthday."

David spun and clutched Sam to his chest, speaking hoarsely. "A greenhouse, Sammy?"

"I hope that it's all right," Sam said concernedly. "Not too much of a surprise."

David dabbed the corner of his eye with a hanky. "No, no. It's just *fine.*" He eyed Sam affectionately. "You always said..." He pursed his lips, unable to finish.

"What?" Sam asked worriedly. "What is it, Dad?"

"When you were a boy...a teenager, really. You gave me that IOU." David's face hung in a frown. "I guess you don't remember."

"For this?" Sam asked, perplexed, glancing around. "No."

David patted Sam's back. "Doesn't matter," he said, straightening himself on his cane. "This is the best birthday gift, ever. And holy moly..." He smiled brightly at the women in the room. "Will you look at that cake!"

"Mom made it," Pepe said.

"Your mom is very talented," David said with a happy gleam in his eye.

Angie walked toward the cake, preparing to light the candles. That was when she noticed they'd forgotten to bring matches. She'd remembered everything else, from serving utensils to plastic forks and paper plates.

"Oh dear," she said to Sam. "Looks like we forgot the matches."

"No problem," Sam said. "I'll go and get some."

"They're in the sideboard in the dining room," David said. "Top middle drawer."

Sam sauntered into the house, feeling awfully pleased. His dad was so happy with the greenhouse. He could tell. Sam couldn't wait to move the rest of the plants into it and help David set things up just as he wanted them. No matter what went on in the past, Sam and his father were making a new start now, and he was glad of it. He walked through the kitchen and into the dining room, his heart feeling light. Friday night had been so special with Angie. Although they hadn't specifically said the words out loud, Sam knew in his heart that he loved Angie, and she loved him.

Sam didn't want anything for Christmas this year. He'd already received the best gifts of all: the love of an amazing woman and the warm acceptance of her family, reparation of his relationship with his dad, and the renewal of his friendship with Ken. They'd bonded anew while working on the greenhouse project together, and Sam had been extra grateful for Ken's kind assistance. It would have taken Sam twice as long to build the greenhouse on his own, and he might not have had it ready in time to surprise his dad.

Even if Sam didn't get his memory back, he'd find a way to move forward without it. He was already driving and easily getting around town. He'd also been able to acclimate reasonably well to his job. He understood he couldn't stay at Angie's forever, which was why he'd arranged to move out right after Christmas. Naturally, Pepe liked having him around. The cute kid was used to being surrounded by women, so it was understandable that he liked having a man in the house. Yet, Sam had already made himself enough of an imposition. While Angie, her mom, and Lita were too polite to say so, he was sure that having another body in the center of the living room was disruptive for them day to day.

That wasn't the sort of future Sam envisioned for himself, Angie, and her family. In his mind's eye, he was starting to see something different. A big house with a yard... A sprawling ranch-style abode with no steps for Lita to navigate and plenty of bedrooms for all. And, ultra importantly, a fenced back yard for Pepe's *dog*. Sam grinned to himself, thinking of the way Pepe said that word, rendered with emotion and awe.

Although Sam's recollections had a gap in time, he'd been able to slowly piece together who he'd been over the years. He'd accessed old e-mails and photos on his phone and computer, as well as his social media accounts, during some of his downtime at work and at Angie's. These had been weird experiences, but informative. It was like studying up on a historical figure, only that person happened to be him. Well, not Sam *now*. But Sam *then*.

The Sam from the past was somewhat different from how Sam viewed himself at present. The old Sam was much more businesslike. Driven. He also didn't appear to have much of a social life, apart from a few former girlfriends who'd moved onto new relationships, according to social media.

Sam reached the sideboard and slid the top middle drawer open, finding the matches located beside a stack of corkboard coasters. He pulled the matchbox from the drawer, noting it felt nearly empty. But that was okay. All they needed were a couple of matches to light the cake candles. Sam could pick up more matches for David the next time he was at the store.

He started to close the drawer when the memory of another birthday party came crashing back to him. It was his dad's birthday, and they'd been celebrating in this very room. Sam saw his seventeen-year-old self in his mind's eye reaching for the matchbox in the sideboard drawer.

A store-bought cake sat on the table along with a birthday card Sam had gotten David. Sam's heart caught in his throat when he remembered the specifics of that card. It was a silly one with a beagle on the front wearing sunglasses and a party hat. Inside, it said, *Wishing you a dog-gone good birthday!*

Sam's neck burned hot and his palms went clammy when he recalled what he'd written on the card.

I.O.U. one completed greenhouse for all your plants.

Deliverable when I'm grown and have a great paying job.

Love ya, Dad. Happy Birthday!

Sam's vision clouded over, and the dining room light seemed to pulsate above him. He was trembling from head to toe. Sam gripped the sideboard to steady himself while clutching the matchbox in his other hand. An icy chill tore through his veins, and then Sam was broiling hot again. Sweat dribbled down his temples and the hairs stood up on the back of his neck.

Then—in a whiplash journey through time—Sam *remembered.* Remembered giving his dad that I.O.U.

because he'd been saving up for college and had used the little extra savings he'd had on college application fees just weeks before. Remembered slogging his way through university and barely scraping by financially. Remembered vowing to do better and earn a good living with his degree. Remembered growing distant from his father when resentment took hold at a college where everybody had better clothes and better cars than Sam...

Remembered that old hurt he'd experienced as a boy when he'd been shipped away to boarding school, and the way he'd buried that pain deep until his college days when those old wounds began to fester. There were girlfriends and casual dates...friends and acquaintances...some from high school, others from college and beyond, all overlapping like scattered images in a video collage.

Next, Sam was opening his store...and—finally—he was in the emergency room at the hospital with Angie. Sam stumbled backward and caught himself on a chair. It was all too much. The worst part of it was how it made him feel inside. All torn up. Angry. *Unhappy with who I am...was.*

Sam shook his head hard, trying to make sense of it, but the unsettling emotions clung to him like mist hugging the waters of a frigid lake. They squeezed his heart harder and clawed at his middle, leaving Sam feeling like he'd taken a sucker punch to his gut. Maybe he'd been wrong to want to remember. Maybe forgetting had been preferable to this. Because the reality of his missing years was unpalatable. Crashing down on him in wave after wave of raw regret and searing loneliness. The ache was so visceral, it was no wonder he'd tried to forget it. Sam stared up at the ceiling and bellowed in anguish. He wanted his new life back. But it was already too late.

In a matter of seconds, it had been ripped away.

"That's when Sammy made me that bear painting," David said with a chuckle. He sat in the greenhouse on a folding chair beside Lita's wheelchair. Angie, Elena, and Pepe were gathered around him. The air fluttered with balloons and bright streamers, and faint streaks of snow were starting to speckle the glass-domed ceiling.

David had been telling the group about all the great birthday gifts Sam had given him over the years, noting that this marvelous greenhouse surprise topped them all. There was one other memorable present: a paint-by-number painting Sam had made for David when Sam was around seven. It had turned out to be a much larger project than Sam had imagined, and the kid had fallen asleep while trying to complete it the night before David's birthday.

Sam's mom had tiptoed into his room like a sprightly fairy and finished the painting for Sam, so he'd have it to give to his father the next day. "You can tell which part is hers and which part is Sammy's if you take a close look. Jocelyn's work stayed within the lines." He chuckled again at the fond memory, and everyone else smiled.

"That painting sounds really cool," Pepe said, glowing. "I *love* bears."

"Where is the painting now?" Elena asked kindly. "Do you have it in your house?"

The bear painting, of course. A wave of shame washed over Angie when she realized what she'd done: nothing but criticize that piece of art since her first day on the job. *And it reminds Sam of his mother.*

David curiously glanced at Angie before answering Elena's question. "Why, it's at Sam's shop. I knew how much it meant to Sammy, so I gave it to him as sort of a 'housewarming gift' when he opened his store."

"How sweet," Elena said, and that only made Angie feel worse. The minute that mistletoe wreath came down, the bear painting was going back up, and she wasn't going to say one more word about it. Sam teased her about bossing him around, and Angie saw that he was right. In spite of her imperfections, he'd managed to love her anyway. And she desperately loved Sam, so she was determined to do better. Be kinder and more accepting, just like Sam had become of her.

Angie didn't know how she and Sam were going to work out a future between them with his memory situation. But she badly wanted to. He'd been so good to her and wonderful to her family, and when he'd kissed her at his condo, he'd sent Angie to the moon. She sighed involuntarily as Sam entered the greenhouse. That was when she realized he'd been gone an awfully long time. He also looked a little different. Winded and pale. She hoped he wasn't getting sick.

"Sam?" she asked worriedly. "Are you all—"

"I remember," he rasped hoarsely, and all heads turned in his direction. Dark circles haunted his eyes, seeming to have surfaced from out of nowhere. "I remember everything."

"Yay!" Pepe shouted, but he was the only one who looked happy.

Sam appeared withdrawn, and the rest of the adults watched him with concern.

Angie strode up beside him and lightly touched his arm. "Maybe you need to sit down?"

"Yeah, I..." Sam glanced around the greenhouse and blinked hard. "Sitting down sounds good."

Elena carried over a folding chair and opened it for him.

As Sam took his seat, he said humbly, "I'm sorry. I didn't mean to ruin the party."

"You haven't," Angie replied, though her heart ached with worry. This wasn't the reaction she expected at all. Why wasn't Sam feeling joyful?

"Well, this is great news," David said, attempting to lighten the moment. "What a very happy birthday indeed." He carefully surveyed his son. "It's probably just the shock, Sammy. Lots of information at once." He grinned encouragingly. "You'll get your sea legs."

Sam raked a hand through his hair then spoke unconvincingly. "Sure."

Angie reassuringly placed her hand on his sweater sleeve, but Sam brushed it away. Hurt zinged through her like a white-hot electrical jolt. Angie pursed her lips and pulled herself together for David's sake.

"So, now," she said, forcing a smile. "Should we do presents first, or cake?"

"Presents! Presents!" Pepe bounced up and down on his heels, and David agreed.

"That sounds like a fine idea," he told the child with a twinkle.

The rest of the party went off okay, and David thoroughly enjoyed opening the small gifts from Angie and her family. Elena had knitted him a scarf, while Lita had made him a beautiful painting of three monarch butterflies. Pepe had created a fancy card for David out of construction paper, complete with lots of stickers, and Angie had brought him a week's worth of homemade soups in individual containers for him to store in his freezer and have on hand.

Through the flurry of activity, Sam scarcely said a word. He did join in on the singing of "Happy Birthday" before David blew out the candles though. When Pepe asked David what he'd wished for, David winked and said, "Ah-ah, can't tell you. Otherwise it won't come true."

As Angie picked up the paper plates, she wondered about her own wishes. She'd wished so hard for Sam to get back his memory. Now that he had, she felt scared because Sam seemed so different, and she didn't know what would happen next.

"Come on, Dad," Sam said, helping David out of the folding chair. "I'll walk you back to the house and you can point out which plants you'd like moved in here."

Elena had already wheeled Lita out to Angie's SUV, and Pepe had gone along to help them with opening doors.

David dipped his chin at Angie. "Thank you for a

very nice party. That cake was the best. I know I'll enjoy those soups, too."

Angie hugged David goodbye. "My pleasure. Happy Birthday!"

She stared up at Sam, and it was like looking into the eyes of a stranger. Angie's heart broke right in two because she knew what he was about to say.

"I'll come back to your place in a bit to grab my stuff."

Angie returned to her apartment with a heavy heart. Lita and Elena appeared long-faced too. It took Pepe more time to understand the impact of Sam recovering his memory.

"That was a fun party," he said, dashing in the door. He shrugged out of his coat then turned his gaze on Angie. "When's Sam coming home?"

The simple question caused warm tears to spring to Angie's eyes. She turned away and grabbed a napkin from the holder on the kitchen table before Pepe could spot them. *Home. We did make a home for Sam here, and now he's going away.*

Angie dabbed at her tears and blew her nose hard. "He's not, sweetie." She drew in a shaky breath. "I mean, not going to stay."

Pepe's face hung in a frown. "Because he's better?" he asked, his little brow crinkling.

"That's right." Angie nodded, willing her tears away. She should know better than displaying her emotions in front of Pepe. She'd only make him and everybody else sad. And Lita and Elena looked pretty disheartened already.

"I can start dinner," Elena offered kindly after depositing her purse in the living room. "Are we still having leftovers?"

Leftovers sounded good tonight. It had been a full day, and the afternoon had been extra busy with David's party. "I think we still have plenty of *piñon* left," Angie said, remembering the Puerto Rican layered dish made with ground pork, cheese, and *plátanos*.

"I'm surprised Sam didn't eat it all," Elena said, laughing. Then, she stopped herself, adding quietly, "He loved that."

Pepe watched the adults with sad eyes as Lita wheeled herself into the living room.

"Wait," Angie asked her. "Where are you going?"

"To sign my picture for Sam," Lita said.

Pepe tugged at Angie's hand. "So, Sam's going back to his place?"

"Yes, baby."

"Will I still get my two Christmas stockings?"

Angie bent low to hug her son. "Of course, honey. Of course." But in her heart, Angie really didn't know.

Someone knocked at the door, startling Angie. *That can't possibly be Sam already?*

"I'll answer," Elena said. Then her face lit up in surprise. "Ernesto," she said, clearly stunned. "You're early!"

"Early?" Angie and Ernesto asked at once, each clearly perplexed.

Ernesto handed Elena a pretty bouquet. "We did say five?"

Elena accepted the flowers, blushing. "I thought it was seven?"

Ernesto glanced around, noting Angie and Elena still wore their coats. "Oh, dear. You're just getting back from somewhere. My mistake," he said gallantly to Elena. "I'm sorry. I can come back later."

"Ma," Angie said under her breath. "Go, *go*."

"*Angela*," Elena murmured between clenched teeth. "Shhh."

"What were you planning, Ernesto?" Angie asked him, grinning.

"We said a coffee. *Un cafelito.* But if you were expecting a meal—" he said to Elena.

"It's a little late for coffee," Angie butted in. "Maybe you should have wine?"

Elena smiled, but shot Angie a daggered look. "We can have decaf."

"I tried to take your mother out earlier," Ernesto explained to Angie. "But she keeps a very busy schedule."

"I know," Angie replied, fighting the urge to giggle. *Elena had a date? A coffee date, and she told no one?*

Elena stared down at her outfit, apparently mortified. She'd dressed nicely enough in slacks and a sweater for David's party, but apparently she'd intended to get more dolled up for her date with Ernesto. "I'm not really dressed to—"

"You look beautiful, Elena," Ernesto said, and Elena's blush deepened. "But if you'd like, I can return at—"

"*Elena*," Lita declared with clear exasperation. "You don't send a man away who brings flowers."

Ernesto had closed the door part way, but he

opened it again, peering into the living room. He grinned at Lita and then at Elena.

"Go on, Ma. *Go*," Angie urged. "You already have your coat on."

Elena's face was flush with excitement as she stared down at the flowers. When she looked up, she met Ernesto's eyes and said shyly, "Okay, but let me grab my purse!" Then, she retrieved her bag and scuttled toward the door, where Ernesto stood waiting.

Angie took the flowers from Elena and waved as her mom and Ernesto departed. "You kids have fun!"

Angie was glad she'd had the brief reprieve with Ernesto and Elena because seeing those two potential lovebirds together had lightened her heart. The evening meal seemed a little quiet with just her, Lita, and Pepe at the table. Lita appeared to be eating extra slowly, and Pepe, who was normally a chatterbox, was atypically somber.

"I miss having Sam here," he said sadly.

"I know," Angie answered. "And Grandma."

Pepe met her gaze square on. "But Grandma's coming back."

Angie wanted to promise that Sam would be back too. After he moved out tonight, they'd surely all remain friends. But Angie didn't want to make false promises to her little boy. At this point, she didn't know what the truth was.

Just as she thought that, the doorbell rang.

"That's Sam," Pepe cried, leaping to his feet. He

reached the door before Angie and yanked it open. "Sam," Pepe said, wrapping his arms around Sam's waist. "We missed you!"

Sam looked down and tousled Pepe's hair. "I haven't been gone that long, little buddy," he said, chuckling. But his laughter sounded forced, uncomfortable. Angie was sure this was awkward for Sam. Before, he'd agreed to stay through Christmas, but now that would make even less sense. This whole day had been a shock to all of them, and most especially to Angie's heart.

"I packed up some of your things before dinner," Angie said. She tried to read Sam's eyes, but there was a cold mask where the warm man she'd loved had been.

"You didn't have—" He spotted the hanging bag for his suits draped over the back of the sofa, and his closed suitcase standing nearby. "Thank you."

Sam greeted Lita, who was still seated at the kitchen table. "I apologize for interrupting your dinner."

"If you want to stay..." Angie began lamely, knowing he wouldn't.

"I appreciate the offer, but I'd better push off." He glanced back into the living room. "Do you mind if I look around to be sure I haven't left anything?"

"Go right ahead," Angie said, hating the tremble in her voice.

Sam checked the hall closet and a couple of bureau drawers, and then peeked into the hall bathroom. "Seems like you got everything," he said to Angie. "Thanks."

He was so cool in his demeanor it was like he and Angie barely knew each other anymore, when only yesterday they'd been so close. This was beyond awkward, and Angie couldn't stand it. And yet, she intuited she needed to give Sam space. He'd only recovered his memory this afternoon and was likely still processing things.

Lita wheeled into the living room and grabbed the drawing of the cardinal pair off her card table, holding it out toward Sam. "Please," she said with a warm gesture.

Sam accepted the gift and smiled wistfully. "Thanks, Lita."

Pepe barreled in from the kitchen holding the picture he'd made of the two of them building a snow fort. "Take mine, too!" he shouted plaintively.

"Thanks, little buddy. I will."

As Angie walked Sam to the front door, she braved a question. "So, when will I see you?"

Sam tilted his chin and spoke so matter-of-factly it stung. "At work, I guess."

Angie nodded and shut the door, then cupped her hands over her mouth, choking back a sob. Then she rushed to the kitchen sink and splashed cold water on her face.

"Are you okay, Mom?" Pepe asked with a worried frown.

"Oh yes, sweetheart," Angie said, although her chin trembled. She bent down to hug Pepe, holding him extra tightly. "Mommy just got something in her eye."

Chapter Twenty-Two

THE NEXT WEEK AT SINGLETON'S Jewelers, everything returned to normal and Sam was glad. He needed the familiarity of his routine to keep him grounded, when the rest of his world seemed to be turning upside down. Sales were strong and the shop stayed extra busy, both with new shoppers and the old ones picking up custom-ordered or -fitted gifts. David had phoned a few times to check on him, but Sam had let the calls ring straight through to voicemail. Just like in the old days. But Sam had made progress with his dad, and he didn't want to jeopardize that. Which was why he intended to stop by and visit with David this evening after work.

Pam and George were polite but distant. Sam guessed that the two of them were dating now, but they both remained professional and kept their personal relationship from interfering with their work. He didn't think he could manage that same kind of balance with Angie. She'd been very quiet this week—not her usual bossy self, and Sam worried that he'd hurt her feelings. He probably should apologize, but he didn't know how or for what. Everything about his life felt familiar—but wrong. His morning walk wasn't nearly as enjoyable without Angie by his side, and he missed her company in the evenings. He also missed little Pepe. Elena and Lita, too.

The family had been extremely kind to him, but their generosity had painted a fantasy portrait in Sam's mind. He wasn't really one of them. They'd merely been charitable about taking him in until he could regain his health, and now he had. Even though Angie had asked him to stay through Christmas, that was back when Sam had amnesia. Once he'd regained his memory, she hadn't mentioned it again. He would have felt wrong about staying on anyway. With his memories restored, it was time for him to stand on his own two feet and get back to normal. As much as *normal* was possible anymore.

Sam walked back to his office passing George in the break room as George fixed himself a cup of coffee. "Where's Angie?" Sam asked, not seeing her in back.

Pam was on the floor helping a pair of customers, but other than them, business seemed to be experiencing a temporary lull.

"She went to run a quick errand," George said, looking up. "She said it wouldn't take more than ten minutes."

"Okay, thanks." Sam entered his office and sank down in his chair. Through the window he could see the snow that had started this morning was picking up steam, and today was December 23rd. Chances were very good for a white Christmas.

He considered the Christmas stocking at his place, wondering what to do about it. Since Pepe had already heard he had one, Sam decided he should fill it and drop it over at some point. Or, he could fill the stocking earlier and bring it into work tomorrow, so

Angie could take it home to Pepe and have it there on Christmas morning. Maybe that was the right idea.

Sam knew he needed to talk to Angie so they could clear the air. They'd both become really involved with each other when Sam wasn't quite himself, and each had said some serious things. He understood that none of that was real now. Angie hadn't fallen in love with him, but with a mere facsimile of the man Sam really was. And the real Sam wasn't a person someone like Angie could love. He was far too selfish, way too flawed. Angie and her family deserved better, and they'd find it some day. He was sure of it. Yeah, Sam had learned and grown from his time spent with Angie and her family, but at the root he was the same man he'd always been. No one could change that completely.

Sam looked toward the doorway when he heard Angie entering the room. Her coat and hair were dusted with snow, and she held a huge rectangular package in her gloved hands. Sam shot to his feet. "Here, let me help with that," he said, lifting the hefty object out of her grasp. "What's this?"

"Your painting." She smiled, but there was sorrow in her eyes. "I had the frame cleaned for you."

He carefully tore back the brown paper packaging, and emotion flooded through him. "Thanks, Angie," he said past the sore spot in his throat. "That was very nice of you."

"When Christmas is over," she said, "and the wreath comes down, we can put it back up."

"I thought you hated this painting?"

"No," she said softly. "Not anymore."

Sam considered the painting gratefully then set

it on the floor, angling its frame against his desk. "Angie. We haven't talked."

"I know." Her dark brown eyes glistened. "I thought you needed space."

"I've had a lot to sort out."

"I get that."

"You and your family were great to me," he said hoarsely. "You don't know how much I appreciate all you—"

"You don't have to thank me, Sam."

"Oh, yes. I do." Sam set his chin. "You and I said some things."

"I thought we felt them, too."

"Yes, but...that was different. We were different. At least, I was."

"I'm beginning to believe that's true." Her disappointment was so clear, Sam felt about two feet tall.

"Angie—" He reached out for her, but she pulled away.

"What is it?"

"It's about Pepe. And his stocking. Should I drop it by or bring it into work?"

"I don't know, Sam," she said dismissively. "Do what you want to do."

Angie held her breath and exited the office as quickly as she could. She'd thought that by taking care of the painting, she'd make herself feel better about her current situation with Sam. Instead, she only felt worse. She knew she couldn't have imagined their mutual attraction. She'd fallen hard for Sam, and he'd appeared to be smitten with her. Then again, that had been when Sam *wasn't himself.*

Angie strode into the showroom, her gaze snagging on the mistletoe wreath behind the Singleton's Signature Diamond Collection. She'd actually started to believe some of that mistletoe magic *had* rubbed off on her. How silly and gullible, she'd been, thinking Sam had changed permanently for the better. The door chime tinkled, and Angie looked up seeing Mr. Jeffries had entered the shop.

"Mr. Jeffries," she said pleasantly. "It's so good to see you."

"You, as well, dear." He grinned warmly. "I just wanted to drop by and thank you."

Angie gasped in surprise. "You mean, you've already given those holiday presents out?"

"Only to my wife, Madeline—a little early." His gray eyes twinkled. "She was delighted with the ruby pendant and drop earrings."

"I'm so glad."

"I let her in on the other gifts, too," Mr. Jeffries confided. "I wanted to get her opinion before wrapping them, and she was thrilled. Madeline said I'd chosen exactly right." He nodded in gratitude. "I couldn't have done it without you."

Angie's heart clenched at the echo of those words. *I couldn't have done it without you.* Hadn't Sam told her precisely that when they'd nearly kissed that morning at his condo? While that may have been Sam's opinion at the time, he clearly seemed to be getting along well enough without her now. Angie didn't know what she'd done wrong, or how she could have fixed things.

By giving Sam space, she'd merely encouraged him to grow more distant. And being distant from Sam made Angie feel so hollow and sad inside.

"Dear? Are you all right?" Angie noticed the worried look in Mr. Jeffries's eyes. She also became aware that tears had formed in hers.

"Oh, yes. Sorry," she said, wiping them back with an embarrassed flush. "I'm just so...*happy* I was able to help." Which was absolutely the right thing to say if "happy" hadn't come out sounding mournful.

Mr. Jeffries glanced toward the register where Pam was ringing up a purchase. George was busy in back, and Sam had apparently stayed in the office. When he turned his attention back on Angie, Mr. Jeffries said sympathetically, "The holidays can be very stressful. When's the last time you took some time off?"

"Time? I...er... I'm not sure."

"That's exactly what I thought. I tell you what. We have a little ski chalet we won't be using this season—"

"Thank you, Mr. Jeffries. That's very kind. But I've got a family."

"Well, take them!"

"My grandmother's in a wheelchair."

"The villa's handicap accessible," he said, apparently not ready to take no for an answer. "It's all supplied with the basics. The kitchen's stocked with staples, too. You'd only need to bring a few groceries and your suitcases."

"I'm afraid none of us ski."

"You have a little boy, don't you? Pepe."

Angie was touched that Mr. Jeffries remembered. "Yes, that's right."

"Well, there's no better place to play in the snow.

We've got a nice stone hearth there for you to sit in front of and warm up afterward."

Mr. Jeffries was making his offer incredibly tempting. "I only have a few days off," she explained. "I have to be back at work on the twenty-seventh."

He smiled warmly, understanding that he was convincing her. "It's just a twenty-minute drive from here. Right outside of town at the Hopedale Valley Springs Ski Resort."

Angie thought of what fun it would be to provide her family with this mini vacation. Elena had the next few days off, and today was Pepe's last day of school. She'd attended his school's Christmas pageant last night. Angie imagined having a real mantel to hang Pepe's stocking from, and that cinched the deal.

"Are you sure it's not an imposition?" she asked worriedly.

"Ms. Lopez, it would make my heart light. The Mrs. will be thrilled with the idea, too. We hate seeing the chalet go unused, especially at Christmastime. It's really magical there. It's just not quite large enough for all our crew that's coming home this year." He eyed Angie questioningly. "It's only got three bedrooms..."

"Three bedrooms is fine," she said with a grin.

"Delightful. I'll drop by tomorrow with directions and the key."

Sam went through the printouts Angie had given him in preparation for their last-quarter tax accounting. She'd made some projections taking them to the end of the calendar year and said she'd tweak those after

January 1st once they had the actual numbers. Sam turned the last page and then pushed the stack of papers aside with a heavy sigh. All week long, Angie had seemed less than thrilled with him, and her coolness bruised his soul. While he had tried to show his appreciation for her stepping in when he'd had amnesia, he'd obviously mucked things up badly.

Angie knew more about the financial side of the business than Sam did. If she had to, she could probably run the store single-handedly. When Sam had lost his memory, she practically had. She'd been patient in helping Sam relearn the parts of his job he couldn't remember, and caring to him outside of work, as well. Angie was a hard worker. Talented. Sam thought he paid her decently, but it likely wasn't well enough, given her family obligations. Maybe if she had a better paying position, and a vested interest in the store, Angie's future would look brighter.

Sam had been managing the business completely on his own, but at what cost? He lifted his cell phone off the desk, finding the stark answer in his nearly nonexistent list of personal contacts. There were some new names and numbers there now, including Ken's. Sam had added Elena's contact information too, since that had been important to have while he was staying at Angie's. The phone vibrated in Sam's hand, and he saw it was David calling. This time, Sam answered.

"Hi, Dad."

"Sammy," David said. "I've been worried about you."

"I know, and I'm sorry. Sorry I haven't returned your calls. It's been kind of a crazy week."

"Settling back into things?"

"That's right."

"How's Angie?"

"She..." Sam peered out of his office and toward the showroom, spying Angie escorting Mr. Jeffries to the door, and he wondered what the older gentleman was doing here. "She's okay."

"Only okay?"

"I don't want to get into it right now."

"Then why don't you come over?"

Sam glanced out the snowy window. "What? Tonight?"

"I'd like for you to see how I've fixed up the greenhouse. It looks really great, if I say so myself."

Sam's heart warmed at the instant connection he felt with his dad. That was a really good thing that had come out of his memory loss. And there was no going back. Though Sam had been shaken at first by the sudden onslaught of remembrances, once he'd pieced things together and had been able to think about it, he understood David had only ever tried to do what was best for him. When he'd shipped Sam off to school, he hadn't meant to push him away. David loved him as a parent does: unconditionally. And Sam had tapped back into his warm affection for his father.

His relationship with Angie was much more complicated. David loved Sam, warts and all. The new Sam, the old Sam...didn't matter which one he was. David was there as his parent. Angie, on the other hand, could never love the man Sam was now. Even though he'd learned, and even if he'd changed, no transformation could be complete enough because Sam still had vestiges of his old self inside him. Hadn't he proved that by neglecting his dad's attempts at communication all week long until now?

Sam responded, trying to inject a note of cheer in his voice. "That sounds good. I'd love to see the greenhouse."

"You can stay for dinner if you'd like," David added hopefully.

"How about if I pick up Chinese?"

"Don't forget the fortune cookies!"

When Angie had dinner with her family that night, she shared the happy news about the chalet.

"Woo-hoo!" Pepe said. "There'll be extra snow there." Next, his face hung in a frown. "But will Santa be able to find us?"

Elena reassuringly patted his arm and winked at Angie. "Of course."

Angie had already told Lita about the elevator that could take them from the ground floor to the elevated main living level, and Lita said she wanted to bring her art supplies in case she spotted some more birds.

"I think it will be a lovely holiday," Elena said to Angie. "How generous of Mr. Jeffries."

Angie carefully surveyed her mom. "This won't interrupt any of your plans?"

"Plans?" Elena asked innocently. "What plans?" Still, her cheeks turned red.

"With, you know..." Angie wiggled her eyebrows, and Lita giggled. "Ernesto."

"Now, stop." Elena squared her shoulders and

picked up her fork. "He's spending Christmas with his family."

"Maybe he could come up to the cabin for a *coquito*?" Angie asked.

"*Si, si*," Lita agreed. "Good idea."

"Can Bobby come, too?" Pepe asked.

"We'll only be there two nights," Angie explained. "I'm sure Bobby will want to be where Santa can find him."

Pepe stared at Angie, confused. "But, you said—"

Angie cut him off by addressing Elena. "But later in the afternoon...it's a twenty-minute drive."

"No, Angie, no," Elena said firmly, though her face was bright red. "It's too soon, *mija*. We've only had one coffee date."

"Two," Lita corrected, holding up her hand, and Angie chuckled.

"Okay," Angie said. "Maybe some other time."

"Yes," Elena said coyly. "Maybe." After a minute, she set her gaze back on Angie. "How was work this week?"

"Oh, you know." Angie lifted a shoulder. "Usual."

Elena wore a motherly frown. "And Sam?"

"I guess..." Angie set her chin, steeling her emotions. "He's getting his life back."

"His old life, you mean?" Elena asked quietly.

Angie studied her half-eaten plate of food, thinking she wouldn't be able to finish her dinner. A poor appetite wasn't normally a problem for her, but it had been this week. "Yes."

"When will we see him?"

"I haven't got a crystal ball, Ma."

Elena laid a hand on her arm. "It's okay, sweetheart.

We all miss him." But it wasn't okay. It really wasn't, because Angie felt like her heart had been shattered to bits.

"Excuse me," she said, dabbing her mouth with her napkin. "I'll be right back."

Then she left her family sitting long-faced at the table, so she could shut the door to her room and weep in private. Angie had to stop this, and she knew it. Sam was getting his life back and she needed to reclaim hers, too. Tomorrow was Christmas Eve, and she'd start fresh. Wake up perky and hopeful and put on a good face for her family. If anyone deserved to have an excellent Christmas, they did.

Sam and David sat in the greenhouse eating Chinese food with chopsticks out of paper cartons. They both drank hot tea from coffee mugs Sam had found in David's kitchen.

"I like this," David said, digging into his lo mien. "It's just like the old days. But better." He stole a peek around the nicely arranged space, which now had dozens of healthy plants lining the shelving. David had put out a few Christmas decorations, too. Small garden gnomes wearing Santa hats adorned some of the pots. The colorful Christmas lights Angie had put up around the outside of the room twinkled cheerily against the glass, which was flecked white by the snow outside. David's birthday streamers and "Happy Birthday" sign were still up, but his balloons had become deflated, hovering near the ground.

"Want me to take down the birthday stuff after we eat?"

"No." David shrugged happily. "Let's leave it up for a few more days. I'm enjoying it."

Sam reflected on those "old days" his dad had mentioned. The two of them had gotten along quite well when Sam had been a boy, and David had been a very good father. David must have been caught up in his own reverie too because he mentioned something about how he used to take Sam to the library.

"I bet Pepe would like to see those trains," David said. "If he hasn't already."

"Don't know," Sam replied. "Angie stays pretty busy with family things on weekends. I'm not sure if she's had time."

"You should see that she does it, then." David motioned with his chopsticks. "Better yet, maybe you could take him?"

"Who?"

"Pepe," David said, as if that were obvious. He leaned forward with a twinkle. "You and Angie seem to be getting along."

Sam shifted uncomfortably in his chair. "Dad, it's not like that."

"What do you mean? I thought the two of you—"

"Nope."

David perused him sadly. "What about that dinner? The Cornish hens?"

Sam had been doing his best to forget that evening, and failing miserably. "That part went off great." He swallowed hard. "Better than great. Angie liked the food. We had a really nice time..."

"But?" David's brow rose.

"That was then. This is now, okay?"

When Sam set his carton on the card table, David said, "*No*-kay." And he said it with gusto.

Sam gawked at him. "Dad?"

"That's not good enough, Sammy. I saw the two of you together. You were like a lit-up pair of candles. Together you glowed, and each of you made the other one's light stronger."

Sam exhaled sharply. "That's because Angie thought I was someone different. Somebody I'm not."

"Who says so?" David asked him.

"You saw me," Sam said disbelievingly. "I was—"

"Open. Relaxed. Trusting," David supplied.

"Precisely." Sam met his father's gaze. "Totally unlike me."

"I don't think so, Sammy. I think that these past few weeks you've been very much like you. You had that hopeful optimism you used to have—"

"As a *kid*." Sam sighed heavily. "Look, I appreciate what you're trying to do. But things are what they are."

"What's that mean?"

"Angie and her family helped me out during an emergency, and now the crisis is over."

"Is it?" David shot him a pointed look. "It's not too late. Not too late to make things work." He viewed Sam fully. "I've never known a more determined man than you. When you set your sights on something, you go for it. Life wasn't easy for you, but you've done well in spite of that. Nobody is all good or all bad. By God's grace, we're all a mixture of both, and you want to know why that is?" Sam waited, and David continued. "That's what gives us compassion, helps us understand our fellow man. The important thing is to be the best we can be: kind, caring, considerate. We all make mistakes. I know I have. I'm sure you've made them, too. At this point in time, I don't want you to make a really big one. You go tell her, Sammy. Tell Angie how you really feel."

"But, what if she won't..."

"Won't what? Won't accept you because you've changed?"

Sam rubbed the back of his neck. "Yeah."

"Then prove to her you've changed for the better."

Later that night, Sam sat alone in his apartment feeling downcast. The gas log fire flickered in the hearth, and a single Christmas stocking hung from the mantel, while pretty bright lights draped from the walls and a Christmas tree sparkled against the window. Sam understood that his dad had made some good points, but Angie sure hadn't been acting like she wanted to continue a relationship with him. All week at work, there'd been none of her warm, fuzzy vibe. In fact, she'd been cool and distant in contrast to how she'd been before. Then again, nothing was as it was before. Nothing at all. Maybe Sam was partially to blame for pulling away, but wasn't that what was better for Angie?

Lita's pretty artwork hung on Sam's fridge beside Pepe's touching portrait of the snow fort, making the rest of Sam's condo seem extra impersonal and lonely by comparison. Even the cheery Christmas decorations didn't help lighten the atmosphere of the suddenly-too-quiet space.

Sam frowned and absently picked up the remote for his sound system, thinking some upbeat Christmas music might lighten his mood. But when he switched it on he pressed replay by accident, and the chords of "Unforgettable" began. Suddenly, Sam was flooded with memories.

He shut his eyes, imagining Angie in his arms as they danced to the music. She really was unforgettable, and he would certainly never forget that night. It was the first time he'd kissed her, after so many close calls, and he'd basked in an emotion he'd never known before: romantic love. Sam grasped that no other relationship had ever come close to what he'd shared with Angie. And now, everything wonderful had gone away. He hung his head as the song ended. Then—just to torture himself—he played it again, and then a third time.

Sam stared into the fire's glow, thinking over what his dad had said about the candles. He and Angie had burned brighter together, it was true. He simply didn't know how to get back what had already been lost.

Chapter Twenty-Three

THE NEXT MORNING, ANGIE GOT dressed for work in her gray skirt and jacket with her bright red pumps and matching handbag. She added the Santa Claus pin to her lapel. Today was Christmas Eve, and things were bound to be extremely busy at the shop. She couldn't wait to get done with her workday and take off for that mountain retreat. She'd busied herself last night, making most of the preparations, which had helped keep her mind off Sam. Perhaps she'd been overly hopeful in thinking their relationship could survive Sam recovering his memory. Much to Angie's dismay, things at Singleton's Jewelers had gone back to pretty much the way they were before Sam's fall.

Still, she didn't regret helping him. She and her family had been there for Sam in his time of need, and Angie knew he was grateful for their support. He'd thanked her several times already, and yet—there was this new distance that persisted between them. Angie frowned, thinking she wouldn't have changed things anyhow. Being with Sam had been good for her in a way she was just now understanding. Since her husband Jack had died, Angie had kept her heart securely stored away. She'd told herself it was because of her obligations to her family, especially to Pepe. She was too busy holding things together to entertain notions of having a life for herself. Angie's relationship with Sam had taught her these things didn't have to be mutually exclusive. She could be a good mother, daughter, and granddaughter, while still having time for a romantic partner too.

As much as she wanted to be bitter, Angie couldn't seriously hold a grudge against Sam. It wasn't his fault he'd suffered from amnesia, and his readjustment after regaining his memory had to have been hard. She only wished he'd included her during the transition. But he hadn't. Sam had completely shut Angie out. Her heart ached fiercely, and Angie told herself to buck up. Now wasn't the day to feel sorry for herself. Christmas was a time to count one's blessings. And Angie had so many.

She had a warm, loving family, and a wonderful little boy. She also had a really good job, which she enjoyed and helped pay the bills. If she could put up with Sam before his accident, she could certainly tolerate working for him now. The amnesia experience did seem to have taken the hard edge off his personality. Yet, in many ways, he was back to the same old Sam. Laser focused on his job and not much else. At least Sam's relationship had been repaired with David. That was another thing Angie found herself feeling grateful for this Christmas, and she was happy that maybe her influence had a little to do with that.

By ten-fifteen, Singleton's Jewelers was packed to the gills. All hands were on deck with George recording data on a tablet as clients picked up their custom-made or -adjusted orders. Pam tirelessly worked the cash register, ringing up purchase after purchase for frantic last-minute shoppers, while Angie stood beside her wrapping each new gift in a pretty package and depositing it in a silver bag with handles that had the Singleton's logo on the side. Sam worked the door, greeting folks when they entered the shop and thanking them for their business as they departed.

Angie was glad things were busy because this allowed her to focus on her work, rather than counting the hours until two p.m., when the store would close for the holiday. She leaned toward Pam as she tied a pretty bow on a box. "So, what are you doing for Christmas?"

Pam smiled shyly. "George is coming to dinner with me and the kids."

Angie was surprised because Pam had never mentioned having children before.

"Charles, Louie, and Max," Pam said, apparently reading Angie's stunned expression. "My three rescue Corgis."

Angie laughed in understanding. George, who was from California, had a small family who didn't often get together for the holidays. "That's nice for George."

"It will be nice for me," Pam confided quietly. "My big, nosy family hasn't stopped peppering me with questions about my ex, and I honestly didn't want to put up with that this season."

Angie eyed her sympathetically. "I can't say I blame you, Pam."

Pam's expression brightened. "Anyway! I'm looking

forward to a quieter day. Staying in Hopedale should prove more relaxing."

Angie teasingly wiggled her eyebrows. "And romantic, maybe?"

Pam flushed. "Well, um..."

"It's okay," Angie whispered. "I'm really happy for you." Her gaze snagged on that mistletoe wreath hanging across the way, and Angie thought about the way hearts had opened up this season. Pam and George to each other...then there was the budding relationship between her mom and Ernesto. Sam and his dad's reconciliation. And finally, Angie falling in love with Sam. She cut a sidelong glance at Sam holding back the door for an elderly lady who was leaving in a fur coat. *If things had ended differently... But, they didn't.*

"Hey, are you all right?" Pam asked her, and Angie realized there was moisture in her eyes.

She tugged a tissue from her jacket pocket to dab at them.

"Yeah, just seasonal allergies. Sorry."

"In December?"

"They seem to be worse this year than ever," Angie said.

Next, Pam turned around the topic.

"So," she asked brightly after ringing up another purchase for a middle-aged man with glasses. He declined the giftwrapping, so Angie just tucked the small jewelry box in a bag. "What are you up to for Christmas?"

"I'm taking my family to Hopedale Valley Springs," Angie said, bolstered by the happy thought. "Mr. Jeffries is loaning us his chalet for a couple of days."

"How nice!"

"Yeah."

"I'll bet your little boy will love that."

"It will be nice for all of us to get away," Angie said, gazing sadly at Sam.

Later that afternoon, after Sam had locked up the shop, he stopped Pam and George in the break room as they were preparing to go.

"Hang on," he said, smiling. "I've got something for the two of you."

Pam and George exchanged curious glances.

"It's just a small something. A little Christmas cheer." He ducked into his office and returned with two prettily wrapped Christmas gifts, handing one to Pam and the other to George. "Merry Christmas!"

Pam accepted her present with pleased surprise. "Gosh, thank you, Sam. I...um, wasn't really expecting this."

"That's why it's called a surprise." Sam chuckled good-naturedly. "You can open it now if you'd like." He also nodded at George, who grinned. Then, both Pam and George unwrapped their mid-size square packages, finding a smaller, oblong case had been tucked inside of each.

Pam pulled out the case and flipped it open. "It's a *pen*," she said, marveling at the sterling silver implement. It was engraved with her first name and had the store logo engraved on the other side. In place of the dot on the "i" above Singleton's there was a small diamond chip. "My goodness," Pam said in awe. "Is that a real diamond?"

"It is." Sam smiled proudly while George opened and examined his gift, which was an identical pen with his name on it.

"This is very cool," George said to Sam. "Thank you."

"I hope you'll both enjoy," Sam told them. "Have a happy holiday."

Pam set her gift package on the break table and slipped into her coat. "Thank you, we will!" She and George smiled pleasantly at Sam as they walked toward the back door.

"Happy holidays," George said.

"See you on the twenty-seventh!" Pam added with a wave.

Once they were gone, Angie reached for her coat.

"Hang on," Sam said, stopping her. "I have a little something for you, as well."

Angie's heart beat harder, as she wondered if it might be something personal. Then, she told herself not to get her hopes up. It was likely another pen.

"Sam, you didn't have to—"

"I know. But I wanted to."

She waited while he ducked back in the office and extracted another package from his desk drawer. This gift looked different from the others he'd given to George and Pam. The box was slightly smaller and was wrapped in red paper, while Pam and George's gifts had been wrapped in green.

"Angie, would you..." Sam started to hand her the gift, and then he thought better of it, glancing around the break room. "You know what?" His brow rose plaintively. "Not here. Maybe we should go and sit on the sales floor."

Angie's temperature spiked and her pulse pounded. Sam was acting awfully mysterious. What was so special about this gift that he couldn't give it to her in the break room like he'd done with the others?

She stared at him warily as Sam led her toward the seating area with the white bucket leather chairs and the low glass coffee table. Through the store's front window, Angie saw it was lightly snowing outside.

"Please," he said, motioning to a chair. "Have a seat."

Angie sat, unsure what would happen next.

Once Sam was seated as well, he began. "Angie, I know this week has been a little uncomfortable. I mean, uncomfortable between us," he said sincerely. "And I'm sorry for that. I mean, if it was me, and I'm sure it was—"

"That's okay," she said softly. "You've been adjusting."

"Yes. There was a lot to take in." Sam balanced the package on one knee, steadying it with his hand. "But I've also done a lot of thinking."

Angie's heart skipped a beat.

"I've been thinking that, when I had amnesia, you did an awful lot around here."

Around here? At work? "Oh, er...yeah. I was glad to."

"Much more than I could have asked for. You practically ran the shop single-handedly."

"No," she said unsteadily. "You helped, too."

"Helped, that's exactly it." Sam set his lips in a firm line. "That's what I've been mulling over, and I've come to the conclusion that I can't do this all alone." Sam leaned forward and handed her the gift. "Angie, I want you to be my partner."

"Partner?" she asked lamely, her head spinning. "You mean, business-wise?"

"Of course. What else...?" He read her expression and froze. "I thought you'd be pleased?"

Angie's stomach soured. What on earth had she been thinking? Anticipating a different kind of proposal? "This is all kind of sudden."

"Well, think on it, then," he said kindly. "If the answer is yes, we can work out the details after the holidays."

"Details," she said, her eyes misting. "I see." Angie blinked and turned toward the window to mask her emotion.

"It would mean a nice raise for you, better benefits."

"That's very generous, Sam." She gripped the package in her hands, fearing she was holding on so tightly she might crush it.

Sam eyed her perplexedly. "You can open that present, if you'd like?"

She did with shaky fingers, hoping to hide the fact that she trembled all over. It was a great offer and totally unexpected. Then why did Angie feel so devastated? She lifted the lid to the box, finding an oblong case inside, and her heart sank weightily. It was a pen box, just like the others. When she opened it, she found a gold pen with her name engraved on it. On the flip side, there was a diamond chip in place of the "i" in Singleton's Jewelers.

"It's..."

"Fourteen-carat gold," Sam said, when she looked up. "Nothing but the best for my new partner."

"Partner," she mumbled under her breath. "Huh."

"Angie?"

Angie didn't want Sam to see her cry, but she couldn't bear being around him another second. "Thanks so much," she said, leaping to her feet. She wrapped her arms around his neck in an impulsive hug. "Both for the gift and the offer!" Then she scooted off the sales floor and into the break room, grabbing her coat.

"Wait!" Sam called, striding after her.

Angie scuttled into her office, keeping her back turned to Sam, so he wouldn't see the hot tears streaming down her cheeks. He'd offered her something fantastic, a partnership in his business. But all Angie could focus on at the moment was her breaking heart. She yanked open her desk drawer and pulled out her red purse, dropping it into her canvas shoulder tote. Next, she scooted past Sam as he stood in the office door, gaping at her, dumbfounded.

"What just happened here?" He glanced back toward the show room, and at the package holding the gold pen, which Angie had left on the table. "Angie?"

She darted down the hall and toward the back door. "Merry Christmas!" she called with a sniff.

"Hang on!" he yelled feebly. "What about Pepe? His stocking?"

She paused at the door without turning.

"Can I bring it by tomorrow?"

Angie gulped as tears blistered her cheeks. "Why don't you bring it into work after the holiday?" Then she got out of there as quickly as she could, half fearing and half hoping that Sam would come after her. But the heart-wrenching thing was—he didn't.

Sam felt like the world's most colossal heel. While he'd thought Angie would be pleased by his offer, he'd been absolutely wrong. He ambled back into the showroom, hands in his pockets and his head hung low. A gold pen clearly hadn't been what Angie was anticipating. She'd been hoping for something more. Something personal. Something to indicate how he truly felt about her.

He strolled over to the Singleton's Signature Diamond case and stared down at the display. "*When your love is written in the stars*," he said with a rueful laugh. "Sure."

Then he looked up and saw the mistletoe wreath. Mistletoe, the plant of romance and promise. Sam stared at it, thinking, as a recent memory tugged at the back of his mind. Next, he set his hands on the top of the smooth glass case housing his collection and peered down at the satiny white tray holding his array of Singleton's Signature Diamonds. One, in particular, seemed to gleam brighter than all the others. Then, without warning, its gems brilliantly sparkled. "Whoa."

Sam straightened in surprise and examined the ring more closely. It was his "Rosebud Bouquet" design, the excellently flawless solitaire diamond ring adorned with tiny white gold rosebuds and four gorgeous rubies. That was the ring that had been missing the day Angie claimed that George had been cleaning it. Sam glanced back at the mistletoe wreath and his heart was filled with understanding. Nobody had been polishing that ring. Angie had been trying it on.

Sam raked his hands through his hair, mentally reviewing his stay at Angie's. The flirty banter they'd shared between them, that day they'd played with Pepe in the snow...and that charming sparkle in Angie's dark brown eyes that made his soul ache to hold her and never let her go. He should have known from how she'd looked at him, and all she'd said, that she cared for him, too. Sam hadn't imagined things; the emotions they'd experienced had been genuine. He'd sensed that deep inside. What's more, he'd *felt* it in Angie's kiss. Now Sam was sure she'd felt it, too. No wonder she'd been so different this week at work. And then, to add insult to injury, Sam had given her that impersonal gift. A personally engraved impersonal gift, but still, it was a numbskull move.

Sam checked his watch, noting it wasn't yet two thirty. Though downtown businesses were closing early today, Sam still had time to make a few stops. His dad's words came back to him, resonating soundly as background Christmas music played. *It's not too late, Sammy. Not too late to tell her how you really feel.*

I sure hope Dad is right, Sam thought, grabbing his coat, scarf, and hat, and heading for the door.

Seconds later, Sam stepped onto the snowy sidewalk and gazed up at the pennant fluttering on the nearest lamppost: *Welcome to Hopedale, Virginia,* it said. *Where love springs eternal.*

"Right!" Sam snapped his fingers with assurance and tamped down his hat.

Then, he scurried down the sidewalk through cascading snow.

Chapter Twenty-Four

ANGIE AND HER FAMILY SHARED a cheerful Christmas morning around a blazing wood fire in the huge stone hearth. They were still in their pajamas and enjoying a lazy day. The adults held coffee mugs and wrapping paper littered the floor. Pepe sprawled on his belly, dividing his attention between his new Batman book from Lita and a hand-held video game from Santa. The stuffed stocking beside him contained the telltale signs of Christmas candy spilling out of its hollow.

"Thank you for my new scarf and flower," Lita said, proudly displaying her fringed floral scarf and the pretty complementing silk gardenia tucked into her hair.

"I'm so glad you like them," Angie said happily. "I love these cute Santa Claus PJs." She pointed to her favorite holiday accessory, which she'd clipped to her bathrobe lapel. "They match my pin!"

Angie angled her mug toward her mother. "And, Ma, my new bag is totally cool," she said mentioning the designer shoulder bag resting beside her, which showcased bold bright colors and geometrical shapes.

"And thank you for my Spa Day at Hopedale Valley

Springs." Elena grinned dreamily, cradling her large mug of coffee in both hands. "I *can't wait.*"

Angie, Elena, and Lita laughed and chattered merrily as Pepe busied himself with his presents. For his part, Pepe had gifted the three women in his life with hand-painted jewelry holders, fashioned from clay, which he'd made at school during Holiday Craft Day. All in all, it was a happy holiday, if only Angie could convince herself to stop feeling like something was missing. And that "something" was Sam. Next, she told herself not to be silly. She had so many things to be thankful for. Not the least of which was this generous getaway at this gorgeous chalet.

The Jeffries' A-framed cabin had a huge window overlooking the forest and mountains, and everything was covered with snow. It was a beautiful white Christmas, and Angie felt so blessed to have her loved ones around her. While she was sad about how her personal relationship had ended with Sam, she'd decided she'd be foolish not to take his offer of a business partnership. While she planned to accept after Christmas, Angie had not yet told her family about her promotion. She decided now might be a good time.

"I have a bit of news," she said, taking a sip of coffee.

"Oh?" Elena asked her. "What's that?"

"Sam has offered me a business partnership in his store."

"Wow, Angie." Elena's smile sparkled. "That's a very big deal. Congratulations!" She turned her attention to her phone, which buzzed in her bathrobe pocket.

"Who *is* that?" Angie teased lightly, realizing Elena

had been texting back and forth with someone all morning. “Ernesto?”

Lita raised one finger and said cheerily, “Lovebirds.”

Angie shot Lita a quizzical look. “Ha-ha,” she said. “Ma and Ernesto, yeah.”

Lita waggled her finger from side to side then pointed straight at Angie. “*Lovebirds*,” she said again, this time with a knowing grin.

“Lita?” Angie asked her. “Are you trying to tell me something?”

Instead of answering, the older woman shrugged. Angie turned her attention to Pepe, who was eagerly punching the buttons on a new game.

“How do you like your Santa gifts?”

“They’re the best.” Pepe shot Angie a heart-melting grin. “It’s okay about the *dog*. I’ve got a backup plan.”

When Angie worriedly glanced at her mother, Elena whispered, “Everything will be all right.”

“Hope so.” Angie heaved a sigh, hating the thought of disappointing Pepe. At least with her job promotion, she’d be able to buy a house for them sooner.

Just then, Angie heard a car door pop open. That was odd, since this chalet was fairly isolated, at least five miles from any other house. She glanced concernedly at her mom and Lita. “Did you guys hear that?”

Elena and Lita exchanged innocent looks. “No,” they said together. For some reason, they didn’t sound particularly convincing.

Angie got to her feet and walked to the window over the kitchen sink, which looked out on the chalet’s gravel driveway. Another SUV had just pulled up and parked behind Angie’s. A well-dressed man exited through the driver's door, and Angie nearly dropped her coffee. He wore a nice overcoat and a hat. *Sam?*

Sam glanced up at the house, not spotting her in the window. He held a Christmas stocking in one hand as he trudged through the snow and toward the outdoor wooden steps leading to the wrap-around deck.

Angie stared down at her nightclothes in a panic, then over at the group. "It's Sam!"

"Oh? Is it?" Elena's eyebrows rose in the worst poker-face expression Angie had ever seen in her life.

"Ma!" Angie cried, totally flustered. "You told him where we are? But why?"

"Sam?" Pepe yelped with glee. "Woo-hoo!" He scrambled off the floor, shooting to his feet, but Angie cautioned him.

"You stay put."

Angie grabbed her coat out of the coat closet and squirmed into her snow boots. She didn't want to make a scene in front of her family. But how could Sam just show up here unannounced? Even if he'd been in secret cahoots with Elena, this was all totally news to Angie.

"Where are you going?" Elena asked with wonder.

"To talk to Sam!"

Elena shared a blank stare, and Lita giggled behind her hand. Pepe simply appeared excited. "Can I come with you? Out in the snow?"

"No, Pepe." Angie yanked on her gloves, first one and then the other. "I need a private word with Sam first."

Then, she stormed toward the door, determined to learn exactly what Sam thought he was doing, showing up unexpected—and uninvited—during her family's holiday.

Sam stared up at Angie with surprise when she stopped him on the steps leading up to the chalet. "Well, hey!"

"Hey, yourself!" she said, noting he held a loaded Christmas stocking.

"Oh, yeah. Sorry." Sam's brow furrowed apologetically. "I maybe should have called."

"Maybe?"

"Angie, look," he said as the morning snow pelted him. "We need to talk. Can we go inside?"

"Not until you tell me what you're doing here."

She pinned him with her gaze, and Sam shifted on his feet, gripping the Christmas stocking against his chest. "I wanted to say Merry Christmas." His eyes glimmered warmly, and Angie felt all jumbled up inside.

"You already said that yesterday."

"Yes. But I didn't have Pepe's stocking."

"What?"

"And there are some other things I need to tell you."

"Such as?" Angie set one hand on her hip, but she didn't sound nearly as formidable as she'd intended.

"Such as..." Sam's smile gleamed. "Angie Lopez," he said, his voice growing husky as his volume rose. "I *love* you!" Sam practically shouted it to the treetops, and Angie blinked.

"Sam," she said, her heart beating harder. "Just what are you—"

"I said, *I love you,*" he repeated with passion and conviction. "And I'm terribly sorry I didn't say it earlier. Earlier this week when I had so many chances to tell you how I really feel. But I was afraid, Angie," His Adam's apple rose and fell as he continued. "Afraid you wouldn't want the old me. The real me... The guy who's not perfect in any way except for in one regard—my honest, pure, and overwhelming love for you."

Angie's heart pounded and her pulse raced as her mind careened in a million directions. She'd claimed she didn't want anything for Christmas, but deep inside her heart this had been her secret wish. To have Sam desire her...*love* her. Just as much as she loved him. Angie's eyes grew hot as she struggled to hold back her tears. "Oh, Sam, don't you know?" She tried to say it solidly, but her voice wavered with emotion. "I love you, too. *I love you, Sam.* Yes, I do!"

His jubilant grin could have melted all the snow in the mountains. "I'm *so* very glad." Sam gazed up at her adoringly. "Could you just...?" He gingerly passed her the stocking, and Angie took it while Sam fished something out of his coat pocket.

It was a ring box, and she'd recognize its design anywhere. It came from Sam's Singleton's Signature Diamond Collection. Angie's mind whirled and her heart pounded wildly as hopeful expectation rose up inside her. More snow pelted them, coating Sam's hat and Angie's hair, but she didn't feel cold in the least. Then, Sam's eyes met hers, and Angie felt warm all over.

"Angie Lopez," he said desperately. "For three whole months, you were right there in front of me and I never completely realized how special you are." He gave her a lopsided grin and Angie's cheeks heated. "I guess it took hitting my head to knock some sense into me. The thing is now. Now, I know."

He took her free hand in his, holding her glove. "*Know* how amazing you are. You're warm and wonderful and funny. Stern and strong and—"

"Bossy?" she asked with one eyebrow arched, and Sam chuckled heartily, his heart so obviously light it made hers feel light, too.

"Yeah, *bossy*," he said, grinning. "But that part helps make you a really great mom. And, even though you're not *my* mother, I haven't always totally minded you telling me what to do."

The moisture in Angie's eyes brimmed to overflowing. "Oh, Sam," she whimpered past the tender burn in her throat.

He flipped open the ring box, and Angie saw it was the ring, *her ring*, the Rosebud Bouquet Diamond. Sam's eyes sparkled with love and affection when he said, "When your love is written in the stars... A Singleton's Signature Diamond says—"

Angie gasped. "*Forever.*"

"I hope you'll marry me," Sam said tenderly. "Marry me and become my forever bride. I want to do right by you. By you and your family. Buy us a big house where all of us can live, and Pepe can keep his dog."

Angie clasped her hands to her cheeks as tears poured from her eyes. And then, she could see it: a future with all of them living happily together. Sam was going to make the very best husband and father.

He'd be wonderful to Elena and Lita too. "I'd like that," she said, her lips trembling. "Would like that very much."

"So your answer is yes?"

Angie nodded giddily and tugged the glove off her left hand as Sam removed the solitaire from the ring box, sliding it onto her finger. It caught a bit on her second knuckle, but Sam determinedly shoved it on. They were likely thinking the same thing. If the fit wasn't perfect, George would take care of it.

"We're going to make a really great team," Sam said affectionately. "On and off the job."

This only made Angie cry harder. Sam tugged a hanky from his coat pocket and handed it to her, and Angie used it to wipe her damp cheeks. "Everyone's going to be so happy," she said, sniffing. "Especially Pepe." She burst into tears again, her heart exploding with joy.

"You've got that right." Sam grinned handsomely and indicated the stocking. "Take a peek inside."

"What?" Angie dabbed her eyes again with Sam's hanky, then peered into the stocking he'd filled for Pepe. It was loaded with dog stuff. Doggie treats, a squeaky toy, even a round rubber ball.

"But... I..." Angie gazed down at Sam. "I don't understand. Is this for later? After we're married?"

"Nope." Sam grinned from ear to ear. "My condo doesn't have the same restrictions as your apartment, so I figured Pepe can keep his puppy there in the meantime."

"Puppy?" Angie asked, her heart pounding. "What puppy?"

Sam thumbed over his shoulder at his vehicle. "I've

got a sweet little lab mix in my SUV. He's wearing a big red bow, but he doesn't have a name yet."

Angie beamed at Sam with love and wonder. "Seriously?"

"Shall we introduced Pepe to his *dog*?" Sam winked, and Angie threw her arms around him.

"Oh, Sam. You're....you're... I love you."

He cradled her face in his hands. "That's pretty great, because I love you, too."

Then he kissed her sweetly in the snow, and Angie's whole world became a bright array of rainbow colors. "I can't wait to go inside and tell the others," she said.

"Well, then." Sam's blue eyes twinkled. "Let's not keep them waiting."

When they came through the door, little Pepe looked up and his jaw dropped. "It's a *dog*!" he yelped rushing toward Sam. "A real, live *dog*."

"Sam," Elena said. "How lovely!"

Sam set the puppy on the floor, and it immediately scampered over to Pepe on its stubby legs. The child scooped the dog into his arms, and the puppy licked his face.

"Is he mine?" Pepe anxiously asked Sam and Angie. "Can I keep him?"

"You bet you can," Sam said.

Then, Angie added, "But he'll need to stay at Sam's place for a little while."

"Just until..." Sam glanced at Angie and looked merrily around the room. "After we get the big house."

He slipped his arm around Angie's waist, and she grinned at her family.

"We have some news."

"Angie and I are getting married," Sam said, and Pepe whooped again.

"That's so cool!" Pepe gazed at Sam in a hero-worshipping way. "So you'll be my dad?"

Sam tousled his hair. "I'll give it my best, little buddy." He handed Pepe the loaded Christmas stocking. "Merry Christmas, Pepe. You might want to open this for your new friend there."

"Oh! Thank you!" Pepe said in a high squeal.

After Elena and Lita offered their warmest congratulations and hugs, Elena addressed Sam. "We're having a turkey with all the trimmings. You'll have to stay."

"I'd love to," Sam told her. "Only, I'd planned to have dinner with my dad."

"Well then, he should come here," Angie insisted.

"I was just about to suggest that," Elena said.

"It's not too much of a drive," Angie said, eying Sam. "And we're not eating until later. Maybe you can go and pick David up?"

Sam nodded. "I'll give him a call." He hugged Angie tighter. "He'll be really happy to hear our news."

Angie beamed up at Sam. "We have a lot to celebrate this Christmas."

"It's certainly one I won't forget."

Sam kissed Angie on the lips, and Elena sighed, while in the background Lita crooned, "*Lovebirds.*"

Epilogue

One year later, Pepe stood on a stepladder to put the angel on top of the Christmas tree at their new house on Mulberry Lane. The expansive four-bedroom, four-and-a-half bath ranch had a large fenced backyard and was just down the street from David's place, which made it easy for all of them to get together. Sam reached forward and held onto the child's waist, keeping him steady. Pepe was getting a little too big to sit on Sam's shoulders, but he couldn't quite reach the top of the tree without assistance.

"You doing okay, little buddy?"

Pepe grinned over his shoulder. "Yeah, Dad."

He righted the angel on the tree's uppermost bough then carefully climbed down the ladder. His dog, Bruce Wayne, sat patiently waiting for Pepe to descend. The moment he did, the dog got to his feet and approached Pepe, happily wagging his tail. "Good boy, Bruce," Pepe said. "Thanks for being our helper."

"Thanks for inviting me over to help decorate your tree," Ken chimed in from nearby. He held the *coquito* Angie had prepared for him as the Christmas tree lights shone cheerily and snow felt outside the darkened windows.

Sam placed a hand on Ken's shoulder. "We're so happy you could join us."

A comforting fire blazed in their red brick hearth, and two stockings hung from the mantel. Sam and Angie hadn't wasted much time giving Pepe a baby sister. Her name was Magdalena, and she'd been born in November, roughly nine months after Sam and Angie's February wedding. The sweet baby with wispy dark hair and bright blue eyes kicked contentedly in the bassinet parked beside Lita's wheelchair. When she cooed, Angie picked her up.

"Would you like to hold the baby?" she asked David, knowing he never passed up the opportunity.

"I'd be delighted," he said, setting his cane aside. Angie passed Magdalena to David, where he sat on the sofa beside Elena. Elena grinned pleasantly at David and then at Ernesto, who was seated in an armchair to her right.

"This is going to be a marvelous Christmas," Elena said. "So much to be thankful for."

Ernesto caressed her with his eyes and said, "Yes," causing Elena's cheeks to tinge pink.

"Merry Christmas, everybody!" Angie said, raising her eggnog.

"*Feliz navidad,*" Lita and Ernesto chimed in together.

Sam raised his own glass and beamed at the group. "Here's to good friends and family," he said. "And to making new memories together."

Angie stood next to Sam by the Christmas tree, and Pepe grinned up at them with his dog at his side. "Merry Christmas," he said sunnily, and Angie's heart melted. This was more than she could have dreamed of: a really perfect life.

Sam wrapped his arm around her shoulders and held her close, and Angie felt blanketed in happiness and warmth. Everyone was full of good cheer, and she and Sam had recently learned from Pam, who'd caught Angie's bouquet at her and Sam's wedding, that she and George were engaged.

Angie wasn't sure what had caused such good fortune to befall those she loved and held dear. Perhaps it was the grace of God... simple destiny, or the pervasive joy of the season... Maybe it even had something to do with the mysterious mistletoe wreath that had hung at Singleton's Jewelers last year. Quite possibly, it was all of those things together, wrapped up like a cheery Christmas package in a lovely red ribbon.

Angie gazed down at Pepe then affectionately up at Sam, her heart filled with contentment. How she'd gotten here didn't matter in the end. What counted was where she'd landed: with her very own *happily ever after* in Hopedale, Virginia. And Angie Lopez Singleton was mindful of her blessings.

The End

Arroz Con Pollo (Chicken and Rice)

A Hallmark Original Recipe

In *An Unforgettable Christmas*, Angie sees a whole new side of her business-minded boss, Sam, after he develops amnesia. In fact, Sam and Angie come oh-so-close to kissing—right before they're interrupted by Angie's mom, who's fixed them a delicious dinner of *arroz con pollo*. We hope you'll love our version of this classic dish.

Yield: 6 servings
Prep Time: 1 hour, 25 minutes
Cook Time: 35 minutes
Total Time: 2 hours

INGREDIENTS

- 6 bone-in, skin-on chicken breasts (or 12 bone-in, skin-on chicken thighs)
- 1 tablespoon olive oil
- 1 yellow onion, chopped
- 1 orange bell pepper, chopped
- 1 green bell pepper, chopped
- 1 tablespoon capers, drained
- 1 tablespoon minced garlic
- 2 cups long grain rice
- 1 (15-oz.) can tomato sauce
- 4 cups chicken broth
- 1 cup frozen peas, thawed
- 1 cup pimento-stuffed olives
- 1 tablespoon chopped cilantro

Chicken Seasoning Rub:

- 1 tablespoon smoked paprika
- 1 tablespoon dried oregano
- 1 tablespoon ground cumin
- 2 teaspoons kosher salt
- 2 teaspoons garlic powder
- 2 teaspoons onion powder
- 2 teaspoons chili powder
- 1 teaspoon ground coriander
- ½ teaspoon ground turmeric
- ¼ teaspoon ground cayenne pepper
- 2 tablespoons olive oil

- 1 tablespoon cider vinegar
- 1 to 2 tablespoons water (as needed to thin seasoning rub)

DIRECTIONS

1. To prepare chicken seasoning rub: combine all ingredients in small bowl and stir to blend.

2. Brush seasoning rub evenly over chicken pieces, cover and refrigerate for 1 hour.

3. Preheat oven to 375°F.

4. Heat 1 tablespoon olive oil in a large, deep oven-proof frying pan. Add chicken pieces and cook on medium-high heat for 5 to 8 minutes, or until golden brown on all sides. Transfer chicken to a plate and reserve; drain excess oil in pan.

5. Add onions, bell peppers and capers to frying pan; sauté on medium-low heat for 5 minutes, stirring frequently. Add garlic and rice and sauté for 2 additional minutes.

6. Add tomato sauce and chicken broth; bring to a simmer. Remove from heat; arrange browned chicken pieces in a single layer on top of rice.

7. Cover and bake for 25 to 35 minutes, or until chicken pieces are fully cooked and rice is tender.

8. Remove pan from oven; fluff rice with a fork, top with peas, olives and cilantro; cover with lid and let sit for 5 minutes before serving.

Thanks so much for reading *An Unforgettable Christmas*. We hope you enjoyed it!

You might like these other books from Hallmark Publishing:

A Royal Christmas Wish
A Down Home Christmas
The Christmas Company
A Timeless Christmas
At the Heart of Christmas
Christmas In Evergreen
Christmas In Evergreen: Letters to Santa

About the Author

New York Times and *USA Today* bestselling author Ginny Baird writes sweet, uplifting, contemporary romance stories with a little bit of humor and a whole lot of heart. Ginny, who is of Puerto Rican heritage, is delighted to share this novel with her readers, as it speaks directly to the heart of her family in so many ways. When she's not writing, Ginny enjoys cooking, biking, and taking long walks in the woods with her Labrador retriever. She cherishes her supportive husband and big blended family, and loves having the entire brood at home for the holidays. To learn more about Ginny and her books, sign up for her newsletter, or connect with her on social media, please visit her website: http://www.ginnybairdromance.com/

Turn the page for a sneak peek of

LIZZIE SHANE

Chapter One

"WAKE UP, SLEEPING BEAUTY!"

I groaned as eighty decibels of enthusiasm landed on top of me in the form of my roommate.

"Today is the day we take New York by storm!" Margo crowed while I burrowed deeper beneath the covers in self-defense, hiding under my pillow as she continued to bounce. "The day all of our struggles turn into charming stories we can tell about how we overcame adversity to triumph magnificently." I braced my feet on her hip and attempted to shove her off the bed, but my feet slid off her slippery pajamas. She seized on my moment of distraction to yank the pillow away from my face. "Watch out, world, we're coming for you! Margo Gonzalez with her audition and Jenny James with her interview."

Oh, no. "My interview." My eyes popped open and I stopped my oh-so-subtle efforts to remove Margo from the bed. "What time is it?"

The light in my room was entirely too bright for seven a.m.—which was when my alarm should have gone off. I scrambled for the bedside table, searching for my phone.

"Seven-oh-five," Margo said. "You left your phone in the kitchen and when I heard the alarm, I figured you needed a more hands-on wake-up system. Also, your sister called."

Seven-oh-five. Margo had flipped on the overhead light; that was why my room was so bright. My ability to breathe returned. I wasn't late. Yet. "Which sister?"

"I dunno. The perfect one? You want breakfast?"

"As if that narrows it down," I grumbled as Margo bounded out of the room without waiting for an answer.

My sisters Chloe and Rachel—the doctor and the mayor—were the twin paragons of our hometown. Rachel had been student body president practically from birth, and Chloe had taken the local Mathletes team to a national championship before graduating early and completing med school at the top of her class. They'd each married their high school sweetheart—one of whom was literally the boy next door—and moved back home to work at their dream jobs and raise perfect children.

And there I was, just Jenny. Still trying to figure out what I wanted to do with my life.

Though maybe this interview would be a start.

I scrambled out of bed and dressed quickly, bypassing the color that dominated my closet and buttoning up in what had become my standard interview uniform: a sleek gray power suit. It was supposed to make me feel confident and professional, but as I tugged nervously on the cuffs, I wondered if the outfit was jinxed. I hadn't had a lot of luck with interviews so far...but this time would be different. This time, as Margo had said, we were going to take New York by storm.

Emerging from the narrow confines of my bedroom, I detoured around the poofy white explosion of tulle currently taking up so much of our living room that it should start paying rent. Margo's wedding dress was too big to fit in either of our microscopic New York closets, so it had become our de facto third roommate—camping on the couch.

By the time I hit the kitchen, Margo was dishing up pancakes and dancing along to the Christmas music coming from her iPhone speakers. "You're a saint," I told her as she handed me my phone.

"Enough of a saint for you to grab my costume for tonight when you pick up yours?" she asked hopefully, pouring me some coffee. "I'm supposed to meet with the caterer after my audition."

I groaned—half with bliss at the pancakes and half with dread at the thought of the party tonight. "I forgot we had to wear costumes. What are we this time?"

"Santa's elves. But with any luck, this will be the last time we have to serve hors d'oeuvres in elf gear. By next Christmas, I'll be a famous actress and you'll be a wildly successful..." She cocked her head. "What's this interview for?"

"Editorial assistant for a publishing house."

One of Margo's eyebrows popped up. "That's the new dream job?"

"I like books," I said, a little defensively. Because yes, I did like books. But I'd had so many interviews for so many jobs in the past two years that it was hard to keep them all straight—and I'd also never expressed any interest in working in publishing before, so Margo's skepticism was somewhat warranted. "Maybe I'll discover the next J. K. Rowling."

Margo rallied quickly, raising her orange juice in a toast. "To the next big thing in publishing."

"Who is going to pick up the next big thing on Broadway's elf costume when I grab mine," I added.

Margo's dark eyes filled with gratitude. "You're the best. And you're going to rock that interview."

"Thank you," I murmured, trying to absorb some of her confidence.

At least some good had come from my as-yet-unsuccessful attempts to find my place as a New York power player. Margo never would have met Harish if she hadn't been rushing to the rescue with a clean blouse after I'd spilled coffee all over mine right before my interview with his company. The poor man had taken one look at my roommate and been smacked hard with the love stick. He'd invited her to his office Christmas party, kissed her under the mistletoe, and the rest was history.

There was nothing quite like mistletoe magic.

Harish had later lobbied for me to get the job, but after the way I'd flailed during the interview, I wasn't surprised when they decided to go another way.

It was crazy to think that was a year ago—and I was no closer to figuring out what I was going to do with my life. Or where I was going to go when our lease was up at the end of January. Margo would be moving out after her winter wonderland-themed New Year's wedding, but she'd promised to pay her share of the rent until the lease expired. After that...

I really needed this job. I couldn't keep doing odd jobs for the rest of my life. I'd come to New York to prove something—and so far, all I'd managed to prove was that I had an impressive ability to bomb interviews.

Margo caught my hand, sensing my insecurity. "It's gonna be great," she assured me. "*You're* going to be great."

"I hope so. I can't be a catering server forever." I glanced at her over my pancakes. "I'm surprised you're still working the party tonight with all the wedding prep going on."

"I need the cash," she admitted. "Weddings are expensive—and I refuse to have Harish think I'm marrying him for his money. Of course, when I'm a wildly famous actress I'll support us both." She winked, but I knew her well enough to see the bravado covering her own nerves.

"You're going to kill this audition," I assured her, squeezing her hand back. "Break a leg, Bernhardt."

"You too." She grinned. "Or maybe I shouldn't say that. You have a tendency to take those things literally."

I rolled my eyes, but I couldn't argue. My clumsiness was legendary. It only got worse when I was nervous—and trying desperately to make everything go right—which made interviews particularly hazardous. "I'll try not to break anything," I promised her.

"Good. You've got this," Margo assured me.

I tried to hold on to her faith in me forty-five minutes later, as I walked into the lobby of a posh Manhattan high-rise for my interview.

The heels of my sharp, interview-only ankle boots

clicked across the polished floors as I approached the security guard and gave him my name and ID, earning a visitor's badge in return. As I shrugged out of my overcoat, I watched the regular employees swiping their passes to gain access to the elevator bank. I tried to picture myself as one of them.

Would I feel purposeful? Accomplished? Would I finally be able to quit all the odd jobs that allowed me to make rent? Or at least quit a couple of them? Would I know that I was doing what I was supposed to with my life? And someday, after a few promotions, would I maybe even be able to afford a cute little studio that allowed pets?

I rode up in the elevator, trying to picture myself in this place, in this job, searching for some sense that this was where I was meant to be. The elevator doors opened and I slipped out past the serious people in serious suits going to higher floors. I quickly spotted the large glass doors etched with the name of the publishing house and smoothed my jacket, whispering a little pep talk to myself as I approached. When I stepped through the glass doors, the office was quiet, almost like a library, and my nerves returned full force.

The receptionist smiled when I gave him my name—which I chose to take as a good sign—and handed me a clipboard. "These are just a few forms to speed up the process. You can take a seat through there and someone will be with you in a few minutes." He pointed through an archway to one side. "Good luck."

I accepted the clipboard with a smile, went into the next room, and sat down, trying to remember how to breathe properly.

The rest of the seats were empty, and I found myself picturing the other people who had occupied those chairs while waiting for their interviews. People who had undoubtedly been more qualified and prepared than me.

I focused on the forms in my lap, trying to calm the twist of nerves in my stomach, but the first words I saw were *Relevant Experience* and the roiling in my abdomen only got worse. Did dog walker count as relevant? One of my clients' dogs was named Charles Dickens—that had to count for something, right?

I left *Relevant Experience* blank for the time being, turning my attention instead to the parts I could answer. Name. Address. Education. I had just finished writing Liberal Studies in the space for my major when a woman with a warm smile stepped through the archway.

"Jenny James?"

"That's me." I scrambled to my feet as the woman's smile broadened and she extended her hand.

"I'm Kate Telly. I'll be conducting your interview today."

"Great!" I juggled my coat and the forms, shifting them to one side so I could shake her hand, instantly second-guessing the enthusiasm of my response. Should I have been more measured? Coolly confident? And how hard was I supposed to squeeze her hand? I'd heard that handshakes were important—the ultimate first impression—but how did you know if you were giving a good first impression or a terrible one? I studied her face for some clue, until I realized I'd been holding her hand for too long and abruptly dropped it. I looked away, blushing and fervently wishing I could replay the last few minutes and be less awkward and self-conscious.

"Right this way."

I fell into step behind the interviewer as she led me through the hush of the office. It was early and the office staff were still arriving, greeting one another and sliding behind their desks to check their email and start their days. I could do this. I could belong here. At least, that's what I told myself as I followed the interviewer into a small office and took the chair facing her desk.

Bookcases lined two of the walls, overflowing with books of every variety. Behind Ms. Telly, giant windows provided a view of the high-rise next door. Her desk was cheerfully cluttered with photo frames and knickknacks, but she cleared a space at the center and extended a hand for my forms. "Let's see what you've got."

I flushed, feeling like I was back in high school and had forgotten my homework. "I didn't have time to finish..."

"That's no problem," Ms. Telly assured me. "This just gives us a starting point. So." She accepted the clipboard I reluctantly handed over and scanned the top page, zeroing in on the few blanks I'd managed to fill. "What exactly is a major in liberal studies?"

It's what they give you when you change majors every six months and they just want to find some way to graduate you in four years based on the hodgepodge of classes you've already taken.

Embarrassment thickened on my tongue. "It's, uh, it's a little of everything."

"Interesting. As you imagine, we see a lot of English

degrees." She smiled encouragingly, as if my major made me unique rather than unfit for the job.

I tried to smile back, tugging at the cuffs of my suit jacket, the one I'd bought because it made me feel professional. Now, I just felt like I was playing dress up. An imposter in gray wool.

"All right, let's get straight to the fun part," Ms. Telly continued. "What first inspired you to pursue a career in publishing?"

"I, um..." The truth clogged in the back of my throat, blocking all other words, but I could *not* say that I just needed a job, *any* job, and my post-grad career counselor had all but washed her hands of me, throwing this at me in a last-ditch effort to find me something. "I like books?"

Ms. Telly beamed. "That's why we're all here, isn't it? Book nerds unite!"

She was so nice. So incredibly nice. I'd been to interviews with people who were bored or distracted, who had taken one look at my unimpressive resume and mentally dismissed me before we even began, but Ms. Telly was doing everything imaginable to put me at ease and it only made me feel even more like a fraud.

"Which five books would you say had the greatest influence on your life, and how?" she asked with the tone of someone who had asked that question a thousand times, and I swallowed nervously, glancing around the room at the walls *filled* with books.

Suddenly, all I could think was *Harry Potter was awesome* and *I really liked Pride and Prejudice.* I didn't belong here. I wasn't going to discover the next big thing in publishing. I'd never even read *Wuthering*

Heights. You had to have read *Wuthering Heights* to be an editorial assistant, didn't you? That had to have been some kind of rule.

"Um..."

"I know. It's hard to pick just five. Don't overthink it. First instincts."

"*Wuthering Heights*?"

Oh, no. Why had I said that? What if she asked me something about it? Did I even know any of the characters' names?

Ms. Telly nodded, smiling. "Interesting. And how do you feel it impacted your life?"

"Well, you know, the characters were very, um, good." Good was noncommittal, right? It could apply to just about anything.

She nodded, making a note on my forms. "And was it gothic romance in general or *Wuthering Heights* in particular that resonated with you?"

"Oh, you know, generally, the gothic." Why was I lying? If I'd said *Harry Potter*, she might not have thought I was highbrow and fancy enough to work there, but at least I would've known what I was talking about.

"Any other influential works?"

"Yeah, um, Charles Dickens."

Oh, no. It was just getting worse. I knew I'd read some Charles Dickens in school, but at the moment, I couldn't remember a single title. The fact that I walked a dog named Charles Dickens did *not* make me qualified to work in a publishing house. What was I *doing* there?

"Great." Ms. Telly seemed to sense I was floundering and pivoted. "Let's move from the classics into the future. What do you believe is missing in the literary landscape of today and how do you see yourself filling that gap?"

My heart beat faster and my hands started to sweat. I didn't know anything about the literary landscape of today. This was wrong. All wrong.

I stared at Ms. Telly as my mouth seemed to fill with sawdust. She belonged here, surrounded by all these books. While I was a fake.

Tears pricked the back of my eyes and I swallowed hard, refusing to fall apart in the middle of the interview. Words blurred in my mind and a buzzing sound filled my ears. I must have answered somehow, but the rest of the interview was like an out-of-body experience. Before I knew it, the very nice Ms. Telly was rising from behind her desk and shaking my hand again. She escorted me back to the front of the office where the receptionist gave me a smile and I caught a glimpse of another woman in the waiting area, wearing her interview best, her pen flying over her forms like she couldn't write her answers fast enough.

She looked qualified. Like the kind of woman who deserved a job like this. Who *wanted* a job like this. She'd probably been striving for this job since kindergarten just like Rachel and Chloe and Margo and everyone else who knew what they wanted out of life. *She'd* probably read *Wuthering Heights*.

Ms. Telly promised they'd be in touch, though we both knew they wouldn't. I forced a smile and thanked her before escaping through the glass doors. The elevator opened the second I pushed the button and I stepped inside, clutching my coat in front of me with both hands and silently kicking myself. The elevator was empty on my ride back down to the lobby—as if to remind me that everyone else was on their way up and I was the only one going in the wrong direction.

I peeled off my disposable visitor's badge and tossed it into a trash can on my way out of the lobby. As I stepped out onto the sidewalk, the cold air and distinctive scent of New York hit me in the face. The smell and noise of the city had always made me feel excited, with that if-you-can-make-it-here-you-can-make-it-anywhere feeling humming beneath the surface.

But as today proved, I couldn't make it here.

I felt foolish as I started uptown on autopilot, walking rather than taking the subway. It was still early. My phone rang as I walked, and I groaned when I saw my sister's name on the screen. Of course. Her timing was as perfect as ever.

"Hello, Rachel."

"When's your interview?" my sister said, completely bypassing any normal sort of greeting. "Are you headed there now? Remember: project confidence."

It was tempting to lie. So incredibly tempting. But Rachel would know. I was a horrible liar. "I wasn't projecting anything other than incompetence. I already bombed it."

"Oh, Jenny." Rachel sighed heavily. "What was it this time?"

I veered around a group of tourists gawking at the Plaza Hotel and jogged a little to catch the light at the crosswalk. "I froze, okay? Because I always freeze."

"Maybe you didn't come across as badly as you thought. You always think you're doing terribly."

"I told her I love *Wuthering Heights*, and when

she asked why, I said that the characters were, and I quote, 'good.' That's it. That's all I could think of."

"*Do* you love *Wuthering Heights*?"

"I've never *read Wuthering Heights*."

Rachel groaned. "Oh, Jenny."

"Why did you call me so early this morning?" I challenged, trying to distract her as I skirted the edge of Central Park, dodging the lingering piles of snow on the sidewalk from the last storm. "Why were you even awake at five in the morning your time?"

"My daughter has decided she doesn't believe in sleep." I heard the exhaustion in her voice. "And I wanted to wish you luck on your interview. Don't change the subject. Why did you tell them you loved a book you've never even read?"

"Because if I'd told them the book that influenced me the most was *Harry Potter*, they would've laughed me out of the office."

"You don't know that. And isn't it better to fail as yourself than succeed by trying to be someone you aren't?"

"I didn't belong there, Rach," I insisted. "Even before I started lying about books, it didn't feel right. Publishing just isn't my thing." At least I hadn't broken anything or spilled anything on anyone. It was all about the little victories.

"Did you really give it a shot, though? Or did you sabotage yourself by counting yourself out before you even walked through the door? Again."

"Rachel..."

"Has it occurred to you that maybe you're putting too much weight on this decision? Pick a job. Any job. I feel like you're waiting for lightning to strike and a giant neon flashing sign saying *this is who you are* to appear, but life isn't like that. Sometimes figuring out what you're meant to be is about making a choice, not waiting for a sign."

"Says the woman who has known what she wanted to be since birth. Besides, I'm not waiting for a sign."

"Are you sure?" Rachel challenged. "Are you even dating anyone?"

I frowned at the phone. "What does that have to do with anything?"

"It's all part of the same problem. You're waiting around for some fairy tale and until you realize that isn't possible you're never going to let yourself have something real. No one gets the fairy tale. There's no such thing as perfect. Not with jobs and not with guys."

"I don't want a fairy tale," I protested. "I don't. I just... I want to know where I belong. I want to *feel* like I belong. You've had that forever. I just want it to be my turn. And yes, I want someone to kiss beneath the mistletoe, who falls madly in love with *me*. I want a guy who looks at me the way Eliot has always looked at you. And the way Danny looks at Chloe. Like Mom and Dad, and Margo and Harish. Is that really so much to ask?"

"Of course not, but we just worry that you're waiting for Prince Charming when he doesn't exist."

"I'm sure all the real-life princes in the world would be horrified to hear you say they don't exist, but I promise I'm not holding out for one."

I didn't want a prince. I just wanted someone who gave me that *zing*. That feeling that I was exactly where I needed to be with the person who fit me like a puzzle piece.

Speaking of princes...

I glanced up, taking in my surroundings and smiling as I realized that I'd automatically navigated to the one place guaranteed to make me feel better. I turned up the street. "Though I am on my way to meet a prince right now."

"Jenny—"

"I know, Rachel," I interrupted my big sister. "Whatever you're about to tell me, I know. I love you, but I'm going to fix my own life, okay?"

"Maybe if you came home. New York isn't for everyone—"

"Goodbye, Rachel."

I disconnected the call before my sister could continue her lecture. I didn't need to hear her tell me that I couldn't really afford to live here on my own after Margo moved out. That I should retreat back to our hometown in Iowa with my tail between my legs—a failure. The one James girl who'd never made anything of herself.

I didn't want to think about any of that.

I pocketed my phone, moving faster now that I knew my destination. I was on my way to meet a prince, and that was all that mattered. The one male in all of New York who looked at me with absolute devotion.

I pushed open the doors to Paws for Love and the jingle bells over the door rang, drawing the attention of the volunteer working inside.

"G'morning, Mercedes."

"Hey, Jenny," she called out, giving me a quick smile before turning her attention back to the lopsided

Santa hat she was trying to balance on a pit bull mix's head. "You here to see your prince?"

"That I am," I confirmed, unbuttoning my coat. "Do you need a hand first?"

Mercedes and I both volunteered at Paws for Love. Lately, she'd been updating the website with adorable holiday-themed photos in a campaign to find more of our furry residents forever homes during the holidays. This time of year, so many New Yorkers felt stressed or lonely and could use a little more love in their lives, but there were always more furry angels in the shelter looking for love than there were families to adopt them. Lucky was one of our newest residents. The one-eared pit bull mix gazed adoringly at Mercedes, his little tail wagging frantically at the attention so his entire body seemed to shiver with happiness.

"No, thanks, I've got this guy," Mercedes assured me, stepping back to pick up her camera as Lucky wriggled with the effort not to leap up and follow her. "Have fun with his highness."

"I will."

I typed the code into the door and headed toward the kennels. Real estate in the city was always at a premium, so the dogs were tucked in two or three to a run. They yipped when they saw me, wagging and bouncing as I called greetings to each one. I plucked a red ball out of a toy bin as I passed and tucked it into the pocket of my winter coat with a smile already growing on my face.

I'd begun volunteering at Paws for Love six months ago, but five weeks ago, everything had changed when I'd met *him*.

A bona fide prince.

No matter what Rachel and Chloe might think, I haven't been holding out for Prince Charming. But when he walked into my life, everything changed.

I rounded a corner and there he was.

"Hello, Your Highness!"

My prince looked up at the sound of my voice, his eyes lighting at the sight of me, filling with an affection so sincere it couldn't be faked—

And then he barked.